DEAD, WHITE, AND BLUE

The Juniper Junction Holiday Mystery Series: Book Two

AMY M. READE

Pau Hana Publishing

BOOKS BY AMY M. READE

STANDALONE BOOKS

Secrets of Hallstead House

The Ghosts of Peppernell Manor

House of the Hanging Jade

THE MALICE SERIES

The House on Candlewick Lane

Highland Peril

Murder in Thistlecross

THE JUNIPER JUNCTION HOLIDAY MYSTERY SERIES

The Worst Noel

Dead, White, and Blue

THE LIBRARIES OF THE WORLD MYSTERY SERIES

Trudy's Diary

Dutch Treat (Coming soon)

PRAISE FOR AMY M. READE

Trudy's Diary: "I especially enjoyed the mystery within a mystery and how the author wove these components throughout the novel. Congratulations to Ms. Reade on a successful mystery that kept me reading long into the night!" From SD, reviewer

The Worst Noel: I won't soon forget this Christmas adventure in the snowy Rockies, and I will miss the winsome characters-- all of them so well-defined that I just know they are even now going on with their lives beyond the last page of the story." From Iris Chacon, reviewer

Murder in Thistlecross: "Amy Reade's series has a touch of gothic suspense, always fun, and this particular entry has the extra added attraction of the old Clue board game (later a movie that was equally delightful) wherein the various suspects move around the castle and the sleuth has to figure out who killed who, how and where." From Buried Under Books

Highland Peril: "This is escapism at its best, as it is a compelling mystery that whisks readers away to a land as beautiful as it is rich with intrigue." From Cynthia Chow, Kings River Life

The House on Candlewick Lane: "As in most gothic novels, the actual house on Candlewick Lane is creepy and filled with dark passages and rooms. You feel the evil emanate from the structure and from the people who live there ... I loved the rich descriptions of Edinburgh. You definitely feel like you are walking the streets next to Greer, searching for Ellie. You can feel the rain and the cold, and a couple times, I swear I could smell the scents of the local cuisine." From Colleen Chesebro, reviewer

House of the Hanging Jade: "House of the Hanging Jade is a suspenseful tale of murder and obsession, all taking place against a beautiful Hawaiian backdrop. Lush descriptions of both the scenery and the food prepared by the protagonist leave you wanting more." From The Book's the Thing

The Ghosts of Peppernell Manor: "If you're a fan of ... novels by Phyllis A. Whitney, Victoria Holt, and Barbara Michaels, you're going to love *The Ghosts of Peppernell Manor* by Amy M. Reade." From Jane Reads.

Secrets of Hallstead House: "Thank you, Amy, for taking me to a new place and allowing me to imagine." From Phyllis H. Moore, reviewer

Cover design by http://www.StunningBookCovers.com

Pau Hana Publishing

Print ISBN: 978-1-7326907-4-5

Ebook ISBN: 978-1-7326907-5-2

Printed in the United States of America

For Megan, Paul, Olivia, and Madelyn

ACKNOWLEDGMENTS

I had so much fun writing this book, in large part because of the research involved. I gathered some great information about jailhouse policies from former corrections officers Beth and Ralph Rivello. Thank you, Beth and Ralph, for sharing your vast knowledge with me and for your patience with all my questions. And huge thanks are due to Jeni Chappelle, my editor, who always makes my books better.

Thanks are also due to Jim Holman and his daughter, Laura Holman, for their generosity to The Parkinson Council. At an auction benefiting The Parkinson Council in March, 2018, Jim and Laura won the opportunity to name a character in an upcoming book. They chose the name Orson Weaver, whom you'll meet in the story.

And last, but not least, I want to thank my husband John, who is always my first reader. His advice is always invaluable.

CHAPTER 1

Lilly used the graduation program to fan herself with a hand that trembled ever so slightly.

"I don't know why people say dry heat isn't bad," she grumbled. "Hot is hot. I don't care how dry the air is."

Her best friend, Noley, nudged her in the ribs. "You're looking at it all wrong. Think about how much better it is to have a late June heat wave than an early January deep-freeze."

You should talk, Lilly thought with a hint of envy. *You probably aren't even sweating.*

Bev, Lilly's mother, leaned across Noley's lap. "Lilly, stop your complaining. This is Tighe's day. No one cares if you're uncomfortable."

"Thanks, Mom," Lilly shot back. Bev's unfiltered words were probably right, though.

Lilly glanced at Noley out of the corner of her eye. Noley was grinning.

When Bev looked away and began talking to the strangers on the other side of her, Noley turned to Lilly again and said in a low voice, "It's not the weather that has you upset--it's that Tighe's graduating. He's not leaving forever, you know. You'll always be his mother."

Tears sprang to Lilly's eyes, as they had so often in the past two weeks. It seemed any mention of Tighe made her weepy. She pulled a tissue from her handbag and dabbed at her eyes, sniffing.

"I know. It's just that now the countdown begins in earnest to the day he leaves home and heads off to college."

Lilly's daughter, Laurel, was sitting on Lilly's left side. "Mom, don't cry. Again. You still have me."

"I know, Laurel, and I'm so thankful for that. But you'll be leaving a year from now." She choked on a sob and the tears fell faster.

"Mom, you're supposed to be happy. Don't let Tighe see you crying. He'll be upset."

Laurel had a point. Lilly didn't want her eyes to be red and puffy when Tighe met up with the rest of the family after the ceremony.

"You're right, Laur. I'll stop. I'm sorry."

Laurel reached for Lilly's hand and held it in a tight grip. *When did she become the comforter and I the comforted?* Lilly asked herself, shaking her head.

"Why are you shaking your head?" Laurel asked.

Lilly smiled. "You're growing up."

Laurel rolled her eyes. "Mom, no more blubbering. Please."

Lilly laughed before the tears could start afresh. "I won't."

The first heavy notes of the high school band's rendition of *Pomp and Circumstance* began to blare across the field. The murmuring of the crowd in the bleachers dulled and parents, family, and friends all focused their attention on the graduates making their way from the back of the school onto the artificial turf.

The boys were in bright royal blue graduation gowns that could probably be seen from outer space; the girls' gowns were white. Lilly searched the graduates for Tighe. She knew he would be near the beginning of the class because they were marching in alphabetical order and his last name started with a "C." He had also decorated his cap with a basketball and a hoop.

"There he is!" she cried, waving at him. She could tell he was looking for his family, but he didn't see them.

"Mom, be quiet," Laurel said in a low voice. "You're embarrassing me."

Lilly rolled her eyes and sat up a little straighter so she could get a good picture of Tighe. She had threatened to wear a big, floppy hat so he could see her in the stands, but Noley had talked her out of it. She aimed her phone at her son and started snapping pictures at a furious rate.

"Mom, don't you have enough pictures? You took a thousand at home," Laurel said.

"You can never have enough pictures," Lilly said.

Once the graduates were seated and the band had stopped playing, the principal got up and made some long-winded remarks. By the time he was done talking, the graduates were restless in their seats, as were all the family members and friends in the stands. When would they get to the good part, the part where the students were called up one by one to receive their diplomas?

Finally, after several other people, including members of the Board of Education, the valedictorian and salutatorian, and a member of the Parent-Teacher Organization had spoken at mind-numbing length, it was time for the presentation of the graduates.

Row by row they stood, waiting for names to be called. Lilly was ready with the video on her cell phone when Tighe's name was called in the principal's deep baritone.

"Tighe Matthew Carlsen."

Lilly stood up to get a better video. Chills ran up and down her spine and goosebumps dotted her arms when she heard Tighe's name. She glanced at Beau, who was watching his son with rapt attention. She thought she even saw a tiny smear of moisture on the corner of his eye. Could it be that he had developed a hint of sentimentality since returning to Juniper Junction?

Lilly continued to film Tighe as he walked back toward his seat. His eyes scanned the stands and he found her. He waved, his smile wide, and held up his diploma. She waved back and gave him a thumbs-up, feeling like the two of them were alone in the stadium for a fleeting moment.

She sat down as the next name was called. Beau leaned across Laurel. "Our boy did it." He grinned.

"Yes, our boy sure did," she said, suppressing a grimace. She knew she shouldn't be petty, but was Tighe really as much Beau's "boy" as he was hers? After all, she had raised him from toddlerhood to his senior year in high school without Beau's help. Why should Beau be taking any credit on graduation day?

Noley elbowed her. "Ignore him," she said through clenched teeth.

Bev leaned forward so she could look at Lilly. "Okay, that's it. Can we go now?" she said in a shockingly loud voice. Or maybe it just seemed shockingly loud to Lilly. She looked at her mother with something akin to horror.

"Mom, shh! We can't go until all the other graduates have been called up," she hissed.

"God, this is boring," Bev said, rummaging in her purse. Several people sitting around them snickered. Lilly turned to them.

"I'm so sorry," she whispered.

"She's only saying out loud what the rest of us are thinking," one man said. The people sitting on either side of him nodded their agreement. Bev finally located a mint and unwrapped it noisily.

Lilly turned her attention back to the class. She knew what was going through their collective minds--*let's get out of these hot gowns, whose party is everyone going to first,* and *when can we eat?*

She and Noley had planned a party for a few hours after the ceremony. Gatherings that involved Noley always promised to be delicious, since she was a sought-after cook, recipe developer, and small-event caterer.

Lilly knew Tighe would want to go to the homes of a few of his friends before his own party started, plus Hassan was flying in from Minneapolis and she knew he didn't want to miss Tighe's party. He had apologized to Tighe for not being able to make it to the graduation ceremony and he had promised to be there afterward. Lilly smiled at the thought of Hassan, her boyfriend since just before Christmas.

Then she frowned. *Boyfriend* was such a teenage word. Partner? No, they weren't in business together. Significant other? Maybe, but she didn't want to refer to him as an "other." Companion? Maybe. Special friend? No, that just sounded weird. Escort? No, he wasn't a gigolo.

Her thoughts turned back to the ceremony, where the principal was intoning the names of the "M" kids.

Halfway there, she thought.

By the time the ceremony was over and the families of the graduates had flooded the football field for photos and hugs and bouquets of flowers, the sun was dropping lower into the western sky.

Tighe peeled off his graduation gown as soon as the obligatory photos had been taken with every family member in attendance. "Mom, can I go to Mike's house? He and I are going to hit a couple parties, then we'll be home. His parents are coming to our party, too."

"Sure," Lilly said. "See you at home." Mike lived less than a block from the school--Tighe would be there before the rest of them even got to the parking lot.

Tighe slung the graduation gown over his shoulder and Lilly watched him saunter over to Mike and his family.

She allowed herself one sad thought--about the metaphorical nature of her son moving away from her to take care of other business--before a stern voice in her head told her to get a grip.

Noley sidled up to her. "Hey, let's get going. We've got a lot to do before people start getting to your house."

Lilly was grateful for any activity that would take her mind off the momentous nature of the day's events. At least temporarily.

They walked toward their cars with Beau and Laurel in tow. Bill, Lilly's brother, had promised to drive Bev to her home to rest for a bit before bringing her over to Lilly's house for the party. Since he was on duty until early evening, he had missed the graduation ceremony, but he met them in the parking lot and took Bev home in his police cruiser.

"Are you picking up Hassan at the airport?" Beau asked. "I can go get him if you want."

It was a nice gesture, Lilly supposed, but the last two people she needed having a conversation without her strict supervision were her current boyfriend-partner-significant-other-companion-special friend-escort and her ex-husband.

"He's renting a car, but thank you," Lilly said.

Lilly, Laurel, and Noley had all arrived in Lilly's car; Beau had his truck. As Noley slid into Lilly's front seat, she noted, "It's nice that Beau is so good about wanting to be friends with Hassan."

"Hmm," Lilly replied.

"Don't you think so?" Noley asked.

"I guess so. It's just kind of weird, you know? Being friends with him is okay, but I suppose I want to keep him separate from the Hassan part of my life."

"Is Dad coming over now?" Laurel asked from the back seat.

"In a little while."

"Good," Laurel said. Lilly smiled. As difficult as it had been at first having Beau back in Juniper Junction, Laurel and Tighe had both come to know him a little better. Laurel, especially, seemed interested in including Beau in family events and talked about him often. There were times it hurt Lilly's feelings, since she had brought up the kids almost single-handedly after Beau had left them over fifteen years ago, but she always tried to remember that having a father was new to Laurel and she was trying to cram a lot of growing-up experiences into a short amount of time.

Lilly pulled into the driveway and heard, rather than saw, Barney leaping up to the top of the fence in the backyard.

"We're home, boy!" she called. "Ready for a party?"

Barney barked his glee at having people who would play with him, and Lilly opened the fence to the yard. Barney ran up to her, his tail wagging at the speed of a metronome on steroids.

"Go get your ball," she said, leaning over to tousle the fur on his head. Barney turned tail and raced across the backyard and returned in a disappointingly short amount of time. He dropped a slobber-covered tennis ball at her feet. She threw it into the bushes on the other side of the yard, then asked Laurel to take over. Laurel was only too happy to stay outside with the dog instead of having to slave away in the kitchen for a party that wasn't even in her honor.

Lilly was taking the caramelized French onion dip out of the refrigerator when the phone rang.

"Hassan!" Lilly cried when she answered it. "Great! See you soon." She hung up and turned to Noley.

"Is he on his way?" Noley asked.

Lilly grinned. "He'll be here in a little while."

"Okay, let's get things done in here so you can spend time with him when he gets here. You know, smooching and all that."

Lilly laughed and turned bright red. "Stop it. I don't want Laurel to hear."

"Oh, I'm pretty sure Laurel knows you and Hassan kiss," Noley teased.

"I know, but…" Lilly stopped as her phone rang. She hit the Talk button without looking at the caller ID. "Hassan?"

She didn't say anything for a moment. She just listened, and felt the color draining from her face as her jaw went slack.

"What?" Noley whispered.

Lilly shook her head slightly and gripped the phone tighter. "Are you all right? Where are you?" she asked, her voice high and taut.

"Thank God. Stay where you are. I'll be over to pick you up in just a few minutes." She hung up the phone and turned to Noley.

"That was Tighe. He's at Mike Foster's house, over by the school, and the house next door is on fire."

Noley's eyes widened. "Is he all right?"

Lilly nodded. "The firefighters had everyone go and stand down the block. I've got to go get him and bring him home. He sounded a little panicked."

"Okay. I'll take care of things here. You go." Noley was practically pushing Lilly out the door. Lilly grabbed her purse and car keys on her way outside. She quickly told Laurel what was happening and then hurried to her car.

CHAPTER 2

Lilly drove as fast as she dared toward the Fosters' house. As she turned down their block, she was not surprised to see a phalanx of fire trucks, emergency vehicles, and crowds of onlookers choking the street. The sight gave her chills. The police were keeping people away from the vicinity of the burning home, but the gawkers were there, nonetheless.

Lilly parked the car as close as she could to the Fosters' house, then hopped out and stood on tiptoes, scanning the block for Tighe. She finally spotted him, clustered with a group of other teens, safely down the block and across the street from the burning home.

"Tighe!" Lilly called, waving her arms. But the noise on the street was deafening and he couldn't hear her. He wasn't looking in her direction, either, since all eyes were focused on the raging fire. Some of the firefighters were running to and fro, getting tools from the trucks, while others trained the massive hoses on the flames licking out of the home's windows like angry tongues.

Lilly made her way to where her son stood. When she tapped him on the shoulder, he turned in surprise. She enveloped him in a hug. "Can you believe this?" he asked.

Lilly could only shake her head. Watching the fire roar, Lilly was both terrified and mesmerized. Embers from the blaze flitted through the air toward the Fosters' home, but the firefighters had soaked their house with water to prevent it from burning.

The Fosters were standing nearby, watching the scene with their neighbors. Debbie Foster, Mike's mother, was crying. Lilly told Tighe to stay where he was while she pushed through the throngs of people to reach them.

"Hi, Debbie. I can't believe this is happening," Lilly said.

Debbie looked at Lilly, slightly dazed, then seemed to gather herself. "Hi, Lilly. I can't believe it, either. It's just awful."

"Did the family make it out okay?" Lilly asked.

"No one is living there right now," Debbie said. "The house has been on the market for a few months."

"Thank God no one was inside," Lilly said, breathing a sigh of relief. Debbie nodded.

I'm going to take Tighe home now and I just wanted to let you know so that no one thinks he's gone missing."

"Thank you for letting me know, but I'm not sure the police are going to let him go home just yet."

Lilly blinked in surprise. "Why not?"

"They asked all the kids to stay put. I guess they have some questions about how the fire started."

Lilly gasped. "You're not saying they think one of the kids did it."

"Oh, no, nothing like that, I'm sure. I think they want to know if any of the kids saw anyone on the property before the fire started."

Lilly stood with Debbie and her husband for several more minutes, then noticed a police officer making his way toward the group of kids huddled with Tighe.

"I'm going over there to see what that officer is saying," Lilly told the Fosters.

They followed her gaze and fell into step behind her as she walked toward the officer, who was taking a small notebook out of his pocket.

Lilly arrived at the tangle of kids just as the officer pointed at Tighe with a stubby pencil. "I'll start with you," he said. "Notice anyone or anything out of the ordinary at the house next door to the Fosters?"

"No, sir," Tighe answered.

"Anyone on the street, maybe walking by, around the time you noticed the fire?"

"No."

The officer proceeded to ask Tighe a long list of questions, but Tighe was unable to offer any useful information. The officer noted Tighe's responses in his notebook and handed him his card. "Call me anytime, day or night, if you think of anything," the officer said.

"I will," Tighe promised.

"Can I take him home now, officer?" Lilly asked.

The officer nodded, having already moved on to the next kid to be questioned.

Tighe stayed close to his mother as they threaded their way back to her car. He didn't say anything until they were on their way home.

"I've never seen a fire up close like that. I mean, I've seen bonfires and stuff, but never anything like that. It just went up in flames so fast."

"And you didn't see anything? Anyone?"

Tighe shook his head, a faraway look in his eyes.

"Did any of the kids see anything?"

Tighe shrugged. "Maybe. I hadn't been there long when the fire started."

"Thank God there was no one living there."

"I know. It could have been so much worse."

Lilly glanced at the clock on the dashboard. She was

surprised at how much time had passed since Tighe had called her.

"We're almost ready for our guests to arrive, so I'm glad I got you out of there," Lilly said. She sniffed the air. "You smell like smoke. You should probably change your clothes before people get to the house." Then she paused.

"Do you still want people to come over?" she asked.

Tighe nodded, his thoughts obviously elsewhere. Lilly reached out to touch his shoulder. "You okay, honey?"

"Yeah, I'm okay. Just thinking. Will Uncle Bill know anything about it? The fire, I mean."

"He's got the evening off so he can come to your party, so unless it's something they can't handle without him, he probably won't know anything about it until he goes to work tomorrow. But we can ask."

Tighe went up to his room to shower and change his clothes as soon as they got home. Noley and Laurel buzzed around Lilly after Tighe went upstairs, wondering what had happened. Lilly gave them the nutshell version and was careful to stress that Tighe was still processing the experience and might not welcome a lot of questions about it.

"Gran called," Laurel said, changing the subject. "She wants to know if Fred can come."

Lilly slumped against the counter. It was going to be hard enough to keep Barney calm when the guests started arriving--adding one more dog to the mix spelled almost certain disaster.

"I'd prefer it if she left Fred at home," she answered. "You want to call and break the news or shall I?"

Laurel shrugged. "Does it matter? She's going to do what she wants."

"Not if Bill tells her he doesn't want the dog in the car," Lilly pointed out.

"Wrong," Noley interjected. "He's still mad that you got her that dog, so he might let Fred come just to spite you." She grinned and Lilly knew she had no choice in the matter--Fred was coming.

"Whatever. As long as he stays outside--he has an accident every time he's over here," Lilly said, her hands on her hips. "Now, enough about Fred. Let's start taking things outside." She handed Laurel a big bowl of potato chips, hefted the bowl of onion dip that was still sitting on the counter, and followed Laurel into the backyard. Noley came out a moment later with a platter of vegetables and hummus.

"Did you make poppers, Noley?" Laurel asked. "Yours are really good."

"I sure did," Noley replied with a smile. "Tighe requested them specifically. I made some with jalapeños and some with sweet peppers."

Lilly and Laurel made several more trips outside with food while Noley assembled burger fixings in the kitchen. It wasn't long before there was a shout from the driveway. Lilly could see the top of Beau's blond head coming through the gate into the backyard.

"Dad's here," Laurel said, her eyes lighting up.

"Good. He can light the grill. People will be here any minute now," Lilly grumbled. She knew she should be more gracious, but it grated on her nerves every time Laurel seemed excited or happy to see her father. She knew jealousy was ugly inside and out, but she simply couldn't help it.

Tighe came into the kitchen just as Beau came in from the backyard. Beau reached out to shake Tighe's hand and noticed immediately, contrary to his usual powers of observation, that Tighe was upset about something.

"What's wrong, man?" Beau asked. "This is your graduation day! You should be dancing!"

"I'm happy," Tighe said. "I'm just preoccupied, I guess."

"What about? A girl?" Beau asked, bumping his shoulder against Tighe's and winking.

"No, a fire," Tighe said.

Beau got serious. "What fire? Was there a fire somewhere?"

"Mom, can you explain? I don't really want to talk about it," Tighe said, reaching for the back door handle. "I'm going outside to get something to drink." He closed the door behind him.

"What's this about a fire?" Beau asked Lilly.

"He went to a graduation party at a friend's house and while he was there a neighbor's house went up in flames. Pretty quickly, as far as I could tell. By the time I got there, the whole street had been cordoned off."

"Did anyone get hurt?" Beau asked.

"No, but I think it's given Tighe a scare," Lilly answered. "He'll be fine once people get here. Now get out there and start the grill, would you? And be on standby in case I need you to go to the store."

Beau left and Noley turned to Lilly. "Bill called. He's on his way with your mom. They have Fred." She gave Lilly a sympathetic smile. "Look at it this way--at least Barney likes Fred. If they didn't get along, you might have a real disaster on your hands."

"I have a feeling I'm going to have a disaster on my hands no matter what."

It wasn't long before guests started to arrive, and everyone came bearing gifts and good wishes for Tighe. Lilly watched him anxiously, hoping his fake good mood would be replaced by a real one. Eventually it was--she was pleased when she noticed his shoulders and neck finally beginning to relax.

Bill and Bev arrived with Fred in tow. While Bev found a place to sit in the yard, Bill came into the kitchen. Lilly gave her brother a pointed look. "You couldn't get Mom to leave that dog at home?"

"And ruin her fun? Never."

"Just because I got her the dog and you didn't think of it, that's no reason to be spiteful."

"Who's spiteful? I just want Mom to enjoy herself and the way she chooses to enjoy herself is to bring Fred to parties."

Noley was standing at the sink with her back to Lilly and Bill. "Would you two stop bickering? I need help," she said.

Bill walked over to her and kissed her cheek. "Sorry. What do you want us to do?"

Noley began ticking off jobs on her fingers. Lilly took a tray of sliced fruit outside while Bill opened a couple bottles of wine and headed to the patio to serve the guests who were just arriving. Lilly noticed that Barney had already had his fill of strangers and was lying down in the corner of the yard.

In contrast, Fred's first act of mischief was to knock the bowl of onion dip off the table and devour its entire contents before anyone noticed what was happening. It was Laurel who looked over toward the food table and noticed Fred's tail wagging from under the tablecloth. She picked up the corner of the tablecloth to find Fred's head in the empty bowl.

"Fred!" she cried. "Mom!"

Lilly hurried over to where Fred sat on the patio, licking his chops without a care in the world.

"Mom, dogs aren't supposed to have onions! He'll die!" Laurel exclaimed. Her eyes filled with tears faster than Fred had engorged himself with the dip.

"All right, let's stay calm. You take Fred into the house and sit with him. Try to keep him quiet. Go online, would you, and see if you can find out what to do when a dog eats onions? We may have to take him to the vet."

"What's going on?" Bev asked, coming up to the group. "Where's Fred?"

"He ate the onion dip, Mom," Lilly said, trying to keep her voice even. She didn't know what frustrated her more--hosting a dog that ate the onion dip or having no more onion dip to serve to the human guests.

"I don't blame him. The onion dip is delicious!" Bev exclaimed.

"Mom, dogs aren't supposed to eat onions. They can make him sick."

"Oh, my God!" Bev cried. "Where is he? Is he all right?"

"He's in the house with Laurel. She's going online to see what she can find about dogs that eat onions."

"Why did you leave the dip so close to the edge of the table?" Bev asked, her eyes blazing.

Lilly counted to ten. Twice. She took a deep breath. "Mom, it wasn't my fault. It wasn't anyone's fault, except possibly the person who was supposed to be watching Fred." She gave Bev a pointed look.

"Well, who was supposed to be watching him?" Bev asked.

"Forget it, Mom. Would you just make sure people have drinks? Tell them where the water and sodas are."

Bev sauntered off and Laurel appeared at Lilly's side. "Mom, Fred threw up all over the kitchen floor."

Lilly groaned. "I don't suppose you cleaned it up?"

"Ew. No way. That's disgusting."

"Okay. I'll take care of it."

"The good news is that he seems to be feeling better. He's jumping all over the place in there."

"Not in the vomit, I hope."

Laurel shrugged. Lilly closed her eyes in a private appeal for calm and headed toward the kitchen. Noley was standing near the back steps.

"Nol, would you please keep everyone out of the house for now? Apparently there's an accident I need to clean up."

"Fred didn't pee in the house again, did he?"

"No. He vomited."

"Gross! I'd offer to help, but I'm afraid that's not my thing."

"That's fine. I'll do it." Lilly went into the house and was struck by the odor that permeated the kitchen—undigested onion with a hint of bile.

Taking a deep breath through her mouth, Lilly reached

under the sink for the paper towels and rubber gloves. She knelt on the floor next to the first pool and ripped off a larger-than-necessary number of paper towels. Closing her eyes and taking another quavery breath, she reached forward and mopped up a towelful of the vomit. She retched. Her salivary glands were working overtime and her body was sweating. She retched again.

She ripped off another long sheet of toweling and repeated the action with a second puddle. She retched again and reached for the trash can.

CHAPTER 3

"What's going on?" The deep voice, which had come from just inside the back door, startled her. She hadn't heard the door opening because of all the noise issuing from her own throat.

"Hassan!" she cried, looking up from her spot on the floor. She breathed through her nose by mistake and retched again. She swallowed and could feel her face burning bright with embarrassment.

"What are you doing?" he asked. Then he noticed the various plops of vomit on the floor.

"Oh, God. Has Barney been sick?" he asked, his face showing his concern. He loved Barney.

"No. This is all Fred."

"What happened?"

"He ate onion dip. All of it, I might add. We didn't make any extra."

"So we go to the store and buy some. No big deal," he said, crossing the floor and leaning down to kiss her. She wiped a stray hair from her sweaty forehead.

"I'm sorry I look so horrible," she apologized.

"You look gorgeous, as always," Hassan said, smiling at her with those beautiful white teeth. His face, olive-toned and handsome, was a sight for sore eyes.

She blushed again. "We can't get onion dip from the store. It won't be as good."

"Who cares? The important thing is that there's something to dip the chips in, right? And where's the graduate? I haven't seen him yet."

"He's outside, mingling. You go find him while I finish up in here."

Hassan went in search of Tighe while Lilly finished the ugly job of cleaning up the mess Fred had made. Noley came into the kitchen with an empty tray and proceeded to fill it again with finger sandwiches from the refrigerator.

"Smells good in here," she said, sniffing the air. "Like flowers."

"That's my cleaning spray. Thank Fred."

"I will. Sorry I didn't do my gatekeeping job very well, but I figured you wouldn't mind if Hassan came in." She winked.

"Not at all," Lilly said as she washed her hands. "How's everything going out there?"

"Beau has waylaid Hassan and is regaling him with tales about his new girlfriend."

"Beau has a new girlfriend?" Lilly asked. "Let's hope she's better than the last one."

"I'm sure Hassan can tell you all about her if you ask."

"I'll pass, thanks," Lilly said with a wry smile.

Hassan came into the kitchen a few minutes later.

"I understand you've heard all about Beau's new girlfriend," Lilly said.

"I suppose so. Her name is Nikki and she's God's gift to men, or at least Beau. He seems quite smitten." Hassan smiled.

"Good for him," Lilly said.

"I found Tighe," Hassan said. "That's why I came back inside. Is he all right? He's doesn't seem like himself."

"He's had a long day," Lilly explained. "I'll tell you all about it later." She led Hassan outside. They walked over to Noley and Bill, who were standing with Bev. Hassan kissed Bev on each cheek.

"Such a gentleman," Bev said, gracing Hassan with her most coy smile.

Bill's phone beeped. He looked down at the screen and frowned. "I've got to take this," he said, moving away from the group and heading up the steps into the kitchen.

The rest of them chatted for several minutes before Bill came back. "Lilly, can I talk to you inside?" he asked.

"Sure," she said, suddenly wary. His tone of voice was serious, even worried, and she wondered why. She didn't have to wait long to find out.

"Did Tighe tell you anything about a fire he saw earlier?" Bill asked.

Lilly heaved a sigh of relief. She could handle this.

"Yes. In fact, I went there to pick him up. He's fine, though. Why?"

"Someone said they saw him leave the party for a few minutes. The fire started not long after that."

For a moment Lilly didn't comprehend what Bill was trying to say. More likely, though, she didn't want to comprehend it.

"So?" she asked, her voice betraying just a hint of defensiveness.

"So, where did he go? Did he tell you?"

"No. He didn't mention it. I'm sure he just went to the bathroom or something."

"Listen, that was a buddy of mine on the force. He called with the heads-up because he knows I'm at Tighe's party tonight. They're going to want to question him again."

"But they've already questioned him once," Lilly said, struggling to keep her voice calm. "They already asked him about the party."

"They want to present Tighe with a slightly contradictory statement from someone else who was there and find out if his story changes."

"But what if it does? What if he just forgot that he went inside to go to the bathroom or get a drink or something?" Lilly could hear her voice rising, but she was powerless to stop it.

"Take it easy, Lil. They just want to talk to him. They don't think he did it."

"Are you sure?"

Bill took just a fraction of a second longer than he should have to answer Lilly's question. She grabbed his arm. "Bill? Do they think he did it?"

"No. Just don't worry about it right now. I don't want to ruin Tighe's party."

"I'm worried," Lilly said.

"Don't be. Tighe only graduates from high school once, so go out there and make sure he's having a good time. I'm sorry I even brought this up to you."

"I wish you had waited," Lilly said angrily.

"So do I."

Lilly returned to the backyard, where more guests had arrived and had made their way over to Tighe to congratulate him. He was standing in the middle of a small crowd of people, looking pleased but tired. Lilly smiled to herself as she watched him. He had grown into such a fine young man. She felt an arm slip around her shoulders.

"You all right?" Hassan asked.

She nodded. "It's something else I'll have to tell you about later. Hope you're planning to stay for hours." She gave him a wan smile.

"I'll stay as long as you like," he said.

She took his hand and made the rounds among the adult guests. Tighe and Laurel were mingling with the younger set. Lilly shooed Fred away from several guests whom he had targeted for special treatment and scanned the crowd for her mother.

"I wish she had left Fred at home," she grumbled.

"Mrs. Carlsen," came a voice from behind her. Lilly turned.

"Oh, hi, Mrs. Laforge," she said, smiling. "I'm glad you could come to Tighe's party."

"Didn't have much choice, did I?" came her surly neighbor's reply. "There's an absurd amount of noise coming from over here."

Lilly smiled, knowing her neighbor was prone to hyperbole. As parties went, this one wasn't very loud at all.

"How about a glass of wine, Mrs. Laforge?" Hassan asked. He always knew what to do when things threatened to become heated. Lilly forced herself to remember that Mrs. Laforge had saved Barney's life in a blizzard just a handful of months ago.

Just then Fred came shooting over to Mrs. Laforge like a rocket. "There's my widdle Freddy-poo," Mrs. Laforge said, her voice high and squeaky. Lilly rolled her eyes.

"Be careful of that one, Mrs. Laforge," she said. "Freddy-poo got into the onion dip earlier and had quite a bout of, ah, illness afterward."

"What? My Freddy? I don't believe it," she said, her voice low now, as she scratched Fred under the chin. "A little onion dip never hurt anyone."

"Except Fred, and millions of other dogs," Lilly said under her breath. Hassan returned with a glass of wine and handed it to Mrs. Laforge with a wide smile.

"I guessed you to be a white wine person, Mrs. Laforge. Am I right?" he asked.

"You guessed right," she said, straightening up and accepting the glass of wine.

Lilly looked around and caught sight of her mother, who had cornered two teenage girls and was, no doubt, telling them about the good old days when she graduated from high school. The girls kept looking at each other--Lilly knew that look. It was one of desperation, of wondering how they were ever going to rid themselves of the old lady. Lilly knew exactly how they felt, but couldn't ignore the sudden pang of sadness that gripped her. As trying as her mother could be, she didn't like to see her judged by others, and certainly not by a couple of teenage girls.

"Excuse me, Mrs. Laforge," Lilly said, leaving her to chat with Hassan.

She made a beeline for her mother and gently took her elbow. "Mom, could you help me in the kitchen for a minute?" she asked. "Sorry to take you away from the girls here, but I need your advice about something."

The girls looked relieved, and Lilly was glad to remove her mother from the situation. She didn't want to think about the things the girls were probably whispering to each other about Bev.

"What do you need my advice for, Lilly?" Bev asked. Lilly searched her mind frantically for something to say.

"Um, I was wondering if you have your huckleberry lemonade recipe committed to memory. I thought we'd make some and set it out for the kids," Lilly answered brightly.

Bev shook her head. "I have never bothered to memorize it. Why memorize something that's already written down? There's only so much room in my brain and I need it to remember the important things."

"Darn it. Well, would you mind helping Noley assemble a few canapés?"

"Certainly I'll help."

"Thanks, Mom."

Bev sauntered off toward the house, waving to friends and strangers alike.

The rest of the party went smoothly, with the exception of one incident involving Fred and a little accident that several people stepped in.

CHAPTER 4

It was well after midnight when all the guests had finally left. Bill had taken Bev and Fred home and returned to enjoy a glass of wine with Noley, Lilly, and Hassan. The kids were both on their phones in their rooms. Tighe had gone upstairs after the party; he was exhausted, but said he had enjoyed the celebration. He seemed to have let go of the uneasiness that had gripped him right after the fire.

The four adults sat in the backyard, talking in low voices next to the fire pit, which was still flickering. Lilly had told Hassan all about the house fire and how Tighe had been next door when it happened.

"I still don't understand why the police have to talk to Tighe again," Lilly fretted.

Bill sighed. "I don't think it's anything to worry about. I told you. One of the kids just said he remembered seeing Tighe leave at some point during the party, and the next thing he knew Tighe was back and the house next door was on fire."

"Am I supposed to take him to the police station tomorrow, or is someone coming here?" Lilly asked.

"If he remembers where he went, if he actually did go

anywhere, it would probably look good if you went in without having to be called in," Bill answered.

"But then they'll know I've talked to you about it."

"That's okay. In the morning, ask Tighe if he left the party for *any* reason, even to use the bathroom. If he remembers doing that, go down to the station and tell them about it. If he doesn't remember, wait for someone from the station to come to you."

"Okay." Lilly knew she would worry about it all night long.

"Lilly, do you have a costume yet for the Independence Day celebration?" Noley asked. Lilly was grateful for the change of subject, even if it meant talking about the upcoming celebration.

"Yes," she answered, suppressing a groan.

"What's this about? What do you need a costume for?" Hassan asked.

"It's this thing the Chamber of Commerce does every year for the Fourth of July," Lilly explained. "The Main Street merchants dress up as American colonists and there's a big reenactment of the signing of the Declaration of Independence."

"That sounds fun," Hassan said.

"You'd think so, wouldn't you? And it would be if we didn't have to dress up in period costume," Lilly replied.

"Whose idea was this?" Hassan asked.

"I don't even know," Lilly replied. "It's been going on forever. It's one of those things where nobody asks why it's been done--they just say 'it's always been done this way so we're going to keep doing it.'"

Hassan nodded.

"Who gets to be Thomas Jefferson?" he asked.

"Anton Beauregard, who owns the barber shop," Lilly answered. "He's been playing Thomas Jefferson for a few years and he's actually pretty good at it. It used to be Orson

Weaver, the guy who owns the Main Street Diner, but he had to give up the role because he wanted to be at the diner on the evening of July Fourth."

"That diner has great food," Hassan said.

"I agree," Bill said.

"Speaking of Orson and his great food," Lilly said, looking at Hassan. "You should have seen the review of the diner in the newspaper a couple weeks back."

"What?" Hassan asked. "Was it bad?"

"It was awful. I felt so bad for him," Lilly said. The others nodded their agreement. "The reviewer picked the wrong day to visit. Orson wasn't even there. He was out doing something for his mother and he left his staff in charge. When they saw the reviewer come in, they panicked."

"So what happened?" Hassan asked.

"They sat him at a table that hadn't been cleaned yet, so that started everything off on a sour note. Then they messed up his order, served him something he happened to be allergic to, and got the bill wrong. It was a complete disaster. When Orson came back and found out what had happened, he emailed the reviewer to explain and ask for another chance, but the reviewer refused. He told Orson that his experience was real and true and would be reported that way. And that's exactly what he did."

"So did it affect the diner's sales at all?"

"Definitely," Lilly said. "Tourists aren't going in because they're reading the review on travel sites, and even some locals are staying away."

"I feel bad for him," Noley said. "He has always been good about selling my baked goods in the diner. He doesn't have to do that."

"And he's sold a lot of them, hasn't he?" Bill asked Noley.

"Yeah. Several people have called and placed orders because they buy my stuff at the diner and it has my name on it."

"We should do something to help him," Lilly said. "Maybe my last meeting as Chamber of Commerce president should be held at the diner. That would bring more merchants in, and they could pass along a recommendation when someone asks for a good place to eat."

"That's a great idea," Noley said.

"Then it's settled. I'll call Orson tomorrow and chat with him. I'd like to know how he's doing," Lilly said.

Before Lilly went to bed that night she knocked on Tighe's bedroom door.

"Come in," he called.

She stood inside the doorway, trying to look nonchalant. "I'm headed to bed. I just wanted to congratulate you one more time. I'm really proud of you, you know."

Tighe smiled. "I know you are. Thanks, and thanks for the party. It was fun."

"I'm glad you were able to enjoy it after…you know. The fire," Lilly said.

"I wasn't really interested in having the party at first, but then I started feeling more like myself," Tighe answered.

"Good."

"I wonder if the police will be able to find who started it." This was the segue Lilly had been waiting for.

"I'm sure they will, as long as everyone they talk to answers them truthfully," Lilly said.

He gave her a look that was unreadable.

"What do you mean by that?" he asked.

"Nothing," she said with a shrug. "I'm just glad you stayed at the party the whole time. That way you can't be under suspicion."

"Why would you think I would ever be under suspicion?" Tighe asked. His eyes narrowed. Lilly knew he could tell she was fishing for information.

"Oh, I don't think you are. You *did* stay at the party, right?"

"Of course! Where else would I have gone?" His frustration was beginning to show.

"I don't know. Maybe the bathroom or the kitchen or something."

He paused. Lilly could see he was thinking.

"I don't think I did," he said.

"Whatever," she said, trying for a casual response. "If you remember leaving the party, we should just amend your police statement, that's all."

"Yeah. I know."

She walked over to his bed and kissed him on the forehead.

"Goodnight, honey."

"G'night, Mom."

She knew she had exasperated him. That had been happening more and more often as he approached the end of his high school years, and she supposed it was to be expected.

The next morning, true to her word, Lilly phoned Orson as soon as she got into work.

"Orson, it's Lilly. How's everything going?"

"It's going okay, Lilly. Thanks for asking." Orson's voice was low and flat. Lilly knew he was lying.

"Are out-of-towners starting to come back?"

"Not yet, but hopefully they will. I've been asking my regulars to put reviews online, so that helps."

"I'm calling to see if we can host a Chamber of Commerce event at the diner," Lilly said.

"Lilly, you don't have to do that."

"I know, of course, but I'd really love to have my retiring-from-the-Chamber party at the diner. Can you do it?"

"Absolutely! When is it?"

"Mid-September. We can talk about details as it gets closer. I just wanted to put it on your radar. Thanks, Orson."

"Thank *you*, Lilly."

She hung up the phone just as Harry, her shop assistant, walked in through the back door of the jewelry shop.

"Morning, Harry," Lilly said.

"Good morning. It's hot out there!" he exclaimed. He went right to work, pulling items out of the vault and taking them into the main room in the shop to set up the displays for the day.

That man is a Godsend, thought Lilly. After the disaster of employing Taffy the previous Christmas, Harry had been like a breath of fresh, non-crazy air. The nephew of her mentor, Robert, Harry was as knowledgeable about the jewelry business as anyone Lilly knew.

Lilly had known Harry when he was a child, but he had moved with his parents to Arizona before reaching middle school. When Robert retired to Arizona to live closer to his sister and brother-in-law, Harry had returned to Juniper Junction just as Lilly was ready to take the plunge and hire another assistant. And though Harry had only been working at the shop for a few months, Lilly already thought of him as family. He was tall and lanky, with light brown hair that fell over his left eye whenever he bent down. He had a wide smile that the customers, especially the ladies, loved. Lilly was thrilled to have him working with her.

"Harry," she said when he came into the back room for more display pieces, "I've got an assignment for you."

"What is it?" he asked eagerly.

"I want you to take part in the Independence Day festivities on Main Street."

"What festivities?"

"You've been away from Juniper Junction for so long you probably don't even remember what goes on for July Fourth."

He squinted his eyes, thinking, then shook his head. "Nope."

"Well, you're in for a real treat. The merchants on Main Street dress up in colonial costumes and toward evening there's a reenactment of the signing of the Declaration of Independence."

"That sounds fun!" he exclaimed.

Lilly chuckled. "That's not the word I use to describe it."

"Why?" he asked.

"Because it's hot and sweaty in those costumes. I can only hope the costume shop washes them between wearings." She effected a shudder for Harry's benefit. He laughed.

"What costume shop do we use?" he asked.

"A big one in Denver. I've already placed my order. I'll call one in for you over the next day or two. You can go onto their website and choose the costume you'd like."

"Cool!" He bustled around the back room, readying more displays. "Maybe I'll be Thomas Jefferson," he said excitedly.

"Taken!" Lilly called back. "You'll have to choose a peon. All the big 'whigs' have been assigned," she added, using her fingers to make quotation marks in the air. She laughed at her own colonial humor. "Ha! Get it?"

Harry walked toward the front of the shop, grimacing and shaking his head. "That was so bad." Lilly kept laughing.

One of the reasons Lilly loved having an assistant, besides being able to spend more time with her mom and her kids, was that having Harry around allowed her more time to do the ubiquitous paperwork and marketing for the shop. Trusting Harry the way she did, she was confident he would be able to handle things while she worked in the office, which is what she did that morning.

But she didn't count on Mrs. Laforge coming into the store before lunch. Lilly was working on ideas for a Christmas in July promotion when there was a tap on the office door. Harry stuck his head in.

"Sorry to bother you, but there's someone out here who's insisting on talking to you."

"Who is it?" Lilly asked.

"I don't know. An older lady," Harry said.

"All right. I'll talk to her." Lilly stood up and followed Harry into the front of the store, where she was surprised to see Mrs. Laforge standing in front of the diamond necklaces.

"Hi, Mrs. Laforge. How can I help you?" Lilly asked, using her sweetest voice.

Edna Laforge whirled around and glared at Lilly. Lilly had the sinking feeling Mrs. Laforge was not in the store to buy baubles.

"You can help me by telling your kids to be a little quieter," she grumbled.

"Are the kids being loud?" Lilly asked, surprised. She had assumed they would both sleep late because it was the first day of summer vacation.

"Isn't that what I just implied?" Mrs. Laforge sneered.

Lilly took a deep breath. "I hope you didn't trouble yourself to come down here to tell me. You could have called, you know."

"I know that. I happened to be in the neighborhood doing some shopping. Heaven knows I had to get out of my house before that racket got any worse."

"Thanks for coming in, Mrs. Laforge. I'll phone the kids and ask them to be quieter."

"And tell them to keep that dog from barking, too!" The older woman swept out of the shop, a scowl on her normally-scowling face. Lilly could practically hear her harumphing as she walked up the block.

"Friend of yours?" Harry asked with a chuckle.

"My neighbor. She's not happy if she's not complaining about something."

"I heard what she said. I can't believe your kids would disturb the peace like that."

"I'll give them a call and find out what's going on." Lilly went back to the office and sat down at the desk. She dialed her house and waited for someone to answer.

CHAPTER 5

"Hello?" It was Laurel, and she sounded out of breath.

"Laurel, Mrs. Laforge was just here complaining about you two. And Barney, of course. Is there anything going on that I should know about?"

There was silence for just a moment too long on the other end.

"Laurel? Answer me."

"It's nothing, Mom. Don't worry. Tighe and I were fighting, that's all."

Lilly narrowed her eyes as if Laurel could see her. "If you were ten, I'd believe you. But you two don't fight like that."

"Well, we did today."

"What was the fight about?"

"Taking Barney for a walk."

"Don't lie to me, Laurel."

"Mom, everything's fine. I've got to go."

"Wait--" Lilly said, but there was a *click* on the other end.

She sighed. The kids couldn't really be fighting, could they? They were getting too old for that nonsense. Still, what with his senior year ending and so many changes coming up soon, Tighe had been on edge lately. It would only get worse after that house fire. Mrs. Laforge would just have to cut them some slack.

At lunchtime Hassan came in just as she was taking the last bite of the sandwich she had brought from home.

He kissed her and hugged her, then held her away from him. "You are just beautiful, you know that?" he asked with a broad smile.

"No. Tell me again."

"You're beautiful. And I have a surprise."

"What is it?" Her mind was happily reeling with romantic images of a fancy dinner, flowers, or possibly a weekend getaway.

"I'm going to dress up as a colonist for Independence Day, too," he said, beaming.

Her shoulders fell.

"What's wrong?" he asked.

"Oh, nothing. That's a wonderful surprise," she said.

"You wanted something different, didn't you?"

"No, no. I think it's great," she said without enthusiasm.

"Would you like my surprise better if it came with reservations at eight tonight at the Water Wheel Restaurant?" His eyes twinkled.

"Definitely!" They had gone to dinner at the Water Wheel on their first date and it was their favorite romantic restaurant.

"Hassan, before you go home, would you mind swinging by my house and checking on the kids? I just want to make sure everything's okay. Mrs. Laforge came by to complain about the noise they're making and it just doesn't sound like them."

"Sure. She actually came by here?"

Lilly rolled her eyes in a wordless response.

"I'll head over there now. I've got someone coming over to the house to talk about replacing the carpets with hardwood floors."

Shortly after Hassan had met Lilly and their relationship

started getting more serious, he had bought a house in Juniper Junction so he would have a place to stay whenever he came for a visit. Though he lived in Minnesota, he made time to visit often. Lilly loved helping him decorate, and it had been her suggestion to put in hardwood floors.

She smiled at him. "Thanks. Shall I meet you at the Water Wheel at eight?"

"Sure," he said, leaning in to peck her on the cheek. "See you then. I'll call if there's anything amiss at your house."

She gave a little wave as he left the shop, then drank the last of her iced tea and leafed through some invoices until the next customer came in.

As the afternoon grew longer and she didn't hear from Hassan, she figured everything was fine at home. She wanted to ask him what the kids had been doing, but she decided to wait until dinner. She always kept a spare dress in the back room of the store in case she had a spur-of-the-moment Chamber of Commerce event, and it came in handy to go out to dinner, too. She hastily put it on after closing the store and drove to the Water Wheel.

Hassan, as always, looked gorgeous. His ivory Oxford played up his Middle Eastern features. Lilly sometimes couldn't believe her good fortune in finding someone who was so easy on the eyes.

He waited until she had pulled her car next to his, then opened the door for her. She reached for her purse and then stood looking at him, beaming, while he closed the door for her. He reached for her hand.

"How was your day?" he asked.

"Great, except for Mrs. Laforge. How were the kids? Good, I assume, since I didn't hear from you."

He nodded. "Everything seemed fine. The place was quiet. When I went inside Laurel was at the kitchen table eating lunch and she said Tighe was up in his room. I didn't go up to bother him."

"I'm sure he's still tired from last night," Lilly said. "I wonder if they were really fighting."

They walked into the restaurant, where the sounds of soft jazz and clinking silverware mingled with the delectable aromas coming from the kitchen.

"That Edna Laforge drives me crazy," Lilly said. She couldn't stop thinking about her neighbor's complaints.

"We're on a date, remember?" Hassan asked, squeezing Lilly's hand. "If I wanted to spend my time thinking about Mrs. Laforge, I would have invited her."

Lilly laughed. He was right. She wasn't at the Water Wheel to worry about Mrs. Laforge's problems; she was there to enjoy a quiet dinner for two with Hassan, which is exactly what she did. After they had enjoyed a leisurely dinner and shared a dessert, they remained at the table, talking and laughing as though they were the only two people in the world. It was just the sort of relaxing evening Lilly needed after the emotionally-draining graduation week and the fire.

It was late when Hassan left for his house and she for hers. She wondered what the kids had done all day.

"I'm home, guys!" she called from the bottom of the stairs.

No answer.

"Tighe! Laurel!" she called. "Where are you?"

Again, no answer.

Barney raced into the kitchen to greet Lilly, and as she stroked his ears, she dialed Tighe's cell number.

"Hello?"

"Tighe, where are you? What are you doing?"

"I'm at Mike's house."

"Why didn't you text me to tell me where you were going?"

"I forgot, Mom. I'm sorry."

"Where's Laurel?"

She could practically hear him shrugging. "She went

downtown, I think. Her phone battery is dead, though, so before you even ask, that's why she didn't text you."

"Why was Mrs. Laforge so angry this morning?"

"Because there was a commotion in the street and it was loud for a few minutes."

"What kind of commotion?"

"Just some people in the street yelling. No big deal."

"Laurel said you two were fighting."

Tighe didn't answer.

"So which is it?" Lilly asked.

"I don't know," Tighe said.

Someone's lying, Lilly thought.

"All right. When are you coming home?"

"I won't be long."

"What are you doing over there? Does it still smell from the fire?"

"Mike and I are just hanging out. And yes, everything smells terrible."

"Why don't you and Mike come over here?"

Tighe sighed and she could hear the exasperation in his voice. "Because I'm already here, Mom. I promise I'll be home soon."

"Okay. Love you."

Lilly put on a pair of pajamas and was making herself a cup of hot tea when Tighe came home.

"Hi, Mom."

He opened the refrigerator and rummaged around until he found a jar of olives and a brick of cheese.

"Hungry?" Lilly asked.

"Yeah, and tired. I have to work in the morning," he answered, reaching into the jar and pulling out two olives before he sliced two thick pieces of cheese. Tighe had gotten a summer job at a flooring store outside Juniper Junction and had only worked a couple shifts before school ended.

"Can you wake me up before you go to work tomorrow morning?" he asked.

"Sure thing," Lilly answered. "Sleep well."

Tighe popped the olives into his mouth and headed for the stairs.

He tripped going up the stairs.

"Ow!" he exclaimed.

"Are you all right?" Lilly asked.

"Yeah. Just preoccupied, I guess."

Poor kid is still in shock over that fire. He shouldn't have gone back over to Mike's, Lilly thought with a sigh. The back door opened and Laurel came in.

"Where have you been, young lady?" Lilly asked.

"I went to a movie downtown," Laurel said. "With Nick."

Lilly had mixed feelings about Nick. Sure, he had been a huge help when Lilly had needed it most over the holidays, but she always felt a little off-balance around him. She never quite knew what his intentions were regarding her daughter.

She pushed those conflicting thoughts aside with an effort and smiled at Laurel. "Was it good?"

"Loved it."

Lilly cleared her throat with an *ahem* sound. "Laurel, leave me a note next time you go out and your phone is dead. I was worried not knowing where you were."

"Mom, you worry too much," she said, rolling her eyes.

"Do I." It was more of a statement than a question. Lilly could hardly wait for the day when her own daughter had children of her own and would know what real worrying was all about.

"Laurel, is Tighe okay?" Lilly asked.

Laurel had been reaching for a cupcake in the refrigerator and she paused just long enough for Lilly to notice.

"He's not." Lilly said, answering her own question.

"I didn't say anything," Laurel protested.

"You didn't have to. I could see it in the way you reached for the cupcake."

Laurel closed her eyes as if she couldn't stand her mother's mother-ness any longer. "Mom, he's fine. Don't worry about him."

"Promise?" Lilly knew asking one teenager to make promises about the well-being of another teenager was ill-advised.

"Promise. I'm going to bed."

"Eat that cupcake downstairs, Laurel."

Laurel sighed and gobbled the cupcake over the kitchen sink before dashing upstairs.

It was like she couldn't get out of the kitchen fast enough.

CHAPTER 6

Lilly didn't sleep a wink that night for worrying about Tighe and the fire. Was it possible he knew something about it? He hadn't been himself since the fire, but was that really so unusual? What kid would act normally if he had witnessed a house burning down?

Lilly was getting ready for work when Tighe went downstairs for breakfast the next morning.

"Hi, Mom."

"Hi, honey. Listen, there's something I want to talk to you about real quick."

Tighe groaned. "Mom, I have to be at work by eight."

"I know. I just wanted to make sure there's nothing you remember about the fire that you may have forgotten to tell the police."

"Why do you keep asking me about this?" he asked in a voice suddenly tinged with anger. Lilly didn't answer.

He gave his head a little shake. "I told the police everything."

"You didn't even leave the party to go to the bathroom or anything?" Lilly prompted. She knew she shouldn't be asking such a leading question, but this was her son, for heaven's sake. She was going to do everything she could think of to help him. And she knew the police wanted to talk to him, whereas he had no idea.

Tighe raised his voice. "I don't know. Probably. Why?"

"Don't yell at me, young man."

"Why do the police care if I went to the bathroom?"

"Because you told them you didn't leave the party."

"But even if I went to the bathroom, I was still at the party."

This was getting ridiculous.

"Tighe, did you go to the bathroom or didn't you?" Lilly's voice rose a notch.

"Mom, what's wrong with you?" Tighe gave her a most disrespectful look of disdain. Lilly had had about enough.

"I was trying to keep from telling you this, but since you insist on arguing with me, someone told the police that you left the party for a few minutes right before the fire started." Her shoulders slumped and she fixed Tighe with a look of pain and hurt.

His look mirrored hers. "Who said that?" he asked.

"I don't know. So did you leave the party? For any reason?"

He bit thoughtfully into a banana and chewed slowly. "I did use the bathroom, but I can't remember when it was."

"Well, you weren't at the party for very long before the fire broke out. Could it have been just before that happened?"

"I guess it must have been. Everything is jumbled up in my memory."

"I don't doubt it. That was a traumatic experience. But, Tighe, the police want to talk to you again."

Tighe's voice turned plaintive. "Can't Uncle Bill just tell them I used the bathroom?"

"They need to hear it from you. Why don't I drive you down to the police station later today and you can amend the statement you gave them at the scene?"

"Okay. I've got to go to work. This sucks."

"It sure does. But try not to say *sucks.*"

Tighe shook his head and went out the back door, his shoulders sagging. Lilly followed him shortly afterward and went to work.

She was in her office going through paperwork when Noley came in later that morning.

"That new bistro that finally took over Herb Knight's yoga studio after he died is doing a bang-up business. There's a line out the door," Noley said.

"Have you been in there yet?" Lilly asked.

"No. Have you?"

"No. I've met the owners, though. They joined the Chamber of Commerce before they even opened the bistro, so they were at an event a month or so ago."

"What are they like?"

"They're a husband-and-wife team. Their names will come to me in a minute. They were both educated in Paris and they moved here from New York City 'to get away from the rat race,' they said." Lilly used her fingers to make quotation marks in the air.

"That's pretty far to come to get away from the rat race."

"I think they vacationed here once or something. They loved it and decided to come back. Oh, I remember now. Their names are Armand and Cerise Deveau."

Noley paused. "Wait a sec. Deveau? I know someone by that name--Kathleen Deveau. I can't stand her."

"Maybe they're related," Lilly said.

"Hmm," Noley answered.

"They seem nice enough. Want to go over there for lunch? My treat. I can introduce you," Lilly offered.

"Sounds good. I'll come back in an hour or so," Noley asked.

"See you then."

A short time later Lilly took her laptop to the front of the store. "Harry, I'm placing your order now for the Independence Day costume."

"Cool!" Harry exclaimed. Lilly smiled. She loved his enthusiasm. She only wished she shared it.

He came to look over her shoulder as she placed the order for his costume. "Are you sure this is what you want?" Lilly asked. "Once I hit *Send* you have to wear it."

"I'm sure. What's wrong with it?" He sounded a little bit hurt.

"Nothing," Lilly hastened to assure him. "It just looks so hot. Long sleeves, a hat, the works. You're sure?"

"Positive. Hit *Send*."

She clicked the button on the screen and closed the laptop. "It should be here in plenty of time," she said. "I hope the weather doesn't get any hotter or we might lose you to the heat."

Harry chuckled. "I never knew anyone who hates the heat as much as you do."

Lilly rolled her eyes. "I didn't always hate the heat. It's a female thing, if you know what I mean."

Harry cocked his head to one side. He obviously wasn't familiar with the finer points of womanhood.

Lilly laughed. "Never mind. I'm going to lunch with Noley in a little while. Can you mind things here?"

"Sure thing, boss," he said with a grin.

"I hate it when you call me that."

"I know."

Lilly shook her head, smiling, as she walked back to the office to grab her purse. Noley was waiting for her when she went out into the blinding sunshine on Main Street.

"So is it real French food, or is it Americanized French?" Noley asked as they walked to the bistro.

"I think it's real, but I've never been to France," Lilly said. "You would probably know better."

They walked into the bistro, which was light and bright

and cool. The line snaked in front of the glass-front sandwich case. The small distressed wooden tables were almost full. Curtains hung across the lower portions of the large windows facing the street, and short valances hung above the windows.

"I feel like I'm back in Paris," Noley said quietly. "It's so cute in here."

"I hope the food is good," Lilly said. "I'm starving."

They walked up to the end of the line and looked at the blackboard that hung on the wall near one of the large windows. The day's specials were listed in handsome script.

Avocat sauce crevettes, salade verte, steak frites. Everything sounded delicious. When it was their turn to order, Lilly chose the classic *Croque Madame* and Noley chose the onion soup with *Gruyère* and a hunk of bread.

They sat down to wait for their food, soaking in the atmosphere and watching the passers-by out on the sidewalk.

When the server brought their food to them, Lilly smiled at her. "Hi, Cerise. Do you remember me? I'm Lilly Carlsen--I own the jewelry store on Main."

"*Mais oui*, but of course I remember you," Cerise said, setting their food on the table.

"I'd like you to meet my friend, Noley Appleton," Lilly said, gesturing toward Noley.

Noley offered her hand and Cerise shook it. "Nice to meet you," said Noley. "You have a beautiful bistro."

"*Merci*," said Cerise. "I have heard of you," she continued, fixing her gaze on Noley. "You are a baker, no?"

"Well, I do bake, but I'm just an all-around cook, I guess," Noley said. She was being modest--she was much more than just an 'all-around cook.'

"Perhaps we can try your food sometime," Cerise said. She smiled at the two women. "I'll let you two eat in peace. Just let me know if you need anything."

Lilly and Noley nodded at Cerise and tucked into their food as soon as she left the table. Noley took one sip of the soup and leaned back with a contented smile on her face. "This. This is what French onion soup should taste like. Want to try it?"

Lilly shook her head. "No, thanks. I'm going to have a hard enough time finishing my own meal. This is delicious."

"No wonder this bistro is doing so well," Noley said. "If everything tastes as good as this, they're going to be the only game in town before long."

Lilly nodded. "I'll have to bring Hassan here. He likes French food."

They ate the rest of their meal in delighted silence, savoring the simplicity of the French food and the cool light of the bistro.

When Lilly had paid the bill and she and Noley were getting ready to leave the bistro, Armand came out of the kitchen to greet them. He was wiping his hands on a dish towel and smiling and nodding at diners.

"I hope you ladies enjoyed your meal," he said, bowing slightly at the waist.

"We loved every bite," Lilly assured him. She introduced Noley to Armand.

After they shook hands Armand said to Noley, "Your reputation precedes you, *Mademoiselle* Appleton. It is an honor to have such a renowned cook in our bistro. I hope you will grace us with your presence again soon, and I would love to try some of your cooking sometime."

As he spoke, Lilly noticed Cerise watching them through the window in the swinging door leading to the kitchen.

Noley smiled. "Thank you, Armand, but you exaggerate. And of course I would be happy to oblige. I'm sure we'll be back soon, and we can talk again then." She shook hands with him a second time and left with Lilly in tow.

"Pretty smooth, huh?" Lilly asked.

"Some things are so smooth you can choke on them,"

Noley replied with a roll of her eyes. "That was a bit too sickly sweet, don't you think?"

"I thought so. But maybe French men have a different way of speaking to women."

"Not *that* different," Noley said with a grimace. They made their way up the street to the jewelry store.

"Why didn't you ask them if they're related to Kathleen Deveau?" Lilly asked.

"I don't want to dislike them before I even know them," Noley answered.

CHAPTER 7

When Lilly entered the shop Harry greeted her with a wave while he attended to a couple who appeared to be interested in buying a silver chain. As usual, Harry was showing them every possible chain, from delicate to chunky, and his conversation was simultaneously knowledgeable and folksy. The couple were obviously enjoying the process and as Lilly listened a discreet distance away, it sounded like Harry might make at least one, and possibly two, sales. *He's a natural*, she thought to herself with a smile.

The shop phone rang and Lilly hurried to the back to answer it in private.

"Lilly? This is Myra at the Chamber office. I'm just confirming some of the arrangements for the Independence Day celebration so we don't end up with the same problem as last year."

Lilly grimaced. Last year's Independence Day celebration had been marred by the Chamber of Commerce's complete failure to have any food at the event. People were furious. It dampened the spirit of the event, and the Chamber almost had a revolution of its own on its hands. Lilly blamed herself, but it hadn't been her job to make the catering arrangements.

The office assistant for the Chamber did that, and she had dropped the ball, thinking it was someone else's responsibility. Still, since it happened on Lilly's watch, she felt responsible.

"Noley Appleton is catering the event. She's ready. I've talked to her about it several times."

"Great. We've also had a request from a new business that wants to take part. It's the couple who own that French bistro--you know, the ones who took over Herb Knight's yoga studio."

"I know them. In fact, I just had lunch there. What do they want to do for the celebration?"

"They actually asked if they could cater the whole thing."

Lilly couldn't believe her ears. "Cater the whole thing? It's a bit late in the game to be asking to be in charge of the entire event, isn't it?"

"We would have welcomed this a year ago," Myra pointed out in a dry tone.

"True. But I've already arranged the catering. Is there some small job we can give them for this year? Then maybe next year they can take a bigger role." Lilly would have liked to see Noley get the job every year, but it had to be fair; next year Lilly wouldn't be the president of the Chamber and wouldn't have a say in the catering at all.

"There must be something we can give them. Let me think," Myra replied. She was silent for a few moments, then said, "I know. How about asking them to create an ice cream bar? It'll be hot out and everyone loves ice cream."

"Good idea. That shouldn't be too hard on short notice, either. Maybe some chopped nuts, hot fudge sauce, whipped cream, cherries, that sort of thing."

"I'm on it," Myra said. "I'll give them a call this afternoon and set it up."

"Thanks, Myra."

Lilly was able to get some paperwork done before Tighe came in after work.

"Hi, Mom." His voice was flat; Lilly suspected the police investigation of the fire hadn't been far from his mind all day.

"Hi. You ready? This shouldn't take long." *At least I hope not*, Lilly thought to herself.

She drove to the police station and told the desk sergeant why they were there. Tighe hadn't said a word since leaving the jewelry shop.

"Have a seat and I'll see if there's someone who can take his statement," the officer said.

They waited for several minutes before the officer returned. "I can take you back now," he said.

Tighe and Lilly stood up to follow him, but he stopped.

"How old are you?" he asked Tighe.

"Eighteen."

"You can come back by yourself if you want."

Tighe looked at Lilly, who looked back at him. *Is he actually thinking of excluding me?* she wondered.

"There's really no reason for you to come back, Mom. I'm just going to tell them I went to the bathroom. I should handle this by myself." He stood up a little taller and squared his shoulders, placing his hand on Lilly's shoulder as he did so.

"Don't worry about me, Mom. I'll be fine."

"Okay." It was all she could say. She didn't know whether to be proud of him or cry. She turned around and sat down in one of the uncomfortable plastic chairs in the vestibule. She tried scrolling through emails on her phone, but she couldn't focus. She tried reading a magazine. Same result. She tried to guess why other civilians in the police station were there and her breathing became ragged and irregular. She couldn't stand the thought of Tighe being interrogated back there like a common criminal. All he did was forget that he went to the bathroom, for God's sake.

When Tighe finally reappeared, Lilly stood up so fast she dropped her purse and tripped over one of her own feet. Tighe reached for her elbow to steady her, laughing.

"What's so funny?" she demanded. She could feel the heat creeping into her cheeks.

"Nothing." He kept laughing. "Mom, really. You need to calm down. Everything is fine. You'll hurt yourself worrying."

She turned on her heel and marched out to the car with her son following close behind.

"So what happened?" she asked as she pulled into traffic.

"I just told the policeman that I wanted to make a change to the statement I made at the Fosters' house and he said that would be fine. So he handed me a pad of paper, I wrote that I left the party for a few minutes to go to the bathroom, and signed it. He read it and said I could leave. That's all. I'm eighteen, Mom. Almost nineteen. I could handle it alone."

"I know. I just don't like to think of you growing up, that's all." If she wasn't careful, the tears were going to start flowing again.

"Are we having dinner at Hassan's house?" Tighe asked. "I'm starving." She smiled, knowing he was changing the subject so she wouldn't start bawling in the car.

"Yes. We'll stop at home and pick up Laurel first."

"I'll just take my car," Tighe offered. "That way you can stay later if you want."

"That's fine."

They rode the rest of the way home in silence. Lilly was thinking about how quickly her kids were growing up and she assumed Tighe was mentally reviewing his trip to the police station.

Lilly drove over to Hassan's house with the kids following closely behind in Tighe's car.

She was impressed anew each time she walked into the spacious foyer at the house Hassan had purchased in Juniper Junction. For a second home, it seemed pretty grand. She often wondered what his home in Minnesota looked like. When she had asked him, he told her it was nothing more than a bachelor pad, but she was skeptical.

The kids loved his house, too. There was a pool in the backyard and they intended to make good use of it during the summer. They brought their bathing suits from home and Hassan had told them they should keep a spare suit at his house.

"Last one in the pool has to do the dishes!" Hassan called as they made their way through the house. Tighe and Laurel broke into a sprint and Hassan stood aside to let them dash past him and through to the French doors leading to the patio.

Lilly laughed as she walked up to Hassan and kissed him. "You know all the right things to say, don't you?"

"I hope so," he answered, placing his hand in the small of her back and steering her toward the kitchen. "Come on," he said. "You have to see what I got for us to grill for dinner."

They were sea scallops--huge, juicy, and the perfect shade of white. There was a pile of fresh vegetables next to them, ready for grilling.

"Ooh. Scallops are my favorite," Lilly said.

"I know. I thought we could put them in a citrus marinade for a few minutes, then throw them on the grill."

"Noley better watch out if you keep cooking like this. She'll have competition."

"Noley has nothing to worry about, believe me."

Hassan poured two glasses of wine while Lilly got to work washing and slicing the vegetables. Hassan had bought zucchini, summer squash, eggplant, and gigantic onions. Lilly tossed everything in olive oil, sprinkled them with sea salt and pepper, and arranged them on a tray bound for the grill on the patio. Hassan mixed the ingredients for the marinade.

They watched the kids in the pool for a while before making dinner; Laurel was beating Tighe in most of their races from one end to the other. Tighe was the better swimmer; for some reason, he was letting her win. Lilly smiled. By the time dinner was ready, both kids were ready for a break from the pool. Everyone enjoyed a delicious meal before adjourning to the fireplace on the edge of the patio to make s'mores. After dinner Lilly offered to do the dishes despite Laurel having been the last one in the pool.

Hassan joined Lilly in the kitchen. "So, are you going to be my date for the Independence Day celebration?" he asked, nuzzling her ear.

She giggled. "Unless I get a better offer," she teased.

"Get a room, you two," Laurel said from behind them. She laughed. "It's so gross to watch your mom kissing."

Lilly whirled around. "Where did you come from?"

"I have to get home. Nick is coming to get me and we're going to a drive-in tonight."

"Another movie? How are you getting home right now?"

"Tighe's taking me. He's out in the car already."

"Okay. I'll be along as soon as I finish up here," Lilly said.

"All right. See you later." Laurel pecked her mother, then Hassan, on the cheek.

Lilly shook her head when Laurel left. "It's hard to believe how fast they're growing up," she said. A wistful look clouded her eyes.

"It means you've done a great job with both of them," Hassan said. "If they can go out and be independent and do things and make decisions for themselves, your work has been a success."

"I still worry about Tighe," Lilly said. "He seems not quite himself yet after that fire. And going back to Mike's house...I just can't figure out why he'd torture himself like that."

"Who can know why teenage boys do anything?" Hassan asked. "I was one myself, a thousand years ago, and I still don't understand half the stupid things I did."

Lilly smiled at him. She couldn't imagine him doing anything stupid, but the whole teenage boy argument was hard to deny. She drank the last of her wine, washed the glass, and told Hassan she needed to get home, too.

"I wish you'd stay," he said.

"I'd love to stay, but the house is a mess and I need to get some cleaning done. I don't know when I'll get time to do it otherwise," she said. "What with the Independence Day celebration coming up, there's a lot more work to do for the Chamber, and I want this celebration to be the best one Juniper Junction has ever had."

"I have a feeling it will be," Hassan said. He kissed her before she walked down the path of pavers leading to the driveway. She turned around and waved to him. "I'll come by the shop to see you tomorrow!" he called.

She gave him a thumbs-up and drove away.

When she arrived at home, Barney greeted her with a frenzy of affection, as usual. She called for Tighe, knowing Laurel wouldn't be home, and was surprised when there was no answer.

"Tighe?" she called again.

No answer.

She knew it was no use worrying about him, but that didn't stop her. Her fingers itched to call him, but if she called right now it would probably only annoy him. He had reached the point where he didn't appreciate his mother checking up on him every time he was out of the house, and truth be told, that was a hard thing for any mom.

So she did what worried mothers everywhere do--she cleaned with a ferocity that surprised even her. When she had cleaned both bathrooms and mopped the kitchen floor, dusted every room downstairs, and vacuumed the stairs, she put all her cleaning supplies away and figured she'd waited long enough.

It was time to call him, whether it made him mad or not.

CHAPTER 8

"Hi, Mom." Tighe answered on the first ring.

"Where are you?" Lilly asked.

"At Jimmy's house." Jimmy had been on the basketball team with Tighe.

"When are you coming home?"

"I'll be home in a half hour or so. Is that okay?"

"All right. Please text me if you're going to be any later."

"Okay. Bye, Mom. Love you." He hung up.

Lilly sighed. She had to remind herself that he was practically a grown man and she couldn't chaperone his every move. She had to get used to giving him some space to make his own choices and mistakes. She hadn't heard Tighe mention Jimmy's name since the time Jimmy got in trouble for stalking a girl in their grade. She hoped Tighe wasn't making a mistake by getting friendly with him.

She flopped onto the couch and turned on the television, hoping for a decent show that could occupy her mind for a while.

She was just bemoaning the lack of tolerable programming when the phone rang. It was her mother.

"Mom, what are you doing up? It's late."

"I know. My fish is missing."

"You don't have a fish," Lilly said.

"I most certainly do. He's a goldfish. His name is Fred."

"Mom, Fred is the dog."

"I know. I named my fish the same thing so I wouldn't forget."

"Mom, why don't you go to bed? The fish may be back by morning."

"You're just patronizing me." *How can she know I'm patronizing her, but not know she doesn't have a fish?* Lilly thought, shaking her head.

"No, I'm not," she said, instead of voicing her real thoughts. "You're probably tired. Have you seen Bill today?"

"That sweet boy." Lilly almost broke her eyeballs from rolling them. "He came by earlier tonight to check on me. I don't know where he finds the time, what with his job and his marriage to Noley."

"They're not married."

"Of course they're married. You were at the wedding, for heaven's sake. Noley had the most beautiful dress..." Bev's voice drifted off at the memory of something that hadn't happened.

"Mom, why don't I give you a call in the morning? I can take an hour or so from work and take you shopping if you'd like."

"All right. That sounds nice. Shopping where?"

"Grocery shopping."

"Okay, I'll make a list. See you in the morning, dear."

"Bye, Mom." By the time Lilly hung up the phone Bev seemed to have forgotten about the fish, which was a relief. She texted Harry and asked him to open the shop in the morning so she could take her mother shopping. Having an assistant was a huge help in such situations.

True to his word, Tighe was home about a half hour later.

Lilly knew she shouldn't ask him about Jimmy, but she couldn't help herself.

"How's Jimmy these days? Getting into any more trouble?"

"He's not so bad, Mom. He just got in trouble that one time."

"Once was enough. That was pretty serious."

"He really liked that girl."

"That's no excuse for stalking her."

Tighe sighed. "Mom, remember what you used to say all the time? If you can't say something nice, keep your mouth shut?"

"I remember. Do you also remember me telling you that life is a series of choices, so the ones you make better be good?"

"Yes," Tighe answered in a mocking tone.

"Good. Then we're even. We both remember everything I've taught you. Now, tell me about Jimmy."

"What do you want to know?"

"Why'd you go to his house? I thought you two didn't really hang out anymore."

"We don't very often." Tighe shrugged. "But he's okay. We just played video games for a while. I'm going over there tomorrow night, too."

Lilly narrowed her eyes as she looked at her son, trying to decide if he was telling the whole truth. After deciding that he would tell her if there was something she needed to know, she opened the back door to let Barney out one last time. The dog did his business, then came bounding inside for a treat. Lilly turned to Tighe, who was rummaging through the fridge.

"I'm going to bed," she said. "Make sure you turn off the lights when you come upstairs. I have to take Gran grocery shopping tomorrow morning, so if there's anything you want, put it on my list."

"Okay. G'night, Mom."

Lilly and Barney went upstairs and Lilly was almost asleep by the time she lay back against her pillow.

She didn't know how long she had been asleep when she was awakened by voices coming from the patio. Rubbing her eyes, she hurried over to the window, but not before she bumped her shin on the bench at the foot of the bed.

"Ouch! Dammit." Under normal circumstances she would have been terrified to be awakened in the middle of the night by voices coming from just underneath her bedroom window.

But she recognized these voices.

"Tighe! Laurel! Stop it! You'll wake the dead--or at least Mrs. Laforge!" She threw the window sash up, her nostrils flaring. The kids stopped arguing immediately and silence reigned on the patio. Finally Laurel spoke.

"Sorry, Mom," she called softly.

"Sorry," Tighe echoed.

"What's the problem?" Lilly called softly.

"Nothing. We were just having a spirited discussion," Tighe answered.

"Spirited, my foot. You were fighting. Now let me get some sleep." Lilly returned to bed and all was quiet for the rest of the night. She didn't even hear the kids when they came upstairs.

Early the next day Lilly pulled up in front of Bev's house. Bev was waiting for her on the front porch, fanning herself. Lilly was relieved to see her mom--she had half expected Bev to be asleep when she arrived. *She must be having a good day*, she thought.

Bev slid into the front seat and leaned over to kiss Lilly on the cheek.

"Thank you for taking me shopping, dear. I only have a few things to pick up."

"What's on your list?" Lilly asked.

"Your father wants a six-pack of that beer I hate," Bev began, and Lilly groaned inwardly. Her father had passed away years ago. Maybe her mom wasn't having such a good day, after all.

"What else?" Lilly asked.

"Bird seed. And kibble for Fred." So she was referring to Fred the dog, not Fred the fish—good.

"That sounds pretty easy," Lilly said. She turned the radio to a station she knew Bev listened to in the house and they drove to the grocery store.

Lilly experienced a moment of hesitation when she and Bev went into the store. Should she accompany Bev to get the things on her list, or leave her mom to do her own shopping?

She decided on the latter, thinking Bev wouldn't appreciate a shopping chaperone. She liked her independence.

Lilly hadn't even gotten through the produce section when she heard her name. She turned to see who was there, suppressing a groan at having to actually talk to someone.

It was Orson Weaver.

"What are you doing here, Orson? I thought you'd be at the diner this time of day."

"Normally I am," he replied with a grimace. "We ran out of spinach and I had to make a quick run to get more. Anything new?"

"Not really, just here with my mom. Getting our shopping out of the way early."

"How's business?"

Shouldn't he be getting back to the diner with his spinach? Lilly thought with a trace of annoyance.

"Not bad." She knew better than to ask about his.

"Ready for the Fourth of July celebration?" he asked.

She pasted on her best smile. "We sure are. Harry and I have ordered our costumes and we're getting the shop ready, too. You?"

"I'm ready. I'm adding a few specials to the menu in honor of the occasion. You know, stuff like succotash and sweet potato mash with molasses."

"Yum," Lilly said. *How gross,* she thought.

"I hear Noley's catering the whole shebang," he said. "Too bad I'll miss it--I have to be at the diner all evening. Don't want to leave anyone else in charge, if you know what I mean."

"I know what you mean. But someone else is in charge over there right now, right?" Lilly asked.

"Yeah. I gotta get going. See you later, Lilly," he said, and strode toward the checkout lanes.

"Who was that?" Bev startled Lilly.

"The owner of the diner across the street from my shop," Lilly answered.

"Is he married?"

Lilly rolled her eyes. "I don't think so. And I'm taken, remember?"

"Of course I remember. I was only asking."

"Did you find everything you need?" Lilly asked, hurrying to change the subject.

"Almost. I thought I'd pick up a few things for lunch and invite Mildred over." Mildred was one of Bev's neighbors.

"Did you find the beer you needed?"

Bev stared at Lilly blankly.

"What for?"

Uh-oh, Lilly thought. She never knew whether it was better to play along when her mother was confused or explain the truth to her or ignore it altogether. This time her decision to play along had backfired.

"My mistake."

"I should say so. You know I hate beer."

Lilly nodded. "Why don't you finish up and I'll find you?"

Bev nodded and moved away. Lilly hurried to get everything on her list, omitting certain items the kids had added to it, such as copious amounts of junk food and soda.

Lilly found Bev in the paper products aisle. They went through the checkout without incident and headed home.

Lilly helped Bev take her grocery bags into the house, then sped back home to unload her own groceries and get to work.

Laurel was in the kitchen when Lilly got home. She immediately started peering into each bag.

"Did you get what I put on the list?" she asked, her brow furrowing.

"I will not take part in destroying your stomach lining with that garbage," Lilly said. "I bought fruit and cottage cheese, though. Have those." She tossed a plum to her daughter.

Laurel caught the plum and looked at it with disdain.

"Why bother telling us to write down what we want if you're not going to buy it?" she whined.

"I never promised to buy everything you write down. Now stop complaining and be glad you have a mother who looks out for your intestinal health.

"Got to go," she said, kissing Laurel's cheek. "I'll see you after work."

"Love you," Laurel grumbled. Barney, who didn't like to be excluded when there was any kissing going on, wiggled his way between Lilly and Laurel.

"Bye, Barney," Lilly said, leaning down and kissing the top of his head. His tail wagged furiously.

Lilly laughed and went to work.

Harry greeted her when she got to the shop. "Bad news, boss," he said.

"Stop calling me that. What's the bad news?" Lilly had learned that Harry's idea of bad news and hers were quite different, so she wasn't worried.

"Someone from the Chamber of Commerce called. They want you to emcee the events on the night of the Independence Day celebration."

But this time Harry was right--that *was* bad news. Lilly hated speaking in front of people. She had been able to avoid emceeing the event the previous year by having the good luck of coming down with a sore throat the day before, but she doubted she could get so lucky a second year in a row.

"Ugh. Did they say what I have to talk about? I hate speaking in front of crowds."

"The woman said it's up to you, but that she'd call back later and you two can discuss it."

"That's great. Just great. I suppose I'll have to wear that ridiculous costume while I'm up there. Between the costume and my nerves, I'm sure to drop dead."

Harry grinned. "I have faith in you. You'll do fine."

Lilly shook her head and got to work, figuring it would be best to keep her mind off her upcoming speaking engagement.

CHAPTER 9

The next morning Lilly turned on the television while she was getting ready for work and was greeted with news of another house fire. This one, on the outskirts of Juniper Junction, had consumed an unoccupied house, so no one had been hurt. Lilly listened to the news report with rapt attention, wondering what the chances were that two unoccupied houses had been damaged or destroyed by fire in less than a week. She shuddered.

Was there a firebug out there? Though the news report mentioned the first fire, there was no indication that town officials thought the two incidents were related. Lilly knew the general location of the house that had burned down. There were nice old homes out that way. Like the Fosters' neighbors, the owners of the home destroyed in last night's fire had already moved out and the house was for sale.

Chilly prickles stung Lilly's skin.

Something strange was going on in Juniper Junction.

She woke Tighe up for work before she left for the shop. He had been out late the night before, hanging out at Jimmy's house, as she recalled.

When she arrived at work, Harry was already there, putting out displays and humming to himself.

"Morning, Harry," Lilly said, smiling.

"Morning, Lilly. Say, did you hear there was another fire?"

Lilly nodded. "I did. Seems kind of strange, doesn't it, following so closely on the heels of the last one?"

Harry cocked his head and fixed Lilly with a hard stare. "I'll bet you're a conspiracy theorist. Do you think aliens killed JFK?"

Lilly rolled her eyes. "Of course I'm not a conspiracy theorist, and I don't think aliens killed JFK. This is different."

"I think you're looking too hard," Harry said. "It was nothing more than a coincidence. House fires happen all the time. That's why there's a fire department."

Lilly considered that. "Maybe you're right. Maybe I'm too close to the first one since Tighe was there when it happened. Maybe I'm just super-sensitive to fires right now."

"That's probably it. I wouldn't go worrying about some pyro on the loose. You have enough to worry about with the Independence Day celebration coming up."

Lilly sighed. "You're right about that. I've got to talk to Myra at the Chamber and see what she wants me to talk about when I make my grand speech."

Harry grinned. "I don't know why you're so worried. You'll do fine."

"Thanks."

Lilly didn't want to wait for Myra to call her, so she dialed the Chamber office and talked to Myra about the speech while Harry waited on the customers who came into the shop. Later in the morning she joined him.

Hassan came into the shop during the afternoon. The house fire hadn't been far from Lilly's mind all day, and she asked him about it as soon as he came in.

"Did you see the news this morning?"

"Yes. I assume you're talking about the second fire?" he replied.

She nodded. "Doesn't it seem strange to you that there were two house fires in such a short time span? Both were nice old homes and both were unoccupied."

"It's possible, but I don't think you need to get all worked up over it. Whoever is investigating it has no doubt noticed the same similarities. Have you talked to Tighe about it?"

"No. I didn't want to bring it up in case he didn't know about it. I don't want to get inside his head and get him all worried about fires."

"It's on the cover of the paper today, so I'm sure he knows about it if he didn't hear it on the news this morning."

"All right. I'll talk to him about it tonight."

Hassan was carrying a large shopping bag. Lilly nodded toward it. "What's in the bag?"

Hassan grinned. "You'll see. Can I go in the back for a minute?"

"Sure." Lilly gestured toward her office and Hassan went through the door. She heard the lock *click*.

What's he doing?

It didn't take long to figure out what Hassan had been doing in the office. When the door opened again, Hassan swept into the main room of the shop.

He was wearing a black tricorn hat, white breeches, an ivory linen shirt, and a handsome navy blue coat with red facing. Gold buttons marched up the edges of the facing.

Lilly gaped.

"What do you think?" Hassan asked, turning around slowly with his arms spread out. "Pretty convincing, huh?"

"It's beautiful," Lilly said. "You look so authentic. Aren't you going to be hot wearing that outdoors?"

"Probably," Hassan said with a shrug. "But it'll be nothing compared to what the real Revolutionary War soldiers experienced."

"Wow! That looks fantastic, Hassan!" Harry said, coming over and admiring the costume from every angle. "I hope I look that good in my costume."

"What costume did you choose, Harry?" Hassan asked.

"One that a merchant might have worn during the colonial period. You know, waistcoat, breeches, a gold watch. I figured I could tie in the jewelry shop with the costume. Maybe we'll sell some watches, who knows?" Harry grinned. Lilly shook her head affectionately.

"What does your costume look like?" Hassan asked Lilly.

"Just a dress. Nothing as fancy as yours," she said. "In fact, you may want to escort someone else to the celebration."

"Not a chance." Hassan pulled her into a hug, then stepped away. "You know, this thing is a little warm. I'll go take it off."

Lilly laughed. "I thought so. I'll have you complaining about the heat before you know it." Hassan winked at her and disappeared into the office again. She wondered how anyone could wear hot clothes in the summertime. She had never heard Hassan complain about the heat, and he always looked nice.

Men, she thought. *They have it so easy.*

The days marched quickly toward the Independence Day celebration, with merchants decorating their shops, the town's public works department being pressed into service to hang bunting and flags up and down Main Street, and citizens getting into the spirit of the holiday by decorating their homes with red, white, and blue lights, flags, and pinwheels galore.

Juniper Junction Jewelry was no exception. Harry and Lilly changed out the typical black velvet inside the jewelry display cases and replaced it with navy blue and rich red velvet. They hung twinkly lights in red, white, and blue around the interior of the shop and luxurious bunting on the display cases. The shop mirrored the elegant decorations that adorned Main Street.

While festive holiday elegance reigned downtown, Lilly visited Noley two nights before the celebration and found her best friend in a frenzied rush to tweak the catering menu and make sure everything would happen as planned and on schedule.

"What's up? You seem stressed," Lilly said, standing in the middle of Noley's kitchen and trying to figure out which course of action was smarter: helping or staying out of the way.

"I'm totally stressed," Noley admitted.

"Okay, so what can I do to help?" Lilly asked. "Put me to work."

Noley pointed to the sink. "You can start by washing those baking sheets. And thanks." She pushed a strand of hair from her eyes and smiled at Lilly. "Sorry if I seem frustrated. It's just that...I am frustrated. I feel like I may have taken on too much."

"I think you're going to be great," Lilly assured her. "This celebration will be a coup for you."

"Not if I can't get everything done on time."

"Remind me what's on the menu."

"I'm doing a red, white, and blue barbeque theme. There will be pulled pork with two sauces, an Alabama white sauce and red plum barbeque sauce, green salad with goat cheese and blueberries, watermelon pops, and dried cherry cookies. That's all the red, white, and blue there'll be. Then there'll also be baked beans and macaroni and cheese. Nothing really gourmet, but they've asked for enough food for a thousand people. And then there will be food trucks for people who prefer pizza and burgers."

"A thousand people," Lilly repeated, shaking her head. "How are you going to make that work?"

"I've got students from the culinary arts program at the community college helping me out, plus I'm using their facilities and vans to transport everything to the town square. The kids'll serve and I'll help wherever I'm needed. It's just a matter of organization. It'll be fine." Lilly wondered if Noley was trying to convince her or herself.

"Are you paying the kids?"

"No, I'm not allowed to. But they're all getting class credit for helping, and I'll also make a big donation to the culinary arts program."

"Sounds like a perfect solution."

"It would be if the assistant director of the program didn't hate me. It's that woman we were talking about--Kathleen Deveau."

"Why does she hate you?"

Noley sighed. "It's a long story," she said, whisking ingredients for the dark red plum barbeque sauce.

"I've got time," Lilly said. She was up to her elbows in dishwater.

"It goes back years. Kathleen and I went to culinary school together, but we were never friends. We applied for the same job right out of school, working for a Michelin-starred restaurant in Denver, and I got the job. I heard she came back here and managed the dining hall at the community college."

"Not exactly the same caliber as a Michelin-starred restaurant, is it?" Lilly asked.

"No. So I was already not her favorite person. Several years later I applied for the job I have now at Fine Dining Magazine as recipe development director. I was hired after the second interview, during which the interviewer let it slip that Kathleen was up for the job, too."

"So why is she agreeing to do this for you?"

"I think her boss, the director of the culinary program, told her to." Noley sighed again. "It's a win-win-win. I get the help I need, the students get to learn out in the real world *and* they get credit for it, and the school gets a donation. To tell you the truth, I had completely forgotten Kathleen was at the college. I might not have approached the department if I had remembered."

"Hopefully she'll act like a grown woman and play nice," Lilly said.

Noley shrugged. "I hope so, too. We'll see."

"Speaking of people with French last names, I forgot to tell you, Cerise and Armand are doing an ice cream bar," Lilly said.

Noley had stopped whisking and was writing something down on a legal pad, but she stopped with her pencil in mid-air when she heard Lilly's remark. "They are?"

"Yeah. Didn't anyone from the Chamber of Commerce tell you?"

"No. Is the Chamber not happy with what I'm planning?" Noley's eyes widened and furrows appeared on her forehead.

"Of course not! They're thrilled," Lilly hastened to assure her friend. "I think Armand expressed interest in catering the event. The Chamber obviously couldn't say 'yes' because you had already been hired to provide the food, but since he and his wife own a new business in town and there was some extra money in the entertainment budget, Myra decided to give them a token assignment."

"When they found out someone else was already catering the event, the courteous thing would have been to back out graciously," Noley said with a grimace.

"Maybe so, but I think they want to get their names out there."

"Um, do you recall the line to order lunch at their bistro? I would say their names are out there already." Noley was pouting.

"What do you care? You've got top billing," Lilly said, now worried she had spoken out of turn. "I'm sorry, I shouldn't have mentioned it."

"No, I'm the one who should be sorry. I sound like a

spoiled brat. I just want everything to be perfect and I really wanted to prove that I could handle this job."

"No one thinks you can't handle it," Lilly said in a soothing voice. "Like I said, Myra was just trying to be nice because Armand and Cerise are new in town."

"Okay. I'll get over it. Are you done with those baking sheets?" Lilly breathed a sigh of relief when Noley changed the subject. Lilly handed over the clean baking sheets.

"I should get going," she said. "Call if you need help."

"Thanks," Noley said, her wan smile betraying how tired she was. "I'll just finish up and go to bed." Noley hugged Lilly and thanked her for stopping by, then Lilly went home.

CHAPTER 10

July Fourth dawned hot and dry, just as almost every other day of the summer had. Lilly had hoped for a mid-summer miracle, but she wasn't surprised when she awoke to find the windows fogged up on the inside from the air conditioner.

She gave herself the once-over in the bathroom mirror. "Why didn't I outlaw colonial dress the minute I became Chamber president?" she asked Barney, who sat at her feet, watching her get ready for work.

As if he understood her, he shook his head. Lilly laughed. "Exactly," she said, bending down to rub the dog's ears.

When she went downstairs to make coffee, she was surprised to find Tighe in the kitchen.

"What are you wearing?" he asked, staring at her colonial costume.

"All the Main Street merchants dress up like colonists on July Fourth, remember?"

"Vaguely. Aren't you going to be hot?" he asked.

"Of course," Lilly replied. Then she recalled Hassan's words. "But no hotter than a real colonist would have been.

Can you imagine having to wear a getup like this every day all summer?" She shook her head.

"No thanks," Tighe said, taking a huge swig of orange juice from the container in the fridge.

"How many times do I have to tell you to use a glass?" Lilly asked.

"Until I learn," Tighe smirked.

"Funny boy," Lilly said. "Why are you up so early? I thought you didn't have to work today."

"I don't. I'm getting together with Mike and Jimmy today."

"Okay. Can you bring Gran to town square this afternoon?" Lilly asked.

"Sure."

Lilly pecked him on the cheek. "Thanks. I'll see you late this afternoon. Text me when you're on your way."

"Okay, Mom. Bye." Tighe was grabbing a muffin from the bread box when Lilly closed the door behind her.

There were already people out and about as Lilly drove to work. Some people were putting up or adjusting Fourth of July decorations, some were chatting with neighbors, some were out for a brisk walk in the already-sweltering heat. Lilly watched them longingly, wishing she could be wearing shorts and a tee shirt, too.

When she got to the shop Harry was already there, resplendent in his colonial merchant garb.

The first customer of the day smiled when she saw Lilly and Harry's costumes. "What's this all about?" she asked, indicating their clothes with a sweep of her hand.

"Happy Fourth of July!" Lilly exclaimed. "The merchants on Main Street dress up like this every year, then we all close early and go to the town square for a reenactment of the signing of the Declaration of Independence."

"That's a great idea," the woman said. Then she cocked

her head. "Wait. Does that mean restaurants are going to be closed, too?"

Lilly shook her head. "The restaurants usually stay open for people who don't want to go to the celebration, but you should call first, just to make sure."

"We're just visiting in town for a few days and my husband doesn't like crowds, so we won't be able to go the reenactment, I'm afraid," the woman explained. "Can you recommend a good place to have dinner?"

"Believe it or not, the diner right across the street has some of the best food around," Lilly said, gesturing toward the diner.

"Really? I don't usually eat in diners," the woman said.

"Try it," Lilly urged. "I bet you'll love it."

The woman nodded. "All right, if you vouch for the food, my husband and I will give it a try tonight. Thanks for the recommendation." She left after handing Lilly a watch that needed repairing.

Lilly smiled. It felt good to promote another Main Street business, and the diner was in sore need of patrons.

The shop was busy for the rest of the day, and Lilly forgot how hot she was in her colonial getup while she waited on customers and invited all comers to the reenactment celebration that evening.

As soon as the clock in the town square chimed five times, Lilly locked the shop and she and Harry took down the displays for the night. They hurried so they could get to the square before the reenactment ceremony began. Hassan was waiting for Lilly on the sidewalk outside the shop when she and Harry exited onto Main Street. Hassan looked wonderful in his outfit; he took Lilly's arm and the three of them walked to the square together. Lilly's cell phone was tucked into a pocket in her colonial dress; how lucky that she could rely on modern conveniences even though she was dressed like someone from over two hundred years ago.

When they got to the square the crowds were already milling around. Some people had joined the merchants in the spirit of the holiday and dressed up like colonial Americans; others were there to enjoy the festivities in cool summer clothes. There was a reenactment of a Revolutionary War skirmish and people watched that with rapt attention. Lilly, Hassan, and Harry wandered in that direction to join the audience.

Halfway across the large square, Lilly caught sight of the staging area for the food as well as one of the community college's catering vans. She told Hassan and Harry, "I'll meet up with you guys later. I want to see if Noley needs any help."

"Want me to come with you?" Hassan asked.

"No. You've never seen this before, so go enjoy it." Lilly pecked him on the lips and he and Harry left. Lilly threaded her way through the crowd to the van, which stood at the edge of the square with its doors open. Lilly walked around the back to find Noley tugging at a huge plastic bin, her hair pinned up underneath a colonial-style white cotton cap.

"Isn't this stressful enough without getting dressed up for the occasion?" Lilly asked with a laugh as she hopped into the back of the van to help Noley with the bin.

Noley blew a stray hair out of her eyes. "I figured it would be smart to dress up like all the other merchants," she puffed.

"Why don't you let some of the college students do that?" Lilly suggested.

"They're off setting up tents and tables," Noley grunted, pointing in the general direction of the tents.

Several tents had been set up and there was a flurry of activity under them, as young adults clad in Colonial-style white shirts and black trousers hurried to arrange tables and begin setting up the food service areas.

"Okay, so you've got me to help now," Lilly said. "Shall I take this bin over to the students?"

"Yes, please," Noley panted, struggling to pull another large bin out of the van.

"Don't hurt yourself," Lilly warned. "Wait until I get back here and then I can help you."

She hoisted the first bin onto her hip and walked away, noting how annoying it was to carry things while wearing a long skirt.

She handed off the bin to the first student she met and hurried back to the van. She and Noley made several trips to the tents to drop off bins of supplies, then Noley was finally ready to oversee the food preparation.

Lilly watched in amazement as Noley directed the students on how to place the food attractively to entice people to eat.

"Remember," Noley kept saying, "it doesn't matter if the food is free. If it isn't presented well, no one will want to eat it." The students obviously listened to her words of advice because when they finished setting up the food service tables, everything looked professional and elegant, even for backyard-barbeque foods.

White linen cloths covered each table and red, white, and blue fairy lights hung around the insides of all the tents. Tables had been set up for people to sit while they enjoyed the food, and a bluegrass band was tuning up under one of the tents.

One table was laden with chafing dishes that were filled with pulled pork and barbeque sauces. There was one table reserved for condiments, including mustard, vintage bottles of Noley's homemade ketchup, relish, and even sauerkraut. Other tables held chafing dishes full of baked beans and macaroni and cheese, and there were cold troughs full of macaroni salad and coleslaw. In the corner of the tent there was one entire table for the green salad and various dressings. Another table farther away held desserts. Lilly couldn't believe how much work had gone into catering this event.

She suddenly remembered the ice cream bar that Cerise and Armand were supposed to set up.

"Where's the ice cream tent?" she asked one of the students running around.

"Over there," the young woman said, not stopping to chat but pointing to a food tent set up kitty-corner to the edge of the tent where Noley's desserts were displayed.

Lilly had been so busy she hadn't noticed the goings-on under that tent. Cerise and Armand, though not dressed in colonial garb, were decked out in old-fashioned soda jerk outfits, complete with red and white striped shirts, black pants, black armbands, and straw hats. They were bustling around getting their fixings bar set up for hungry townspeople. Lilly couldn't see the set-up very well, but it looked like they had a large number of available toppings and sauces to put on ice cream. She made a mental note to check out their tent after dinner.

Lilly's cell phone buzzed in her pocket. She pulled it out and looked at the caller ID--it was Tighe.

"Hi," Lilly answered.

"Hi, Mom. We're here with Gran. Where should we meet you?"

"I'm under one of the food tents. You'll see me. I'm one of only two people dressed like Revolutionaries. Not including the band, of course."

She could hear the smile in Tighe's voice. "Okay, we'll be there in a few minutes. Gran is having a good day, I think," he finished with a whisper.

"Good," Lilly whispered in return.

It wasn't long before Lilly spotted her mother and the kids weaving through the small crowd of people that had gathered near the food tents. Those people were the smart ones, Lilly figured. They wouldn't have to wait in a long line for food, and there was no chance of running out of the delicious offerings before they could fill their plates. And with Noley's catering, this food promised to be a one-of-a-kind backyard-style barbeque.

"Over here!" Lilly stood on her tiptoes and waved so the kids could see her. They moved toward her, each on one side of their grandmother, keeping the crowds from closing in around her. *If I can raise kids who treat their grandmother that way, I've done a pretty good job,* Lilly thought.

Tighe and Laurel sat with Bev for a few minutes before Lilly could come over and relieve them of duty. When she had a minute to wander over to their table, she was surprised to find Bev dressed in a long skirt.

"Mom! You dressed up this year!" Lilly exclaimed.

"I thought it was about time I participated," Bev said. "I draw the line at wearing one of those scratchy dresses like you're wearing, but I figured I could at least wear a long skirt."

"I love it," Lilly said. She turned her attention to the kids. "Why didn't you dress up?" She winked.

"You've got to be kidding. I'd be laughed out of school," Laurel said, rolling her eyes.

"Yeah. I might get laughed out of college and I haven't even started yet," Tighe said.

"Are you two going to see the reenactment?" Lilly asked.

They both nodded.

"Well, you'd better get going. I'll take Gran over in a few minutes," Lilly said. "I'll just help Noley with a couple finishing touches and then we'll head over."

The kids left, going their separate ways when they were outside the food tent. Lilly was sure Laurel was meeting Nick and she figured Tighe would meet up with Mike and Jimmy. She still wasn't sure about Jimmy, but they couldn't get into much trouble in such a crowded place.

CHAPTER 11

She bustled around, helping Noley set out stacks of plates and utensils, before taking her mother by the arm and leading her away from the food tents and toward the corner of the town square where the reenactment would take place.

"Aren't you hot in that dress?" Bev asked as they made their way across the grassy square.

"You bet. I'm dying," Lilly said. "I don't know how women wore these things in the summertime."

"This skirt is as hot as hell," Bev said, nodding.

"Mom!" Lilly turned to face her mother. "You never talk like that."

"I do when it's this hot," Bev retorted.

Lilly chuckled and they kept walking. They were moving slowly because of the heat and their long skirts.

Lilly spotted Hassan before he saw her, so she was able to get a good long look at him without feeling self-conscious. He was so handsome dressed in his costume, looking every bit the sophisticated colonial gentleman. His dark hair and dark eyes complemented the ivory linen shirt, and he wore his tricorn hat at a jaunty angle, unlike most of the other costumed men in attendance, who wore their hats flat on their heads.

As if he could feel her eyes on him, he suddenly turned and looked in her direction. He gave her a wide grin when he spotted her and her mother. He moved toward them after saying a few words to Harry, who was standing next to him.

"You're just in time," he said in greeting as he leaned down to kiss Bev's cheek. She beamed at him.

"I need to show you off to my friends," she said, looking around. "I wonder if any of them are here."

Hassan laughed. He took Bev's other arm and he and Lilly escorted her to where Harry was still standing, saving them good spots to watch the reenactment.

"Hello, Harry dear," Bev said, offering him her cheek.

"Bev, you look very festive and … independent," Harry said with a smile.

"I should think so," Bev said with a sideways glance at Lilly. "*Some* people think I can't go anywhere on my own."

"Mom, that's not why we're with you. We just thought it would be fun if we all went together."

"All who?" Bev asked. "I don't see the kids anywhere."

Lilly searched her mind for an answer, realizing that her mother knew full well that Lilly was afraid to leave her to her own devices in a crowd. "This is an adults-only fun time."

"I don't participate in that kind of fun," Bev said primly.

"Mom, that's not what I meant! I mean it's just us adults, that's all."

Bev arched her eyebrows at her daughter.

"Look, there are people headed up to the stage," Hassan said, pointing. Lilly breathed a sigh of relief, happy that her mother might ignore her for the next several minutes.

Thomas Jefferson led the other actors onto the stage and there was a smattering of applause as people began to realize the reenactment was beginning.

The crowd became noisier at first, as people told their friends and family the show was about to start, then a hush fell over the people of Juniper Junction, citizens and tourists alike, as Thomas Jefferson unrolled the piece of parchment he was carrying.

He cleared his throat and stood facing the people, then read the words from the scroll in a booming voice.

"When in the course of human events it becomes necessary for one people to dissolve the political bands which have connected them with another and to assume among the powers of the earth, the separate and equal station to which the Laws of Nature and of Nature's God entitle them, a decent respect to the opinions of mankind requires that they should declare the causes which impel them to the separation.

"We hold these truths to be self-evident, that all men are created equal, that they are endowed by their Creator with certain unalienable Rights, that among these are Life, Liberty and the pursuit of Happiness…"

Thomas Jefferson continued reading the document while people listened in now-total silence. The applause when he concluded with the words "And for the support of this Declaration, with a firm reliance on the protection of Divine Providence, we mutually pledge to each other our Lives, our Fortunes, and our sacred Honor," was deafening.

Lilly never tired of hearing the famous words written so long ago, and they never failed to give her goosebumps.

She held Hassan's hand, wondering if he felt the same way she did. Since he had been born in the Middle East, lived for many years in England, and had moved to the United States as a young man, maybe he wasn't likely to find those words as inspiring as she did.

But when she turned to him, she was shocked to see his eyes glistening with unshed tears. He blinked quickly and looked down at her with a broad smile. "I love this!" he exclaimed. "We have to do this every year."

She gave his hand a squeeze and turned to look at her mother, who was trying to engage the young couple next to her in conversation.

"So, are you married?" Bev asked.

"Mom," Lilly cautioned.

"What? I'm just talking to these young people."

"We're not married, but maybe someday," the man said, winking at his girlfriend. She blushed.

"Whattareya waiting for?" Bev wanted to know.

This took the man aback just a bit. He glanced at Lilly, seeming to sense she might be able to stop her mother from talking before she asked any more embarrassing questions.

But it was too late. Before Lilly could open her mouth Bev spoke again.

"Are you having sex?" Bev asked. The man's eyes widened and the woman tugged on the tail of his tee shirt. Neither spoke.

"Mom! That's private!" Lilly scolded.

"They don't mind, do you?" Bev asked, gesturing to the couple. They had undoubtedly thought she was a sweet old lady until she opened her mouth. They were looking around for a quick escape.

"Uh, actually, we don't discuss those things with other people," the woman said.

"Just be careful," Bev warned. She nodded slowly at the young woman. "You know the old saying, 'Why buy the cow when you can get the milk for free?'" She shook her finger at the poor woman. "Don't be giving that milk away for free, my dear."

The woman nodded, her face red and her eyes wild, like a caged animal. "Have a nice day," she mumbled. She grabbed her boyfriend's arm and they practically raced away from Bev.

"Mom, you can't say things like that to strangers," Lilly said. "You can't even say things like that to people you know. That's private."

"Pshaw. Someone needed to tell that girl the truth about certain men. She seemed very naive, didn't you think?"

"Do me a favor and just don't talk to strangers. Please."

Lilly tucked her mother's arm through hers and pulled her gently toward the food tents. She didn't want to lose track of Bev in a crowd. There was no telling what trouble she could get into.

When they arrived at the food tents, Myra was in a tizzy, having looked everywhere for Lilly.

"You need to get up there and say something!" she said in greeting, pointing toward the dais set up in the center of the food tents.

"Now?" Lilly asked. "I was going to take Mom to get something to eat."

"I'll take care of your mom," Hassan offered. "You go do your thing."

"You know I hate speaking in public," Lilly said to Myra as she guided her mother's arm into the crook of Hassan's arm. She wasn't taking any chances that Bev might get away.

"It's only for a minute," Myra said, giving Lilly a little push. "Now get up there and wow them!"

Lilly grimaced and picked up her skirt to walk through the crowd of people waiting in various lines for food. She crossed her fingers, hoping the Chamber of Commerce had ordered enough food for the event. She knew Noley could handle the care and feeding of crowds, but there wasn't much she could do if the food ran out.

Lilly slowly mounted the steps to the dais, being careful not to step on the hem of her skirt. All she needed was to trip and fall on her face in front of everyone in Juniper Junction.

Once she was standing at the dais, she gripped the sides of it to keep her hands from trembling. She cleared her throat and leaned into the microphone, then blew into it just because she thought that's what she was supposed to do.

"Good afternoon. My name is Lilly Carlsen and I'm the President of the Juniper Junction Chamber of Commerce. I'd like to welcome everyone to Juniper Junction's thirtieth annual Independence Day celebration."

There was a *whoop* and a loud catcall from somewhere in the crowd. Lilly wanted to ignore it, but she couldn't. For just a moment she allowed her eyes to scan the faces where the sound had come from.

That's when she saw Nick, Laurel's boyfriend, and she knew Nick had been the one. Her eyes narrowed.

She wanted to wring his neck. No doubt the boy thought he was hilarious. Laurel was standing next to him and even from a distance, Lilly knew that Laurel knew Nick was in trouble. Laurel slapped his arm and scowled at him. Lilly continued talking.

"The merchants of Juniper Junction bring this celebration to you every year because we believe the spirit of patriotism is still alive and well. I hope you'll take the opportunity to visit some of our local merchants, who have been readying their shops for this event for months now. We're strong believers that the Shop Local movement can do great things in a community and we're proud to be able to bring you this wonderful event that celebrates everything Juniper Junction has to offer you."

She was almost done. There were just two more sentences she needed to squeak out before she could get off the dais and get something to eat in relative obscurity.

But before she could take a breath and continue speaking, a scream echoed from the crowd.

CHAPTER 12

Lilly's head jerked in the direction of the scream as people in the crowd began shouting and gesturing for help. The screaming became louder as more people joined in.

She searched the crowd for Myra, who was nowhere to be seen. Not that she had expected to find any one person in that sea of people--everyone was moving as one away from the screaming.

Lilly leaned into the microphone and called for security, but she wasn't sure anyone had heard her. A few seconds later she was relieved to see three security guards running toward the food tents from the direction of the reenactment stage.

Again, she scanned the crowd, this time for Hassan and her mother or the kids. *Even Nick would be a welcome sight,* she thought. But she didn't see their familiar faces in the pandemonium that was breaking loose around the food tents.

Lilly clambered down from the dais, cursing the colonial skirt that was keeping her from breaking into a full run.

"What's going on?" she asked a man running toward the street.

"Some woman just keeled right over! And I don't think it was an ordinary heart attack because the woman next to her just started screaming and everyone else joined in when they saw what happened," the man exclaimed. "Don't just stand there--run! There could be terrorists here with biological weapons!"

He kept running without a backward glance to see if she was following him. She wasn't. Her heart had skipped a beat at the mention of someone keeling over, and her mind was racing through the possibilities. It could be her mother, Laurel, Noley, anyone. She couldn't waste a single second getting over to the melee to see the victim. Saying a silent prayer that it wasn't someone she knew, she raced through the crowd, trying gently to elbow people out of the way, until she stopped short at the sight of a petite woman lying supine on the grass, the bottom half of her body twisted to one side.

Lilly's eyes traveled from the woman's body to her gray face, and she drew in a sharp breath.

It was Cerise.

"Cerise!" she cried, rushing forward. One of the security guards stopped her from coming any closer while another man was attempting CPR, apparently to no avail. The other two officers were on their walkie-talkies, presumably alerting authorities.

"What happened?" Lilly asked the people standing near her. There was a chorus of murmured *I don't know*s and shrugged shoulders. One woman stepped forward. "I was next to her when she dropped. She just started convulsing and her eyes were really wide, like she was asking for help but couldn't." The woman shuddered. "I didn't know what to do, so I started screaming for help."

Someone had walked up behind Lilly and tapped her on the arm. She whirled around, her adrenaline pumping. She was ready to knock out the first person who touched her.

"Hassan! Mom!" she exclaimed in relief, giving them each a hug. "Do you know what happened here? Poor Cerise!"

"Who's Cerise?" Hassan asked, while Bev just watched, her eyes wide.

"The owner of the new bistro in town. She owns it with her husband. They were in charge of the ice cream tent today."

"This is horrible," Hassan said in a low voice.

"I'll say it is," Bev piped up. "Who's in charge of this thing, anyway?"

"I am, Mom," Lilly said, then she put her index finger over her lips and said *shh* in an attempt to get her mother to stop talking.

"Well, something certainly went wrong, didn't it?" Bev asked. *Obviously, Mom. No one was supposed to die.*

The police had arrived and the crowd was parting before them like the Red Sea. The paramedics followed, pushing a gurney over the uneven ground. They quickly got to work on Cerise and before long had confirmed her death and loaded her body onto the gurney. She would be taken to the medical examiner's office right away for an autopsy, they told the police. Lilly was standing close enough to hear the conversation.

"Mom!" Lilly turned and saw Laurel and Nick running toward her. "What happened?"

Laurel gave her mom a hug and Lilly even accepted one from Nick, too. "I don't know," she murmured. "A woman from town died suddenly and everyone is trying to figure out what happened. I want you to go home. I'll be there as soon as I can get there. Do you know where Tighe is?"

Laurel shook her head.

"I'll text him," said Lilly. "You two get going."

"Okay." Laurel kissed Lilly's cheek and took Nick's arm. The two of them hurried away from the scene.

After they left Lilly turned back to the police and paramedics. "Any idea on the cause of death?" one officer was asking the head paramedic.

He man shook his head. "Can't tell yet. The ME'll have to run a tox test. Cause of death could be heart attack or stroke, though the woman seems pretty young for that."

Tox test? Lilly assumed that referred to toxicology. She wondered what the medical examiner would test for. Alcohol? Probably. But Cerise had been working, so there certainly wouldn't be enough alcohol in her system to kill her. Someone would have noticed if Cerise had been stumbling drunk.

Drugs? Lilly had to admit she barely knew either Cerise or Armand. They could be drug users. But again, if there were enough drugs in Cerise's body to kill her, someone surely would have noticed her behaving strangely.

What else was there? Lilly had no idea.

There were so many questions that would have to be answered. Lilly noticed Myra standing next to one of the police officers, her eyes wide. Lilly texted Tighe, then called him and left a message. Then she left her mother in Hassan's care while she went over to talk to Myra and the officer.

"Is there anything I can do to help?" Lilly asked.

"This woman has been very helpful," said the police officer, indicating Myra with his hand. "But I also have a few questions for you. Did you know Cerise Deveau?"

"Yes, but not well. I'd met her a couple times and I've eaten in her bistro once, but that's about it."

"Do you know if she used alcohol or drugs?"

"No."

"What about her husband?"

"What about him?" Lilly asked. She didn't mean to be disrespectful, but she didn't know what the officer meant by the question.

"I mean, do you know her husband?"

"Oh. Yes, but I don't know him any better than I know Cerise."

"How did they happen to be providing dessert at this event today?"

"Armand called and wanted to do the catering," Myra explained. "We already had a caterer, so I asked him if he and Cerise could set up an ice cream bar. It was really only to get them involved, since they're new in town and expressed an interest."

The officer nodded and flipped his notebook closed. He took two business cards out of his breast pocket and handed them to Myra and Lilly. "If you think of anything that would help, give me a call."

"Thanks, officer," Lilly said.

"Yes, thank you," Myra echoed.

"Aren't you Bill's sister?" the officer asked Lilly.

"Yes," she replied.

He nodded, then turned away. *Ugh,* she thought with an inward groan. *He probably remembers me from all the unpleasantness last Christmas.* She could feel the blush creeping across her cheeks.

Turning to Myra, she said, "I'm sure the police are going to ask questions of some of the people here, then they'll send everyone home. I don't know what to do with all this leftover food."

"Do you suppose the police will want to take samples of it to test?" Myra asked.

"Why?"

"In case there was something in the food that killed Cerise."

Myra's words struck Lilly like a bolt of lightning. She hadn't even given thought to the possibility that something in the food had killed Cerise. Immediately her thoughts flew to Noley, who had worked so hard to pull off this catering job.

Hey, where is Noley?

Standing in one spot, Lilly turned in a tight circle, scanning the remaining onlookers for her best friend.

"Have you seen Noley?" she asked Myra.

"No. She's probably back at the van, getting more food," Myra said.

While the police kept order in the areas around the food tents, Lilly went in search of Noley.

She found her friend sitting behind a stack of paper products in the back of the college's catering van. Her head was on her knees and her hands raked through her hair repeatedly.

"Noley! What's wrong?" she asked.

Noley looked up. Her eyes were red-rimmed and puffy from crying.

"I'm sorry, Lilly. I know you wanted this to be perfect, but I'm just overwhelmed. I'm exhausted. My head is killing me. I asked the kids to take over for a few minutes while I took a break back here."

"So you don't know what's going on out there?" Lilly asked.

"No. Why? Is something wrong?" Noley's voice rose suddenly and she leapt to her feet. "I shouldn't have left the students in charge. What happened?"

"Slow down," Lilly said, putting her hand on Noley's arm. "Cerise is dead."

CHAPTER 13

Noley's mouth fell open and she sat down hard on the stack of paper products. She didn't speak for several seconds.

"What happened?" she finally asked in a breathy voice.

"We don't know yet," Lilly said. "I spoke to the woman standing next to Cerise when it happened. She just said Cerise was having convulsions and her eyes were really wide, like she was trying to ask for help."

"Oh, my God. That's terrible," Noley said, shaking her head slowly. "I just served her a helping of salad not long ago and she seemed fine."

"Maybe she was sick, or maybe it was the heat," Lilly suggested.

"I doubt it was the heat," Noley answered. "I know you think it's hot enough to die, but most other people aren't affected by the heat the way you are."

Lilly shrugged. "It was just a suggestion."

"I know. I'm sorry. It's just that I was already feeling overwhelmed, and now this...I feel like I'm going to have a nervous breakdown." Noley buried her face in her hands. "What if someone thinks it was my food that killed her? You know what happened with one bad review of the Main Street Diner--one person's opinion on a day when the owner wasn't even there was enough to push the diner toward having to close. What if people start suggesting that my food killed Cerise? I'll never work again."

Lilly didn't say anything. What could she say?

"I'm sorry. It must seem so callous of me to be thinking about my job at a time like this, but I just can't help it. I feel terrible for Cerise and Armand, but I didn't know either of them. I'm feeling as sorry as I can for them."

"I understand," Lilly answered, though she really didn't. A woman was *dead*, for heaven's sake. Even if Noley was worried about her own future, maybe she should keep those thoughts to herself.

"Come on," Lilly said. "Let's get back to the tents. People are going to be looking for you and you can't stay hidden forever."

Slowly and reluctantly, Noley stood up and followed Lilly from the back of the van to the food tents. The police were still talking to several people, and small groups clustered together across the grass, talking quietly among themselves.

"I guess we should start packing up this food," Noley said to one of the students standing nearby. "I don't know what we're going to do with it all. I guess we could take it to a homeless shelter in Granger." Lilly thought it was a great idea to deliver food to the homeless in the next town up the mountain, but the student stopped her.

"The police told me that we can't touch the food," she said. "They need to take it to test."

Fear sprang into Noley's eyes. "Test it? For what?" she asked. "Surely they don't actually think this food killed Cerise." She took a deep breath.

"Nol, maybe you should sit down," Lilly suggested. She pulled out the closest chair for Noley. Noley sat down heavily and fixed Lilly with a look of despair.

"Can you call Bill?" she asked. "I need to know why the police need to test my food."

"Sure. I'll call him," Lilly said. She whipped out her cell phone and punched Bill's number. She listened for a long moment, then pushed the *Off* button.

"I'm getting his voicemail," she said. "Maybe he's working."

Noley shook her head. "I'm sure he knows why you're calling. He's just not answering because he knows I'm in trouble."

"Noley, Bill wouldn't do that. If he can help you, he will. He doesn't refuse to answer phone calls just because they might be difficult."

Lilly turned her head to search for Hassan and her mother. She saw them sitting together at a table across the lawn, talking earnestly. Her mother made a sweeping hand gesture and Hassan chuckled and shook his head. Lilly turned her attention back to Noley.

"Listen. I'll get in touch with Bill, don't worry. He may even call you before I can get reach him."

Noley twisted up her mouth, which indicated to Lilly that she didn't believe a word Lilly was saying.

"Noley, as soon as this is over I think you should go home and get a nice, long rest. Turn off your phone, turn off your brain, and get some sleep."

"I will." She sounded miserable.

A police officer had made his way to their table. "Are you Noley Appleton?" he asked. Noley nodded. "I've got a few questions for you," he said, pulling out a chair. Lilly took his action as her cue to leave. She squeezed Noley's hand and headed over to the table where Hassan and her mother were sitting.

She sat down heavily, wishing she wasn't wearing the uncomfortable colonial clothes.

"What's happening?" Hassan asked, covering her hand with his.

"The police are talking to Noley. One of the students who was helping her said the police need to test all of the food Noley made, so she's obviously upset about that."

"Do they actually think Noley has something to do with Cerise's death?" he asked, leaning forward in his chair.

Lilly shrugged. "I don't know what they think. They're probably testing the food just to be on the safe side, but I would be upset, too. I don't blame her. She's so tired from catering this event. She needs some rest."

"She works too hard," Bev said. Lilly nodded.

"How are you doing, Mom?" she asked. She hadn't even thought about her poor mother; she was probably tired and itching to go home.

"I'm just fine. This is exciting!" she leaned forward and spoke the words softly, as if she didn't want anyone else to hear her.

"Death is exciting?" Lilly asked.

"Well, I didn't know the woman, so it's not as if I'm prostrate with grief," Bev answered. Lilly often found herself wishing her mother had more of a filter.

Lilly leaned back in her chair and ran her hands through her hair. "Mom, why don't I take you to get something for dinner and then home? There's obviously not going to be any more food served here, so you'll need to eat somewhere."

"All right," Bev answered.

Hassan broke in. "Lil, do you want to stay and help Noley pack everything up? Even if the police take the food, she'll need to clean up everything else. I'll take your mom to the diner and get her something to eat and I'll get take-out for you."

"That would be great," Lilly said. "Noley would appreciate the help, I'm sure. Mom, is that plan all right with you?"

"Absolutely," Bev replied. "Come on, Hassan, let's go." She allowed him to take her hand and help her up. They both kissed Lilly and were on their way just a moment later. Lilly watched them go, grateful as always for Hassan's help and his willingness to overlook her mother's lapses of politeness. She leaned back in her chair again, this time with her eyes closed. She sat that way for several minutes, wondering why it was taking so long for the police to talk to Noley.

Her cell phone buzzed. She looked at the caller ID--it was Tighe.

She answered the phone without preamble. "Where are you?"

"At Jimmy's house. We came over here once the sh--, um, once the mess hit the fan at the square."

Why Jimmy's house again?

"Okay. You can stay there, but if you decide to leave, I don't want you to go anywhere but home. Laurel and Nick should be there by now."

"Okay. I'll probably head home in a little while."

"Okay. I'll be home as soon as I can get there. Stop somewhere and get dinner if you didn't eat here and I'll pay you back."

As she hung up she noticed Noley walking toward her. The poor thing looked like death on overtime. Her eyes were still puffy and red-rimmed.

Lilly pulled out a chair for her and she sat down with a long sigh.

"Are you okay?" Lilly asked.

Noley shrugged. "I know they think I did it. They think I poisoned Cerise." She leaned forward with her arms crossed on the table in front of her, then lay her head down. "What am I going to do?" she asked in a muffled voice.

"You're going to let me and the culinary students help you clean this place up, then you're going to eat something and go to bed."

Noley started to protest, but Lilly held up her hand.

"No arguments. You're exhausted. Worrying about how

someone died when you had nothing to do with it is the last thing you need right now."

Noley lifted her head and gave Lilly a grateful look. "Thanks. I could definitely use the help cleaning up. It's always the worst part of any event."

The friends made their way to the tent where Cerise had fallen. Police had wrapped crime scene tape around the entire food service area of the town square and the crime scene people were collecting samples from every tray of food, placing each sample in a separate labeled plastic bag. They also took what was left of the food that had been on the plate Cerise was holding when she collapsed.

"It just kills me to see them doing that," Noley mumbled.

"Don't pay any attention to it," Lilly advised. "You know you didn't do anything wrong, so you have nothing to fear."

The students from the community college had already started boxing up the paper products and cutlery, so Lilly and Noley waded into the group and helped them. After that was done and they had obtained permission from the police, they removed tablecloths from all the tables, packed up the chafing dishes, and stored the Sterno pots that kept the dishes warm. After many trips back and forth between the tents and the school's vans, everyone was ready to call it a day.

"Where's your car?" Lilly asked Noley.

"At the college. I drove there in my car and drove one of the vans here."

"All right. I'll follow you to the college, then I'll follow you home, then I'm coming in to make sure you eat and go to sleep."

"Have you heard from Bill yet?" Noley asked, not meeting Lilly's eyes.

"I haven't. Look at me," Lilly ordered. "He's working. He's busy. He's not avoiding you, I promise."

Noley glanced up at Lilly and smiled. "I guess you're probably right. I just get nervous, that's all."

"Well, don't be. He thinks you walk on water, so he's not going to do anything to jeopardize your relationship, believe me."

Noley finally managed a small smile. "Thanks for putting up with me, Lil."

"You're welcome."

CHAPTER 14

Once the students had been safely deposited back at school and the vans had been emptied of foodstuffs, Lilly followed Noley home. The first thing she did upon walking into Noley's house was to go into the powder room and change from the scratchy, uncomfortable skirt into a pair of shorts she had left in her car. She pulled her hair from the cap she had worn all day and put it in a ponytail, then she changed from her peasant blouse into a tee shirt.

She found Noley in the kitchen pouring a glass of water. Lilly leaned against the counter next to her with a sigh. "It feels so good to get those clothes off. Honestly, I don't know how women survived the colonial era in those ridiculous outfits."

Noley smiled. "Just be glad you only have to wear them once a year. Can you imagine if that was your entire wardrobe? Ugh."

"Don't even say that." Lilly pretended to shudder.

Noley stood with her back against the counter and sipped her water.

"While you drink that I'm going to fix you something to eat. It won't be as good as anything you make, but at least you won't have to make it," Lilly said. "Now sit down and let me create something out of your leftovers."

Noley obliged and Lilly got to work making a sandwich. She found apples, ham, Gouda cheese, and the expensive kind of bread. She sliced the apples and put them on the bread, layered the ham over the apples, and shredded some cheese to go on top of the ham. She covered everything with another slice of bread and set the sandwich in a sauté pan on the stove. Before long Noley was enjoying a fancy grilled cheese sandwich, a pickle, and a small bag of potato chips.

Noley ate slowly. "Hey, this is really good," she said.

"Did you think I couldn't make a decent sandwich?" Lilly teased.

"No, I mean this is sort of gourmet," Noley said with a laugh. She hadn't laughed in hours. "Where did you come up with it?"

"I just thought it up in my own wee brain," Lilly answered, pointing at her head. "Now eat before I send you to bed without the rest of your dinner." She turned to the sink to wash the dishes.

"There are some cookies in the jar over there," Noley said. Lilly was glad to hear it--that meant Noley wanted more to eat and that was a good thing.

She reached for the jar and took off the lid. Inside were cookies that sparkled like some of the baubles in her jewelry shop.

"These are gorgeous! What kind are they?" Lilly asked, taking four out. She handed two to Noley and kept two for herself, then sat down across from her friend.

"They're white chocolate chip with chopped apricots, and the sparkles are from sanding sugar."

"Ooh, they're delicious," Lilly said. She knew she was talking with her mouth full, but she couldn't help it. She would be requesting these in the future.

There was a knock at the back door and both women

jumped. Lilly got up first and, laughing nervously, peered through the kitchen curtains. "I guess we're both a little jumpy."

She was happy to see Bill standing on the back landing. "It's Bill," she said.

"Oh, I don't know if I want to see him or not," Noley fretted.

"Why not?" Lilly asked, opening the door.

"Because…" Noley began, but then stopped when Bill came into the room.

"I came as soon as I could get away from the station. I heard what happened earlier. Are you both all right?" he asked, his concern obvious in the tone of his voice. He strode over to the table where Noley was still sitting and leaned down to kiss her cheek.

"We're okay," Lilly answered. "A little shaken up, but otherwise all right." She looked to Noley for confirmation.

"Yeah, we're all right," Noley said, her head bobbing up and down. "I'm just so embarrassed."

"Why are you embarrassed?" Bill asked.

"Because they took samples of all the food I made and I'm sure they think my cooking killed Cerise. Now no one will ever want me to make food for them again." She pushed her cookies away, laid her head on the table, and started to cry.

"Noley! What's wrong?" Bill asked. Lilly didn't know what to do. She wanted to comfort Noley, but she thought maybe it wasn't her place; maybe Noley would rather talk to Bill.

"I just can't believe this is happening," Noley said, without lifting her head. She sniffled loudly.

"It's just procedure," Bill said, pulling out the chair next to her and putting his arm around her shoulders. "The officers had to call the crime scene investigators to do that. Otherwise they'd be accused of improper investigation. They all know you. Not one of them thinks you did anything wrong."

Noley lifted her head. "Promise?" she asked. "You're not just saying that because I'm a blubbering mess?"

"Of course not," Bill said. He still had his arm around her shoulders, and now he held her away from him. "It looks like you could use some sleep."

"She could," Lilly piped up. She figured it was time for her to leave. "Bill, could you see that she gets in bed? Take the alarm away from her so she sleeps as long as her body will let her."

Bill saluted his sister. "Will do."

Noley stood up and gave Lilly a hug. "Thanks for everything. I really appreciate you coming home with me and staying for a while."

"You'd do the same for me," Lilly replied. She picked up her purse from the kitchen counter. "Bye, you two. Noley, I'll call you tomorrow."

Lilly let herself out the back door. She drove home and was pleased to find both kids and Hassan there.

"What a day!" Lilly exclaimed when she sat down with everyone in the living room.

"How's Noley?" Hassan asked.

"I've never seen her so tired," Lilly said. "Bill's there with her now. He'll make sure she gets a good night's sleep. What time is it, anyway? I'm hungry. I had two cookies at Noley's house, but that's it."

Hassan stood up. "I brought you a Cobb salad from the diner. I'll get it from the fridge."

"Mom, is Noley in trouble?" asked Tighe.

"I doubt it," Lilly said. "She didn't do anything wrong. Her food happened to be in the wrong place at the wrong time."

"How did the lady die?" Laurel asked.

"They don't know that yet," Lilly said. "I'm sure there will be a story in the paper tomorrow, but the medical examiner won't release any results before then. Besides, I heard there was going to be a tox test, which I assume reveals if there were any toxins in Cerise's bloodstream. Those results won't be back for a while."

"Do you think maybe the food was undercooked?" Tighe asked.

"I hadn't thought of that," Lilly admitted. "But I don't think so. The pork cooked for hours, and there was nothing else that would have caused someone to get sick."

"I don't know," Tighe said. There was a note of skepticism in his voice. "You hear all the time on tv about vegetables and fruits that make people sick if they're not washed enough. Do you think that woman could have eaten the fruit or one of Noley's salads and gotten sick?"

"I hope not," Lilly said. "Besides, food poisoning makes people throw up, not go into convulsions immediately."

Just then Hassan came into the living room bearing a tray with Lilly's Cobb salad, a tall glass of iced tea, and a piece of watermelon.

"Ah, thank you," Lilly said, settling back into the sofa. She took a long drink of the tea and laid her head back. "That's perfect."

"Mom, your speech was really good. Even Nick said so," Laurel said. She beamed at her mother.

Thank God Nick liked it, Lilly thought to herself. *I was so worried*. She managed to avoid rolling her eyes. She decided it was not the right time to ask Laurel about Nick's catcall during the speech.

"Thank you very much, honey," she said. "I always get nervous before things like that. I'm so glad that was my last official act as the President of the Chamber of Commerce."

Later on, Hassan and Lilly sat in the living room, talking over the circumstances of Cerise's death.

"I heard some people saying she wasn't a very nice person," Hassan said.

"I haven't heard anything. Her bistro has been very

successful in the short amount of time it's been open. Some people are jealous of success. Maybe that's what's behind the things people are saying."

"I wonder if the bistro will stay open."

"I don't know. Her husband runs it with her, or rather, ran it with her. Maybe he'll stick around and keep it open. Maybe he'll go back to New York. There doesn't seem to be much to keep him here."

"No family?"

"Not that I know of, though there is one local woman who might be related to them."

"What brought them here?"

"They were here on vacation and just fell in love with the area, I guess."

"How is Noley doing?" he asked.

"She's wiped out. She was upset earlier, but she seemed to calm down once she got home and was able to relax a little bit."

There was a knock at the front door, so Lilly got up to answer it.

"Bill! Come on in," Lilly said. "What are you doing here? Is Noley all right?"

"She's fine. She fell asleep as soon as she crawled into bed. I came over here because I wanted to talk to you about something."

That doesn't sound good.

"What is it?" Lilly asked.

"Can we sit?" Bill asked.

Lilly motioned for him to join her and Hassan in the living room and the three of them sat down, Hassan and Lilly on the sofa, Bill in an armchair.

"What's up?" Lilly leaned forward with her elbows on her knees.

Bill sighed. "I'm a little concerned about what happened this afternoon."

Lilly tilted her head and squinted her eyes. "You mean because someone died?"

Bill shook his head. "That came out wrong. Of course I'm concerned that someone died. What I'm really concerned about, though, is Noley's role in this whole thing."

"Surely you don't think Noley had anything to do with Cerise's death!" Lilly exclaimed.

"No, no. Of course not. What I'm concerned about is how this investigation may affect her. The police are going to have to talk to her again, and who knows what'll happen when the medical examiner's report comes out? Hopefully it'll say Cerise died of natural causes, but she was a young woman with no medical issues that I've been made aware of."

He paused and let those words sink in.

"Do you mean you think she died by something other than natural causes?" Hassan asked. Now he was leaning forward, too.

Lilly was staring at her brother, wide-eyed. "Do you mean to say you think someone murdered her?"

"Let's not jump to conclusions," Bill cautioned. "But I think we have to be aware that it's certainly a possibility."

"How awful," Lilly murmured.

"If it turns out that Cerise was murdered, things are going to get much hotter for anyone who had anything to do with the set-up and service of food at the celebration this afternoon," he continued. "*And* Noley actually served a salad to Cerise, she told me. That means…"

"Noley will be under police scrutiny," Lilly finished his sentence. "Can't you do anything about it? I mean, you're in the department. They all know you."

"I couldn't do much for you when you were suspected of murder over the holidays last year, could I?" Bill answered Lilly's question with one of his own. "I won't be able to help Noley any more than I helped you. I might be able to slow down the investigation by a day or two, but that's it. After that I have to let things run their course."

"Did you talk to Noley about this?" Lilly asked, fearing the answer.

"No," Bill answered, shaking his head. "She was in no condition to hear hypothetical bad news, even if it is highly possible. Once she's had some time to rest and process everything, maybe you can, you know, sort of prepare her for the possibilities."

"You're a chicken," Lilly accused him. "You just don't want to be the one to tell her."

Bill managed a tired grin and held up his hands in a gesture of surrender. "Guilty as charged."

"Maybe all of this will be moot," Hassan suggested. "Remember, it's entirely possible that Cerise died of something in her system that wasn't put there by another person. And until we know otherwise, it's possible that she passed away from natural causes."

"You're right, of course," Bill said. "I just know from being in this business that the cause of death is not likely to be natural causes." He put his hands on his knees and stood up. "Sorry to be the bearer of bad news tonight, but I wanted you to be aware, Lilly."

"All right. I'll see how she's doing tomorrow. Thanks for coming over," Lilly said.

"Okay. Goodnight." Lilly kissed Bill's cheek. He and Hassan shook hands and he walked down the front path to his car.

Rather than returning to the living room, Hassan followed Lilly to the kitchen, where she washed the few dishes she had used for dinner.

"How are you after everything that happened?" Hassan asked. "Everyone has been so worried about Noley. I'm worried about you, too." He wrapped her in a strong embrace.

"I'm all right, I suppose. Frankly, I'm surprised we haven't been interrupted twenty times tonight by reporters calling."

"Oh, that reminds me," Hassan said with a mischievous look in his eyes. "You'd better put the phone back on the hook after I leave."

"You took the phone off the hook?" Lilly asked with a hoot of laughter. "That's perfect! Thank you," she said, kissing him.

"They may have been trying to call your cell," he pointed out after she pulled away.

"I turned off notifications and the ringer," she said with a smile.

"Smart woman."

CHAPTER 15

Noley called Lilly first thing the next morning.

"Feeling better?" Lilly asked.

"I'm rested, but I don't know if I'm actually feeling any better," Noley replied.

"Why not?"

"Because now I've had a chance to think through what happened and it looks even worse than it did last night."

"Then you're doing it wrong. Things are supposed to look *better* in the morning," Lilly said, attempting a light tone. But she knew what Noley was thinking, and had to admit her friend's dark thoughts might be right.

"Will you have time to talk if I come into the shop today?" Noley asked.

"Sure. What time?"

"Early. Before you open. I'll bring breakfast." Noley made the best muffins, so Lilly jumped at the chance to have breakfast from Noley's kitchen.

"Deal. I'll see you in a little while," Lilly said, then hung up the phone. She didn't bother eating breakfast at home, but she did have a cup of coffee before leaving for work. The kids were still asleep when she left, but she knew they'd be up soon because they both had to work.

Harry got to the shop just a few minutes after Lilly, and she remembered with a pang of conscience that she had forgotten all about him the day before.

"That was some excitement yesterday, huh?" Harry asked, setting his coffee on top of one of the display cases.

"It sure was. What happened to you? I think the last I saw you, you were with Hassan and my mom right after the reenactment."

Harry nodded. "Yeah, then I ran into a friend of mine and we hightailed it over to the food tents."

"Did you get any of the food before...before everything happened?" Lilly couldn't decide on the most tactful way to phrase Cerise's death, but she wanted to find a diplomatic way to figure out if there had been poison in the food.

"Yeah, we both did. It was delicious."

"No ill effects?"

"Of course not. I've had Noley's food before and it's always good. Why do you ask?"

"No reason. I just thought, you know, since it was so hot yesterday people might have overeaten and felt sick." *Could I be any lamer?"* Lilly suppressed a groan.

"No way. The food was great. We didn't go to the ice cream table, though, because I don't like ice cream."

"So were you there when Cerise...fell ill?" Lilly asked.

"No. We had left by then. The lines were getting long for the food, so we left. Did you see what happened?"

"I didn't see it firsthand, but I saw the aftermath. I was up at the podium giving my Chamber of Commerce speech and there was suddenly a scream and all this movement around where Cerise was. I didn't know what had happened until several minutes later."

"Do they know how she died?"

"Not yet. We're waiting to hear from the medical examiner."

Harry opened his mouth to say something else when there was a knock at the front door. Lilly glanced up and saw Noley on the sidewalk, holding up a brown paper bag. Breakfast.

Lilly hurried to open the door. She let Noley in, then locked the door again so no customers would come in and interrupt them while they talked.

"Come on to the back. We can eat at my desk," Lilly suggested.

"Harry, want a bagel and cream cheese? I picked them up at the grocery store," Noley said.

"No thanks, I've eaten already."

Lilly tried to hide her disappointment at the prospect of a grocery store bagel and cream cheese for breakfast. She motioned for Noley to sit in the chair opposite her own, then she sat down behind the desk.

"I brought bagels. I didn't feel like cooking today," Noley said, as if she had read Lilly's mind.

"Why don't you feel like cooking? You always feel like cooking," Lilly said. This was a worrisome development.

Noley shrugged, a bland expression on her face. "Just sick of it, I guess. I'll get the old passion back again, I'm sure, but for now I just feel like buying stuff that someone else has made."

"Is that the only reason?" Lilly asked, raising her eyebrows.

Noley sighed, the expression on her face changing from bland to downright sad.

"No. You know that. What if I poisoned Cerise? What if something I made actually killed her? I couldn't even live with myself, let alone cook for anyone again. I don't want to start killing my friends and family next."

It was so dramatic that Lilly had to chuckle.

"Nol, I hardly think you're going to start killing people off with your food. Everyone loves your food. You'll see--nothing you made killed Cerise. I'm sure of it."

"Well, I'm not. You know how tired I've been lately. What if I made some terrible mistake and put the wrong ingredient in something?"

"This isn't a movie, Noley," Lilly said, leaning forward earnestly. "Besides, if you put something in the food that killed one person, why hasn't anyone else come down with an illness? Or even died? And what mistake could you possibly have made that could kill someone? I don't care how tired you might have been--you wouldn't substitute poison for actual food."

That seemed to give Noley pause. But she thought of an answer quickly.

"Cerise must have been allergic to whatever I put in the food. So naturally, she would get sick before anyone else does." Noley rubbed her temples. "Oh, God, what if more people start to get sick?" There was a rising panic in her voice.

"Noley, pull yourself together. You're falling apart. How about taking a break? I can leave Harry in charge of the store and you and I can go shopping or something this afternoon. How does that sound?"

Noley shook her head. "I can't do it today."

"Why not?" It was none of her business, but Lilly asked nonetheless.

Noley didn't answer.

"It's because you're saving your money in case you have to go to jail, isn't it?" Lilly guessed.

"Yes." Noley's voice was barely perceptible.

"You're going shopping this afternoon and I'm going to make you buy the most expensive dress you can find. Then I'm going to call Bill and tell him to take you to dinner at the fanciest place around."

"But--" Noley protested.

"No buts. I'm in charge here." Lilly opened the office door

and called into the shop. "Harry! Can you come here a minute?"

"Sure, boss. What is it?" Lilly shook her head and chuckled.

"Can you take care of things here while I'm out this afternoon?" she asked.

"You know I can."

"Thanks." She turned to Noley as Harry returned to the front of the shop. "It's settled. Come back here at eleven o'clock and bring your wallet. And your appetite. Lunch is on me today and we're not having bagels."

Noley couldn't help laughing. "Sorry about the bagels. They were pretty awful, weren't they?"

"I was secretly hoping for your blueberry-studded muffins."

"My Blueberry Studmuffins? You should have said something. I have some in the freezer."

"I'll wait until you're ready to cook again, then you can make me some fresh ones," Lilly said with a wink.

Noley left and Lilly opened the shop a few minutes later. The customers who came in during the morning all seemed to have been present when Cerise died and they wanted information.

"The paper said the cause of death hasn't been determined yet," said one woman who came in to pick up a repaired Rolex.

"That's right," Lilly said.

"I thought since you were sort of in charge of the whole thing, you might have some inside information."

"I was in charge in name only," Lilly said. "Other people did all of the actual work. I only know what the papers are saying about Cerise's death," Lilly said. It was a fib, but that was better than ratting out Bill, whose hunch she couldn't seem to banish from her mind.

"Have you heard whether her husband is going to keep the bistro open?" the woman asked.

"No. I suppose he'll need some time to think about it. That's a pretty big decision."

The woman agreed. "For purely selfish reasons, I hope he stays open," she said. "The food is just wonderful."

"Speaking of food," Lilly said. "Did you have any of the backyard-barbeque-themed food yesterday?"

"Yes, and it was absolutely delicious. The barbeque sauces were just inspired. Who catered the event?"

"Noley Appleton," Lilly said. She figured she should start some positive buzz about Noley before anyone had a chance to think her food poisoned someone. Then she gave herself a mental slap. *No one was poisoned. Cerise must have died of natural causes.*

"Oh! I know Noley. She's a delightful person. I didn't realize she was a caterer. I thought she was a recipe developer."

"She is. She also judges cooking contests and writes for cooking columns. But she wanted to try cooking for a huge crowd, so the Chamber of Commerce gave her the job. She got the students from the community college to help. I think they pulled it off beautifully, don't you?"

"Oh, yes. Everything was yummy and the lines were organized. It was all wonderful until, well, you know. Cerise."

Lilly nodded solemnly, then the woman left so Lilly could tend to another customer. She was surprised to see the woman who had asked for a dining recommendation the day before.

"Hello!" Lilly greeted her.

"Hello. I just wanted to come by and thank you for the dinner recommendation. The diner was great."

"I'm so glad to hear it! Say, would you consider posting a review of your meal online?" Lilly asked. *Orson could use some positive reviews right about now.*

"I'd be happy to."

When Noley arrived for their afternoon out, she wore a faraway expression.

"You okay?" Lilly asked.

"I've just heard from Armand," Noley said, her voice dejected. "He's a mess."

"He must be. Why did he call you?"

"To ask me if I could provide the bistro with some desserts for a few weeks, until he can find a pastry chef who can do it full-time."

"So he's staying open?"

"That's his plan, but he says he's going to play it by ear. If it's too much for him, he'll close the bistro and move back east. He'll be closed until after the funeral, but after that he wants to open up again. He says he needs to stay busy to keep his mind off the death of his wife."

Lilly closed her eyes. "I can't imagine what he must be going through," she said. "So are you going to go to work for him?"

"I told him I would do it, of course. I have to help him somehow. The food business is hard enough when a person's *not* in mourning. These next few weeks, especially, are going to be really hard for him. And it's so nice of him to consider me for the job after everything that's happened."

Lilly hugged her friend. "You are the best person," she said.

"The jury's still out on that," Noley replied, her face grim and lined with stress. "After all, I may be the one who killed his wife."

CHAPTER 16

Lilly and Noley left the jewelry store in Harry's capable hands. Their first stop was the spa on the other end of Main Street, where they each made an appointment for a massage after lunch. Next they went to Ruby Red's Couture Salon.

The bell over the door jingled daintily when they went in.

"Hi, girls!" Ruby cried, coming around the counter to greet them. She gave each of them a hug. "What brings you in here today?"

"Noley needs a dress," Lilly said.

"Ooh!" Ruby exclaimed. "What's the occasion?"

"I don't really know," Noley said. Ruby looked confused.

"It's a surprise," Lilly explained. "You know she's dating my brother, Bill. Well, he's going to take her someplace fabulous and she needs something equally fabulous to wear."

"How thrilling!" Ruby cried. If the clothes in Ruby's salon weren't so chic and of such high quality, Lilly doubted she'd be able to stand spending much time in there. Ruby's enthusiasm could be a little on the manic side.

"What can you show us?" Lilly asked.

"I have just the thing," Ruby gushed. She took Noley's

arm and led her over to the side wall of the shop, where the fabric of gorgeous dresses rustled elegantly when touched.

Ruby zeroed in on a cocktail dress that hung gracefully from a padded hanger. It was sleeveless navy blue silk with an empire waist and a chiffon skirt over the silk.

"Noley, that's gorgeous," Lilly said. "You could put your hair up and wear some gold jewelry. You'd look beautiful."

Noley sighed. "I suppose."

"Noley," Lilly scolded, "You don't have the proper dress-shopping spirit."

"I know. I'm sorry. I just can't stop thinking about...you know."

"What's the matter?" Ruby asked.

"She's upset over what happened yesterday at the reenactment," Lilly said, not wishing to share with Ruby the exact nature of Noley's feelings.

"Oh, of course you are, dear," Ruby fussed. "Everyone in Juniper Junction is upset. How is Armand holding up?"

That was one of the nice things about merchants in a small town--they all cared about each other and were concerned about each other. Well, mostly. Eden Barclay and Herb Knight hadn't really been missed by their fellow business owners the previous year.

"He's okay, I suppose," Noley answered. "He's going to try to stick it out and open the bistro again once the funeral is over."

"That's the spirit," Ruby said enthusiastically. "Now, Noley, you go try on that dress."

It was like the designer had Noley in mind when the dress was created. She was devastating in it. The fabric draped perfectly, the color complemented Noley's hair and eyes, and the dress was just the perfect shape for a fancy summer night out.

"She'll take it," Lilly said to Ruby as soon as Noley emerged from the dressing room.

"Wait!" Noley cried. "I haven't even looked at myself in a mirror yet."

But when she turned around to face the mirror on the wall behind her, a faint smile crept across her lips. Even Noley, in her pensive and melancholy mood, knew the dress was perfect.

"Lilly's right. I'll take it."

Ruby beamed. "That's wonderful! And it doesn't even need any alterations. It's lovely just the way it is."

"Now, shoes," Lilly said, turning toward the back of the shop.

"I've got just the ones," Ruby said, and she made a beeline for a pair of strappy, sparkly navy sandals.

Noley tried them on, and sure enough, they fit as well as the dress did. Her smile grew as she stood up and walked in a circle to test out the shoes.

"Wrap these up, too, Ruby," she instructed with a smile. "I love them."

Lilly grinned. She had known this shopping trip would do her friend a world of good. Now all she had to do was talk to Bill and have him make reservations somewhere.

When Ruby rang up the sale Noley balked at the exorbitant total.

"I didn't even look at the prices," she said. "I was concentrating on how everything looked."

"Nol, you never spend any money on yourself," Lilly said. "Now cut it out and give Ruby your credit card."

Noley handed over the card with a grimace. "The spa is expensive, too," she fretted.

"Noley, you make more than I do, and I can afford a spa day every once in a blue moon," Lilly said. "You just don't spend enough to know how it feels."

Noley laughed. "I suppose you're right. I'm really kind of a miser when you get right down to it."

Lilly and Ruby laughed and the two friends walked outside with Noley's packages.

"Where to for lunch?" Lilly asked, checking her watch. "We have plenty of time to eat before we have to be at the spa."

"How about the diner?" Noley suggested. "I'm feeling a little poor right now, so some cheap diner food might be a good thing before I spend another fortune at the spa this afternoon."

"Remember, this is my treat." Lilly said.

"Oh, I forgot. Well, I still feel like diner food."

"Then the diner it is," Lilly agreed.

They set off for the diner, Lilly trying her best to keep Noley's spirits up. She wanted to avoid talking about Cerise--or the reenactment, or cooking, or the police, or catering, or anything of the sort. She wanted to stay on safe topics that would put Noley in a good mood.

"Hi, ladies," Orson greeted them when they entered the diner. "Where would you like to sit?"

Lilly looked around and saw with a sinking heart that there were more empty tables than there should be at this time of day. And the problem wasn't competition from the bistro, because that was closed temporarily. It had to be that nasty review from the paper.

But she didn't mention it to Orson--she was sure he knew exactly why his diner wasn't bustling like it normally was at this time of the season. Instead, she pointed to a booth near the front window.

"Unfortunately, that's one of two tables where you can't sit," he explained, his face clouding. "I've got to fix them. Luckily I do a little woodworking, so I don't have to call anyone to do it for me. It's cheaper that way." Lilly had to admit, the booths displayed a rare kind of craftsmanship, unusual in a diner setting.

"Okay, how about that one?" Lilly asked, pointing to

another empty booth. She liked to be able to watch the comings and goings at her shop across the street, but she would have to forget it this time.

"Right this way," Orson said. He grabbed a couple menus and led the way to the booth. "Can I bring you something to drink?" he asked.

"Iced tea for me, please," Lilly said.

"I'll have iced tea, too," Noley said. "But I'd like a slice of lemon in mine. Not a wedge. And no straw. Thanks, Orson." Orson grinned at Lilly. Noley's restaurant-ordering quirks were legendary in Juniper Junction.

"Why the smiles?" Noley asked good-naturedly. "I just know what I like."

"And so you shall have it," Orson said. "Be right back."

The women perused their menus while he was gone. When he returned, Noley asked about the soup of the day.

"It's split pea," Orson said.

"That sounds good," Noley said. "I'll take a cup of that with no garnish and with oyster crackers instead of Saltines, please. And I'll have half a tuna sandwich. On wheat bread with no crusts. And it would be great if you could bring the soup and the sandwich together instead of bringing the soup first."

Orson smiled another knowing smile and turned to Lilly.

"Just a Greek salad for me," she said.

"Easy enough. Thanks, girls," Orson said.

I hate being called a girl, thought Lilly.

"I hate being called a girl," Noley said. Lilly chuckled.

"That's exactly what I was thinking."

"So what should I wear for jewelry with my new outfit?" Noley asked.

"I think gold goes really well with navy blue," Lilly answered. "Do you have any good gold jewelry?"

"I have a nice bracelet and a pair of thick hoop earrings," Noley said.

"No necklace?" Lilly asked, furrowing her brow.

"No."

"You're welcome to borrow one of mine," Lilly said, then she had a thought. "Wait! I know--I'll lend you a necklace from the shop for the night."

"You wouldn't mind lending me one?" Noley asked.

"Of course not. I think I can trust you to bring it back," Lilly said with a grin.

"Then it's settled. Bracelet, earrings, and a gold necklace. I'm getting excited about my big night out and I don't even know if Bill has planned it yet." Noley chuckled.

"I know he hasn't because I haven't told him yet," Lilly said. "I'll call him tonight. Does he know that you're going to be working with Armand?"

Noley shook her head. "I haven't talked to him since I spoke to Armand. I'll tell him tonight. I think he'll be happy."

"I know he will. He's happy when you're happy."

Orson brought their meals just then.

"I heard what happened at the reenactment," he said, setting down their dishes. "I can't believe I missed it because I was here working."

"It was awful, that's for sure," Lilly said. She noticed Noley squirm. Orson must have noticed, too.

"But I don't want to ruin your lunch with talk like that. Enjoy, ladies."

Lilly and Noley ate in relative silence.

"Dessert?" Orson asked when they had finished.

"Oh, not for me," Noley said. "I'm stuffed. That hit the spot, Orson."

His smile could have lit up the diner if the lights hadn't already been on.

"Me, neither. That was a great salad, Orson," Lilly said. Orson smiled again.

"Thanks, you two. And Lilly, thanks for sending that couple over for dinner on the fourth. They said you recommended the diner when they asked for a recommendation. I really appreciate it."

"Your food is great, Orson," Lilly said earnestly. "Whenever I get a customer who wants a recommendation, I send them here."

"I hope people start coming back soon," he said, the ghost of a frown creasing his forehead.

"Don't worry, they will," Noley assured him.

Lilly paid the bill and they set off for the spa. They wanted to relax in the sauna before their afternoon appointments.

No words passed between them in the sauna. *I don't why I enjoy this,* Lilly thought. *I hate the heat outside.*

They went their separate ways for massages, and met again in the plunge pool afterward.

"I feel like a wet noodle," Noley said, closing her eyes and breathing deeply of the scented air.

"Isn't that the greatest feeling?" Lilly asked.

When they emerged from the spa they went to the jewelry shop so Lilly could check on Harry.

"How's it been going, Harry?" she asked.

"Fine, boss."

"I'm going home for now," Noley said. "I need a nap after that massage. Thanks for taking me out today, Lil. That was exactly what I needed. You're the best." She wrapped Lilly in a big bear hug and went out onto Main Street wearing a smile.

CHAPTER 17

The day of Cerise's memorial service arrived, bringing with it more soaring temperatures. The morning radio host warned that the risk of forest fire was growing every day and that people were being asked to cut down on watering lawns and flower gardens. *Great,* thought Lilly. *All this town needs is more worrying about fire.*

Since Harry wanted to attend the service, too, Lilly had decided to close the jewelry shop for the morning. She got to work early and printed out a "Be back soon" sign that she could hang in the front window, then at ten o'clock she and Harry left the shop and walked over to the church where the service was being held.

The pews were packed with people who had come to say goodbye to Cerise. Armand sat in the front, surrounded by richly-dressed men and women whom Lilly assumed were probably his family and Cerise's family from France.

The service was beautiful. It was not a traditional funeral, since the medical examiner had only released the body the previous day. Cerise hadn't left burial instructions, so Armand decided to have her cremated. When he told Noley about the service on the day he hired her, Armand had told her of his plans to return to France to scatter Cerise's ashes outside the village where she grew up.

After the service the family stood in a receiving line outside the church, greeting and thanking mourners for coming. The church was full of Main Street merchants who felt like they had lost one of their own, despite the bistro not having been open for very long.

Noley had joined Harry and Lilly for the service. As they stepped to the back of the line, Noley nudged Lilly's arm.

"Remember the woman I told you about, Kathleen Deveau?" she asked in a whisper. "That's her, hugging Armand." Lilly craned her neck and saw a woman step away from Armand. She was wiping the corners of her eyes with a tissue. She wore a purple suit and her hair was in a severe bun. She must have felt Lilly's eyes on her, because she looked over her shoulder. Catching sight of Noley, a scowl flitted across her face before she turned around and left the church.

Orson was in line in front of Lilly, Noley, and Harry, waiting to express condolences to the family. Hassan had been unable to attend the service because he was picking up his father from the airport in Denver.

"Any word on how Cerise died?" Orson asked in a low voice.

Lilly shook her head, aware of Noley stiffening beside her. "It'll probably be at least another week," she whispered. Orson nodded, seeming to understand that Lilly didn't want to discuss the issue just then.

"Is Armand going to stay open?" Orson asked. This, at least, seemed a safer topic. Noley relaxed visibly.

"Yes. He'll probably open the day after tomorrow and try to stay open," Noley answered. "In fact, I'm going to be working for him until he can get back on his feet and hire a full-time pastry chef."

Orson didn't get a chance to reply. It was his turn to talk to Armand and the family next. He murmured his condolences and waited for Lilly, Noley, and Harry as they talked briefly to the family, too.

The four of them walked back to work together. Noley had parked behind the jewelry shop and was going straight home. Armand had asked her to familiarize herself with the recipes she'd be using for the bistro, so she was going to spend the rest of the day working on those. They were recipes Cerise had perfected and Armand wanted to honor her memory by continuing to use them exactly as she had.

Orson waved goodbye to Lilly and Harry and crossed the street to the diner. Lilly and Harry opened up the shop and set out the jewelry again. It wasn't long before Hassan and his father walked into the shop.

"Amir!" Lilly greeted Hassan's father with a big hug. He held her away from him and smiled broadly at her.

"Lilly, my dear, you are even more radiant than the last time I saw you," he said.

"Thank you," Lilly said, blushing. "What do you two have planned today?"

"I've got to show him the work we've done at the house. He hasn't seen the floors or the patio," Hassan said.

His father grinned. "I can't believe my son here is such a conscientious homeowner. It's been years since he's shown any interest in anything other than gem hunting. Lilly, you've done wonders with the boy." He threw his head back and laughed while Hassan shook his head good-naturedly.

"I do my best," Lilly said with a smile. Hassan put his arm around her shoulders and kissed her, then he and his father left the shop. Lilly stood in the window and watched them make their way slowly down Main Street, observing how attentive Hassan was toward the older man--walking on outside of his father, keeping his hand at the ready to steady him if necessary. She smiled. She was very lucky to have found Hassan.

After work that evening Lilly called Noley. She didn't want to wait until later, in case Noley was going to bed early. She was supposed to be at the bistro at an unearthly hour.

"I just called to wish you good luck tomorrow," she said when Noley answered the phone.

"Thank you. I'll need it," Noley answered.

"You'll do great. What's on the menu?"

"Earl Grey *madeleines*, honey *madeleines, Éclairs*, *financiers*, *petit fours*, *palmiers*, *pain aux raisins*, *tuile*, *tartes des alpes*, *bichons aux citrons*. You name it, in French of course, and I'm making it."

"Yum. I may have to stop in and do some sampling."

"Don't you dare come in, at least not tomorrow. I won't be able to take the pressure."

"Pressure? What pressure? I'm your best friend!"

"That's where the pressure comes from! Cooking for people I don't know is easy. Cooking for people I *do* know is the hardest thing I do."

"Okay, I won't come in tomorrow. But I can't promise I won't come in at all while you're working there."

"That's okay. Just give me time to get settled."

"Are you excited? Maybe just a little?"

"I'm not excited as much as I am nervous."

"Well, I happen to know you'll do great. I won't keep you--I just wanted to wish you a great day. Call me when you get home tomorrow. I want to hear about your first day."

"I will. G'night."

Lilly hung up the phone.

"Mom! Are you home?" Laurel's voice came thundering down the stairs. Lilly went to the bottom of the staircase and looked up.

"I'm home. Come on down!"

A minute later Laurel came bounding down the steps.

"How was your day?" Lilly asked, kissing her daughter on the cheek.

"Great. How about yours?"

"Good," Lilly answered. "Amir is in town."

"I love him!" Laurel gushed. "Am I going to get to see him before he goes back to Minnesota?"

"Probably. I don't actually know how long he's staying. Where's Tighe?"

If Lilly hadn't been looking at Laurel, she might have missed the fleeting look of panic that flitted across Laurel's face.

"Young lady, tell me where your brother is."

"I don't know."

"The truth, Laurel."

"I mean it. I don't know. Maybe he had to work late."

"What was that look on your face for?"

"What look?" *I might have known she'd play dumb. Sometimes I think those two are too close. I wish one would rat out the other once in a while,* Lilly thought.

"Never mind," Lilly said with a sigh. "It's obvious I'm not going to get anywhere with you. If your brother is up to something, will you tell me?" *The old guilt trip ought to work.*

"Depends on whether he can get out of it by himself," Laurel said. She kissed her mother on the cheek and ran upstairs before Lilly could grab her and force a confession out of her.

Maybe it's nothing that requires a confession, Lilly thought. *I hope not.*

She let Barney outside and waited for him on the patio, sitting in the darkened backyard and listening to the crickets.

A door slammed. Lilly groaned aloud. Mrs. Laforge. That woman's ability to sense when Lilly didn't want her around was uncanny.

A moment later there was a knock on the back gate and it swung open before Lilly could answer.

"Mrs. Carlsen? It's Edna Laforge."

"I know, Mrs. Laforge. Come in. What can I do for you?" Lilly could hear the tired notes of her own voice.

"I need to talk to you about your son and his friends." Loud sigh. "I'm sorry to have to bring this up."

Sure you are.

"It's just--they peel out of your driveway in their cars. It's very dangerous and they're going to hurt someone one of these days. Not to mention the noise it makes, of course. It drives me up a wall." Mrs. Laforge came to stand in front of Lilly. Barney raced up to her and started sniffing her ankles.

"And that reminds me," Mrs. Laforge continued. "This dog. He got out today. If that nice old Mister Gristede across the street hadn't brought him home, heaven only knows where he might be right now. It really would be a good idea for you to get an electric fence and then your neighbors don't have to go running all over Kingdom Come to chase him." She emphasized her last words with a loud *harrumph.*

Lilly closed her eyes and prayed for the strength she would need not to drop kick Mrs. Laforge clear back to her own yard.

"As for the cars, with all due respect, I don't know what you're talking about. My kids have been at work all day. There shouldn't be any cars at our house. And as for Barney, thank you for letting me know he was out. One of the kids must have let him out by mistake. I will talk to Mister Gristede and thank him personally." *And just wait until I find out who left the dog out…*

She stood up and whistled for Barney, who by that time was digging in the bushes. "I'll go talk to the kids and see if I can get an answer for you about the cars." She turned to go inside.

"I don't know how you're going to talk to Tighe when he isn't even home yet."

Lilly turned around to face her neighbor. Had the woman no sense of common courtesy?

"Mrs. Laforge, don't you have anything better to do than keep an eye on my children?"

It was the wrong thing to say.

"If I don't, who will?" Mrs. Laforge asked. She tossed her head and walked back through the gate, slamming it behind her.

CHAPTER 18

Lilly was getting a headache.

She went inside, gave Barney a fresh bowl of water, and called upstairs. "Laurel! Can you come down here, please?"

Laurel's bedroom door slammed shut a moment later and she came downstairs to stand in the kitchen.

"I didn't do anything," she said.

"How do you know what I'm going to say?"

"I don't. It's how you say it. Someone's in trouble."

"Did you forget to let Barney in earlier today?"

Laurel thought for a moment, then said. "I didn't even let Barney out today. I couldn't have forgotten to let him in. Why?"

"Mrs. Laforge just paid me a friendly visit to tell me Barney got out. Apparently Mister Gristede had to chase Barney all over the place to get him to come home."

Laurel shrugged. "That old bat is probably making stuff up. Did she tell you we're too loud when you're not home, too?"

"As a matter of fact, she did."

Laurel looked at her mother, her eyes wide. "I was only joking! We're not too loud, I swear."

"I didn't say you were. But Mrs. Laforge is hearing cars going too fast or something. She's got it in for both of you."

"I can't stand her."

"I know. But try to remember that she saved Barney last Christmas when he was out in the blizzard. We owe her one."

"And we invited her to Tighe's graduation party. There. We're even. We don't owe her anything."

"Okay, okay. Do me a favor, will you? Just keep your ears open when I'm not home. If you hear any cars peeling around the neighborhood, let me know where it's coming from and I'll tell Mrs. Laforge to send her anger that way."

"Okay. Will you tell Tighe or do you want me to?"

"I'm going to text him to see where he is. I'll tell him."

Laurel ran back up to her room and Lilly reached for her cell phone and texted Tighe.

Where are you?
At Mike's.
I thought you guys weren't getting along.
We r now.
What are you doing?
Hanging out.
When will you be home?
Dont no.
You have a midnight curfew.
Cant I stay out late 2nite?
No.
Why not?
I'm not arguing with you. Be here by midnight.
Ok.
Did you leave Barney outside earlier?
Dont think so. Why?

Mrs. Laforge said he got out and a neighbor had to chase him to bring him back home.
Wasnt me. Maybe Laurel.
She says it wasn't her. Do you work tomorrow?
Yes
I'll wake you up before I go to work. Lock the door when you come in tonight.
Ok.
Love you.
Luv u 2.

She would discuss the car issue with him in the morning. She sat down in the living room and watched television for a while, then she let Barney out one last time, then the two of them went upstairs.

Lilly never slept well until she knew both kids were in the house, so she tossed and turned until she heard Tighe come in downstairs. She looked at the clock. He made his curfew by one minute. She smiled and was able to drift off to sleep.

When Lilly awoke the next morning she found that her headache had only gotten worse overnight. She stood at the kitchen sink drinking her first cup of coffee, hoping the caffeine would bring some relief to her pounding head. She poured a second cup and was going to get Tighe up when he came downstairs, still dressed in pajamas.

"You're up early," she said.

"I'm starving. Anything good for breakfast?"

"Cereal and toast."

"Gross."

"Sorry, pal. I'm afraid I gave Cook the week off."

Tighe smiled. "Okay, okay. No need to get snarky."

It was Lilly's turn to smile. "If you want something else, make it yourself. Now, listen. Mrs. Laforge is on another rant about cars and noise. She swears it's coming from this house. Any idea what she's talking about?"

Tighe shook his head.

"Okay. Just be aware of it. I'd like to figure out where it's coming from. And you don't know anything about Barney being left outside yesterday?"

Tighe shook his head again.

Someone was lying to Lilly—again—and she intended to figure out who it was.

When she went in to work Harry was already there, setting up the jewelry displays.

"So did you hear there was another fire last night?" Harry asked, arranging a heavy watch on a velvet wrist.

Lilly spun around to face him, sloshing coffee on her blouse in the process.

"Darn it," she said, trying to dab the stain with a napkin. "No. I didn't hear. What happened?"

"Another vacant house, another total loss of property. But no one was hurt. Thank God," Harry added.

"Where was it?"

"Nowhere near the other two homes, if that's what you mean," Harry said. "Over in the Foothill Acres section of town."

Lilly nodded. That part of Juniper Junction had a large number of lovely older homes. It was horrible to think that the firebug might have struck again. And Tighe had been out again last night…

"Do the police know what happened?"

"They're not saying anything except that they're treating it as suspicious," Harry said. "I'm sure that means arson."

"It's terrifying to think there might be an arsonist on the loose in Juniper Junction," Lilly said with a shudder.

"At least whoever it is seems to be targeting homes that are for sale or vacant for some reason."

"Maybe, but for how long?" Lilly asked.

Again that day, talk in the jewelry shop focused on the third fire and who could have set it. Why would someone do such a thing? It seemed there was nothing else people wanted to talk about all day.

Hassan came in a little after lunch. He kissed Lilly and shook hands with Harry. "Have you heard about the fire?" Lilly asked him.

"I have. It's all over the news," Hassan said gravely. "Have you talked to Bill?"

"Not yet, but I'm going to. I keep forgetting to call him to tell him to take Noley out to dinner, so I need to talk to him, anyway."

"How is she doing her first day on the job?" Hassan asked.

"I haven't talked to her," Lilly said. "I'll call her tonight."

"I was going to stop in and get something for me and Dad to have with dinner," Hassan said, his eyes twinkling. "Do you think I should?"

"I don't know. She banned me from going in because she said it would make her too nervous."

"She didn't ban me," Hassan said with a grin.

"So get over there! Let me know how she's doing." Lilly laughed and steered Hassan toward the door.

Hassan stopped by on his way back home to report that Noley was so busy she hadn't even seen him, which was probably a good thing. He also said the bistro's line was out the door, as usual, and that people were lining up for the pastries and desserts.

Lilly smiled at the news--it sounded like Noley was having a good first day on the job.

When Lilly spoke to her that night on the phone, her friend was exhausted. She hadn't even eaten dinner, though Armand had offered to give her whatever she wanted from the menu. She had been run off her feet all day, but she was thrilled to have stayed busy.

"And how did Armand do with the bistro opening up again?" Lilly asked.

"Pretty well. He didn't have a whole lot of time to mourn

for Cerise, so that was positive. I think it's important to stay busy when something awful happens so that you can keep your mind on other things until you're ready to deal with what happened."

"Did he talk about her at all?"

"Actually, he did. I was a little surprised. But it was all stuff like 'Cerise loved making madeleines because they have such an interesting shape' or 'Cerise loved that old guy who comes for lunch every day.' You know, just small things that he remembered about her and he would mention them aloud. It was nice."

"I'm glad you had such a great day."

"Yeah. The only thing that stunk was when Kathleen Deveau came in. I found out she and Armand are distant cousins."

"Did she say anything to you?" Lilly asked.

"Not on your life. She doesn't speak to me."

"Ignore her," Lilly advised. "Back at work first thing in the morning?"

"Yup. I need to get some sleep."

After Lilly hung up she called Bill. She had several things she needed to talk to him about.

"Hi. What's up?" he asked when he answered the phone.

"I just talked to Noley. Have you spoken to her since she got home from work?"

"Yeah. Sounds like she had a busy day. I'm happy for her."

"I knew you would be. Listen, I'm sure she didn't mention it to you because I was supposed to do it, but how about you making reservations at some really fancy place and then taking her for dinner and dancing some night?"

"Why?" He sounded suspicious. "Is she mad at me? What did I do wrong?"

Lilly laughed. "She's not mad, and you didn't do anything wrong. I just told her that I would talk to you about taking her out for a night on the town. Which town is up to you. She just needs to go out and let off some steam. She's still worried about how Cerise died. She's convinced it was her food."

"Sure. I can do that. When? Where should we go?"

"I don't know when. At this point I think you'll have to wait until Armand hires someone to be his full-time pastry chef because I think Nol's going to be very busy for the next couple of weeks. And as for where, that's totally up to you. You could go to The Water Wheel, but that's not a dancing place. It's more of just a dinner place. How about somewhere in Lupine?" The neighboring town was known for its over-the-top restaurants and lounges.

"Sounds good to me, though I don't really belong in those fancy-schmancy places. But if it's something Noley wants, I'll do it."

"That's the spirit. Now, on to my next question. What do you know about these fires?"

"Nothing." He said it almost before she finished asking the question.

"You're lying. I can tell because you answered me too fast."

"Lilly, you know I can't share information about the investigations."

"Okay, all right. Just tell me that Tighe is off the hook and that the police know he didn't set that first fire. Or any of the others, for that matter."

"I'm pretty sure he's off the hook."

"What do you mean *pretty sure*?" Lilly was aware of the shrillness of her voice.

"Don't worry about it. I told you before, they only wanted to question him again because someone said he had left that party for a few minutes before the fire started and they needed to make sure he could account for his whereabouts. Don't worry. We're on it, and Tighe is not a suspect. I only say 'pretty sure' because I haven't talked to the detective in charge. But I certainly wouldn't worry about it if I were you."

"Promise?"

"Promise."

"Okay. Last question. How's Mom? Have you talked to her?" Lilly asked.

"Actually, I wanted to talk to you about her."

Uh-oh.

CHAPTER 19

"Is something wrong? I haven't even talked to her in a couple days," she said.

"She seems to be getting more forgetful. I mean, twice when I was talking to her yesterday she couldn't think of very basic words. Like 'refrigerator' and 'mailbox.'"

Lilly was silent for a moment while the information sank in. She sighed. "I guess this is all part of the progression." She felt a surge of hatred toward the dementia sweep through her.

"I guess so."

"I'll go see her after work tomorrow. Maybe she can come over here for dinner," Lilly suggested.

"She'd probably like that. I have to work all night tomorrow, so I may not be able to stop and see her. Let me know how she is."

Lilly hung up and turned to Barney, who had come up to her and was resting his face on her knees. She cupped his head in her hands and kissed his snout.

"Barney, you're so lucky you aren't human."

He answered with a *Woof!* and a furious wag of his tail, then began bounding around the kitchen. Lilly laughed. "I know what you want. You want to go for a walk."

At the word 'walk' Barney lost all control and leapt up trying to lick Lilly's face. Still laughing, she clipped his leash to his collar and led him outside. Barney's walks were really more like *moseys*, since he had to stop every two feet and smell the grass, the sidewalk, and whatever detritus happened to be lying on the ground. Sometimes it was a pile of leaves, sometimes it was something far worse.

They had walked around the block and were returning home when a car pulled up in front of the Carlsen house. There were voices, then the passenger door opened. Barney started to growl and strain at the leash.

"No, Barney. Sit." Lilly waited to see who was getting out of the car before approaching the house.

It was Tighe. Lilly walked up to him, with Barney straining at the leash again.

Tighe shut the car door, rapped on the window, and the driver pulled away from the curb a little too quickly.

"Who was that?" Lilly asked.

"Mike."

"Oh. Why didn't he say hello? I haven't seen him in a while."

"He's in a hurry. He has to get home."

"Oh. Where's your car?"

"Mike picked me up from work earlier, so it's still there."

"How will you get to work in the morning?"

"One of the guys can pick me up, or I'll walk."

"Mike pulled away from the curb pretty fast. He's probably the one Mrs. Laforge is complaining about."

"That wasn't too fast," Tighe said.

"Yes, it was."

"Stop it, Mom."

Lilly decided to let the matter go for the moment.

Barney was trying to get Tighe's attention by shoving his nose under Tighe's hand, sniffing his feet, and slamming his tail against Tighe's leg, so Tighe finally reached down to give

Barney's head a vigorous rub. Barney stood, accepting the attention for a moment, then seemed to tire of it and pulled on the leash toward the front steps.

"Have you eaten?" Lilly asked as they all went into the house.

"Yeah, but I'm still hungry," Tighe answered.

"There are snacks in the pantry. I'm going up to bed," Lilly said.

"Goodnight. Love you," Tighe said, leaning in to kiss his mother's cheek.

"Ugh. Where have you been? You need a shower."

Tighe chuckled. "We were outside at Mike's house. I probably smell of outdoors."

"You do. And not in a good way."

Tighe laughed again. "I'll take a shower before I go to bed."

"Thank you. Goodnight. Love you, honey."

The next day dawned stormy and dark. Lilly liked days like that because it seemed bad weather put people in a shopping mood. Despite the rain and the heavy winds, there was a steady stream of customers through the jewelry shop that day. Lilly sold three gemstone pendants and two watches, as well as an engagement ring for a very happy and nervous young man.

When she finally locked the door for the day and she and Harry had put away the jewelry displays, she headed over to Bev's house. It was still raining when she pulled up in front of her mom's craftsman-style bungalow.

She dashed up the front steps and knocked on the front door, then tried the handle. She usually knocked first, then just let herself in. But today the door was locked.

She waited for her mom to come to the door, but after a few moments there was no answer. Lilly knocked again, louder this time, and waited. Still no answer.

Lilly pulled out her cell phone and dialed her mother's number. She could hear the phone ringing inside the house, but there was no answer. Lilly was rifling through her purse to find the keys to her mother's house when a noise made her turn around.

Bev was coming up the steps. She was soaking wet and bedraggled, rainwater streaming down her face, her hair matted against her head. She was dressed in long pants and a short-sleeved blouse and her clothes clung to her as she shivered.

"Mom! Where have you been?" Lilly cried.

"Out for a walk," Bev replied.

"In this weather and without an umbrella? Let's get you inside and into some dry clothes."

Bev waited while Lilly unlocked the door, then Lilly ushered her mother into the living room. "Mom, you wait here while I find you some other clothes to wear." Lilly hurried upstairs and quickly found another pair of pants, a soft tee shirt, and a large bath towel. She also grabbed clean underwear from her mother's dresser and ran downstairs again.

"Here, put these on. You can change in the dining room and the neighbors won't see you," she said. Bev obeyed without a word.

While she changed her clothes, Lilly went into the kitchen to fix two cups of hot tea. As the tea steeped she checked the refrigerator to see if there was anything she could make for her mother to eat. She had intended to invite her mother for dinner with her and the kids, but there was no way she was letting her mother leave the house again.

When the tea was ready and she had prepared Bev a sandwich, Lilly sat down at the table to wait. A few moments later Bev appeared in the kitchen, holding all of her wet clothes and dressed in the dry ones. Her hair was still wet and she was still shivering.

"Mom, you sit down and eat. I'm going to get the hair dryer. If your hair is dry, your whole body will feel warmer."

Bev sat down as directed while Lilly ran upstairs again. She came down holding a hair dryer.

"Do you want me to do your hair for you, or do you want to do it yourself?" Lilly asked.

"I can do it myself."

"Aren't you going to finish your sandwich?" Lilly asked. "You've only had two bites."

"I'm not hungry. Any word about what killed that poor woman at the celebration?" Bev asked. "I would have asked you sooner, but you so rarely come to see me anymore."

"Mom," Lilly said, exasperated, "it's only been a couple days. And I've talked to Bill, so I know you're not sitting alone over here all the time."

"Poor Bill doesn't have the time to keep running over here," Bev said with a sad shake of her head. Lilly could feel her blood pressure rising.

"Mom, I should probably get going," Lilly said. *Before I lose my mind,* she thought. "I'll talk to you tomorrow."

"Goodnight, dear. Thank you for coming over and for the sandwich. It's the thought that counts."

Lilly took a deep breath, counted to ten, and kissed her mother's soft cheek. "Bye."

She was glad she hadn't invited her mother to dinner at her house--she didn't need that stress. But as she got in her car and drove away, Lilly took a deep breath. Her mom couldn't always help the way she was, and Lilly needed to come to terms with that. It wasn't going to be easy.

When she got home Laurel was there and Tighe had phoned to say he was on his way. Lilly was thrilled--the three of them would be able to have dinner together, which didn't happen nearly as often as she would have liked.

She and Laurel busied themselves shaping hamburger patties to throw on the grill, and Lilly sliced a pineapple to grill, too. She figured they could either put the pineapples on their burgers or have them for dessert.

When Tighe came home, though, he looked worn out.

"Do you feel okay?" Lilly asked when she saw him.

"Yeah, I'm just tired. I need to go to bed."

"But it's early. We made burgers. Don't you want one?"

"No thanks, Mom. I already ate."

"Where?"

"I grabbed a slice of pizza after work with a couple guys."

"Oh. Okay. Go get some rest. Love you."

He gave her a perfunctory hug and went upstairs to bed. So much for the small family having dinner together. At least she and Laurel could enjoy some mother-daughter time.

"How long will the burgers take?" Laurel asked. "I told Nick I could go for ice cream after dinner, so I have to hurry."

So much for mother-daughter time. Was it going to be like this all the time after Tighe left for school? Lilly supposed she should start getting used to it. Had she been like this as a teenager? She was saddened to think she might have hurt her mother's feelings all those years ago without realizing it.

She and Laurel ate a hurried dinner and before long Nick was knocking at the front door. Laurel opened it with a wide smile and Lilly felt a sudden twinge of loneliness. She watched them leave, blissfully aware only of each other, and thought about the day when Laurel and Tighe would both be in school.

She swallowed hard and vowed not to let such thoughts burrow into her brain. The kids were still home, and the thing to do was to enjoy every minute with them. That's what she intended to do. She called Noley just to check in and see how her day went, but there was no answer. She was probably still at work.

Since Hassan and his father were busy on a conference call with some gem buyers overseas, she had the entire evening to herself.

And suddenly she didn't know what to do. Should she

make muffins for the kids' breakfasts? Should she sit down and watch television? Should she fold laundry?

None of those options sounded appealing.

When Barney came over and sat next to her feet, his tongue hanging out, she knew what she wanted to do. She would take Barney for a walk.

There was the usual jumping around--by Barney--while she tried to clip on his leash, and they left. The sky was already a darkening purple thanks to the mountain to the west of Juniper Junction that brought sunset to the town a little early.

She and Barney set off toward Main Street, where he loved to walk because so many people would stop and ask to pet him. He was like a politician--he knew just where to go to find the love.

And sure enough, even though most of the shops on Main Street were closed, there were people milling around because the restaurants were still open. Barney pranced down the street, waiting to be approached by his public.

And he wasn't disappointed. At least half a dozen people commented about "the beautiful dog" and wanted to meet him up close. With every "what a good boy!" his tail wagged harder and harder until Lilly thought he would take off and fly around the block.

It wasn't until they were on their way home that Barney wanted to stop every few feet and sniff his surroundings. Lilly usually encouraged him to hurry a little, but on that night she was happy to let him sniff away to his heart's content. The rain had stopped and the sky had cleared, making the first few twinkling stars visible in the dark skies high above Juniper Junction. The air was finally cool and, as always, dry. Lilly was enjoying her time with Barney.

They were almost home when Barney stopped to sniff the bushes in front of Mrs. Laforge's house. He was at it an especially long time and Lilly finally decided it was time to go home. She was getting tired.

"Come on, Barney boy," she said, giving the leash a tug. "Time to go home." She gave the leash another tug, but Barney refused to leave the bushes.

"Barney, what did I just say? It's time to go home."

He wouldn't budge, and his sniffling was getting more intense.

"Barney, what on earth is so interesting under that bush?" Lilly asked, exasperated.

She walked over to where Barney was now lying on the ground, still sniffing, and bent down to physically move his body away from the bush.

But when she got a look at what had so captivated him, she stumbled back in horror.

It was someone's hand.

CHAPTER 20

Stifling a scream, she reached into her back pocket with trembling hands and closed her fingers around her cell phone. She dialed nine-one-one and waited for the dispatcher to answer.

"Nine-one-one. What is your emergency?"

"This is Lilly Carlsen. I've just--or rather, my dog has just stumbled across someone's body. It's lying under a bush." She gave the dispatcher the cross streets and promised to wait there while police and an ambulance were sent to the scene.

"Do you want me to stay on the phone with you?" the dispatcher asked.

"No, I'm all right. I've got my dog here with me," Lilly answered.

She hung up and looked up and down the intersecting streets for the first sign of police lights. Nothing yet.

And then Barney started to whine.

"What is it, Barney?" Lilly asked, almost afraid to know the answer.

She walked back to where Barney was now sitting on his haunches and she heard a low moan. Lilly hadn't even looked at the person yet because she was afraid the body attached to the hand was dead. But it clearly wasn't.

"Hello?" Lilly asked. "Can I help you?" She bent down low to the ground and listened hard for a response. Another moan.

"The police are on their way, and an ambulance. Don't move. You'll be okay," Lilly assured the person. She hoped she wasn't lying.

Finally a voice, thick with fog, spoke.

"Get that dog away from me."

Lilly recognized that voice. "Mrs. Laforge?" she asked, incredulous. Barney gave the hand one last lick for good measure.

"Barney, come here." Lilly gave the leash a tug and Barney finally trotted away to sit a few feet from Mrs. Laforge. Apparently now that his friend from next door was conscious and speaking, he felt his work was done.

She knelt down next to Mrs. Laforge.

"Are you all right, Mrs. Laforge? What on earth happened?"

"I don't remember. I came outside because there was a car parked out front, then I don't remember what happened after that. I can't move my leg."

"Don't move," Lilly repeated. "The police will be here any minute."

As if to confirm what Lilly had said, the women heard a siren just a second or two later. In another moment Lilly could see lights from a cruiser reflecting off the dark houses in the neighborhood.

The car came to a stop and two officers got out, striding over to where Lilly knelt on the grass.

"What happened here?" one of them asked.

"This is my neighbor, Edna Laforge," Lilly said. "I was walking my dog and he actually found her lying here."

"How did you end up here, Mrs. Laforge?" the other officer asked.

"How am I supposed to know? Do you think I came out here for a nap?" the lady snapped.

"She can't move her leg," Lilly informed the officers. "And I think she was unconscious when the dog found her."

"We've got an ambulance on the way. Should be here soon," the first officer said.

"I'm not going in any ambulance," came Mrs. Laforge's querulous voice. "Someone just help me up and get me into my house and leave me alone."

"Mrs. Laforge, if you can't move your leg you really need to go have it checked out," Lilly said. The officers were silent, content to let Lilly convince the lady to go in the ambulance.

"Someone help me up," Mrs. Laforge directed. "If I can walk, I'm going home. If I can't, I'll go to the hospital. Does that make you happy?"

"Yes, ma'am," the first officer said. "But we're not the ones who can help you stand up. You have to wait for the paramedics for that. We don't want to take a chance on making your injury worse."

"Bah," was all Mrs. Laforge said.

The ambulance arrived a moment later and the paramedics quickly assessed the situation. "Your leg could be broken, ma'am. You need to go to the hospital to get looked at."

"I said I would go if I couldn't walk. If you'd been here sooner you would have heard the conversation. Now help me up so I can see if I can walk."

The two paramedics looked at each other. One shrugged and said, "Okay. Let's see if you can stand up."

Mrs. Laforge had remained essentially motionless from the time Barney found her, so Lilly worried that she might be more seriously hurt than she believed. She watched anxiously as the paramedics tried to turn Mrs. Laforge over onto her back before helping her stand up.

Mrs. Laforge moaned again. "Take is easy, will you? My head is killing me."

The paramedics exchanged glances again and one said, "That's it. I'm not doing this. Ma'am, you need to go to a hospital. There's a good chance you have a concussion. I'm not taking 'no' for an answer." The other paramedic, obviously relieved his partner had stood up to the cantankerous old woman, stood back and nodded, his arms crossed over his chest.

"Oh, for Pete's sake. All right, get me into that expensive truck and take me wherever you want to go," Mrs. Laforge said. Lilly could have sworn she heard the faintest hint of relief in her neighbor's voice.

After the police had taken a statement from Lilly and Mrs. Laforge had been loaded into the back of the ambulance, Lilly took Barney home and gave him a treat. He had managed to stay by her side during the entire scene at the corner, so he deserved it.

More than anything, Lilly wanted to go to bed. She was tired from working and visiting her mother and the ordeal with Mrs. Laforge. But instead, she grabbed her purse and got in the car. She was going to the hospital.

When she arrived at the hospital located halfway between Juniper Junction and Lupine, a nurse took her back to see Mrs. Laforge. Lilly heard Mrs. Laforge before she saw her.

"That hurts!" Mrs. Laforge roared. "Stop it or I'll sue you!"

A moment later a doctor pulled back a curtain and stepped into the main area of the Emergency Department. He gave his head a little shake. A nurse followed him and closed the curtain.

"Doctor, this is the patient's neighbor. She found the patient on the ground."

"Okay, thanks. I have a couple questions for you. First, did Mrs.--" he glanced at his notes. "Did Mrs. Laforge lose consciousness that you know of?"

Lilly nodded. "I think she did. She didn't seem to be awake when my dog found her."

"Do you know if she has any medical conditions I should know about?"

"I don't know," Lilly replied.

"Do you have any idea what happened to cause her to fall?"

Lilly shook her head. "Is she badly hurt?"

"I'm not supposed to discuss her condition with you because you're not a family member. Mrs. Laforge gave the nurse her sons' phone numbers. If Mrs. Laforge gives permission for you to receive information, I'll be able to talk to you."

The nurse spoke to Mrs. Laforge and the older woman consented to let the doctor talk to Lilly. He had also telephoned her sons and they promised to get to the hospital as soon as possible. It would be a while, though, because they both lived a fair distance away. Lilly couldn't help being a little bit envious of them--she would have like to live a fair distance away from Mrs. Laforge, too.

She went into the curtained cubicle to sit with Mrs. Laforge.

"How are you feeling?" she asked.

"I'm sore."

"Do you remember what happened?"

"How many times do I have to tell people I have no idea what happened? For God's sake, the story hasn't changed since the last person asked me. That doctor is a menace. Doesn't care that my head hurts. He just keeps poking around up there like he's panning for gold."

Lilly tried to suppress a smile. "I think he's just trying to figure out where you hit your head."

"Be that as it may, it hurts and he's making no effort to be careful. I told him I'll sue him and I intend to."

"What's the last thing you remember?" Lilly asked in an effort to change the subject.

"I remember going outside because there was a car and I heard a loud noise. After that I don't have any idea what happened. I didn't just faint, mind you. I'm as strong as a horse."

And as ornery as a wolverine, Lilly thought.

The doctor came in just then.

"Mrs. Laforge, someone is going to come in to wheel you down to X-ray. You've got some nasty bruises on your thigh and we need to make sure you don't have any broken bones."

"It's about time someone did something to figure out what's wrong with me," Mrs. Laforge snapped. The doctor ignored her and walked out. He was clearly in for a long evening.

As it turned out, Mrs. Laforge had not broken any bones. True to her words, she was almost as strong as a horse. But she had deep bruising that would make it painful for her to walk. She also had a moderate concussion and the doctor decided, probably against his personal wishes, that Mrs. Laforge needed to be kept at the hospital overnight for observation. The old lady was not happy to hear it.

"So I can't go home. Well, maybe the federal government would like to hear about this. Maybe Medicare would be interested to know you're bilking them out of money."

"Mrs. Laforge," the doctor said with a sigh, "I am doing what any other doctor would do under the circumstances, and it has nothing to do with your insurance. You can always refuse to stay, but I wouldn't recommend it."

"Hmph. We'll see," Mrs. Laforge said with a scowl.

"Mrs. Laforge, can I get you anything from home? A change of clothes or a toothbrush or anything?"

The woman heaved a sigh. "I suppose I'll need something

to wear home tomorrow. And I will need my toothbrush, of course. The key is hidden under a flower pot in the backyard. I can't remember which pot just now."

Lilly had to fight the urge to roll her eyes. As she recalled, there were about a million flowerpots in Mrs. Laforge's backyard.

"Can I get some television in here?" Mrs. Laforge suddenly called out. A nurse came in a few moments later.

"Mrs. Laforge, I'm going to have to ask you to stay calm and keep your voice down. And you can't watch tv because you've suffered a concussion."

"Well, that's the silliest thing I've ever heard," Mrs. Laforge grumbled.

The nurse gave Lilly a slight smile.

"Mrs. Laforge, I'm going to head out. I'll be back with your stuff as soon as I find the key."

"All right. And thank you."

Lilly hadn't expected thanks. Maybe the concussion had knocked some manners into Mrs. Laforge.

But then again, probably not.

Once Lilly got to Mrs. Laforge's house, it took her about a half hour to find the flowerpot with the key under it. She was in a foul mood by the time she unlocked the back door and went inside. It had been a long time since she had last seen the inside of Mrs. Laforge's house.

And nothing had changed. The house had an antiseptic smell about it, as though Mrs. Laforge spent a lot of time cleaning. There were plastic flowers in vases and zig-zag afghans on the back of each piece of furniture in the living room. When Lilly went upstairs, she found more of the same. Outdated furnishings and decor and a strong odor of cleaning supplies.

She quickly found a change of clothes for her neighbor, then she went into the bathroom to find a toothbrush, hairbrush, and cold cream. Once she had everything she needed, she went back downstairs.

It wasn't until she had turned off the kitchen light and was ready to leave that she heard a noise coming from the small shed in the backyard. It was a loud clattering sound, and Lilly froze when she heard it. It was the sound of something being disturbed, of something that didn't belong.

She reached over to lock the kitchen door as quietly as she could, then she stood to one side of the kitchen window so she had a view of the shed. Anyone in the shed wouldn't have seen her because all the lights in the house were off, but she wanted to stand out of anyone's line of sight, just in case.

When she saw the person emerge from the shed, he stepped into the circle of light cast by a floodlight on the back of the house. It had been triggered, apparently, by the motion in the yard.

Lilly gasped. It was Tighe's best friend. It was Mike.

CHAPTER 21

Lilly didn't know what to do. Should she call the police? Should she call Tighe? Should she go out and confront Mike herself?

What on earth was he doing out there?

She made up her mind quickly. Yanking open the back door so she would purposely startle Mike, she yelled his name.

"Mike! What are you doing here?"

He had taken off running toward the front of the house when he heard the door open, but he stopped short when he heard his name being called.

"Who's there?" he asked.

"It's Mrs. Carlsen, Tighe's mom. What is going on?"

Mike turned around slowly and faced Lilly.

"Nothing."

"Nothing, my foot. Tell me right now what you were doing in my neighbor's shed or I'll have to call the police."

"I was at your house and I thought I heard a noise out here," he said. "I came to check it out, that's all."

"Please, Mike. I'm not stupid. Don't waste your time and mine telling me a pack of lies. I want the truth. What were you doing in the shed?"

Mike sighed and his shoulders slumped. "Looking for power tools."

"Why?"

"To sell. Please don't tell the cops, Mrs. Carlsen. I won't do it again, I promise."

"Mike, why on earth are you trying to sell stolen things?"

No answer.

"Mike?" Lilly prompted.

"I need money."

"What for? All you need to do is ask and I can lend you some money."

"Thanks, Mrs. C."

"But not until you tell me what it's for."

"I can't."

"Why not?"

Mike shrugged.

"I can't lend you the money if you don't tell me what it's for. It must be pretty serious if you're willing to steal from old ladies to get it."

"It's nothing. Never mind, Mrs. C. Thanks anyway." He looked at his feet and started to shuffle away.

"Wait, Mike. I didn't see your car out front. Do you need a ride home?"

"No, thanks. I'm parked a block away."

"All right," Lilly said with a nod. "Don't let me catch you doing something like this again."

Mike nodded, then turned away and hurried off. Lilly stood watching him go, wondering what he could need money for. Should she tell his parents? She wasn't sure. She figured she would wait and see if Mike did anything else stupid. Should she tell Mrs. Laforge? Most certainly not. There was one person Lilly would be sure to talk to about this, though--Tighe.

When she got back to the hospital she found Mrs. Laforge already being taken up to a room to spend the night. She followed the orderly as he wheeled Mrs. Laforge to her overnight digs. Mrs. Laforge complained the entire way.

"Where did you learn to drive?" she demanded. "That last corner almost ripped my arm off. Don't you have any care for an old lady in pain?"

The orderly apologized and looked like he was trying to bite his tongue to keep from responding to Mrs. Laforge in other, less polite, ways.

"It's freezing in here. No wonder it costs so much to go to the hospital. How else will they pay the electric bill?"

When the orderly finally had Mrs. Laforge situated in her room, he left with an audible sigh of relief. Lilly bustled around the bed, making sure her neighbor was comfortable. She hung up Mrs. Laforge's clothes in a small armoire which stood next to the bed, then she put the toiletry items in the bathroom.

"Mrs. Laforge, can I do anything else for you before I head home?"

"No. I just want to go to sleep," the lady answered. "Do you know when my sons will get here?"

"I'm not sure, but they said they would be here as soon as possible."

Mrs. Laforge nodded and closed her eyes. Lilly walked to the door, then turned around to look at her neighbor. The old lady looked small under the thin bedcovers, and her face held a worried look even with her eyes closed. Lilly watched her for a moment, suddenly feeling sad, then turned again to leave.

"Thank you," Mrs. Laforge said, raising her voice just a little bit.

"You're welcome," Lilly replied.

When she pulled into the driveway at home, she noticed Tighe's light was still on. He must not have gone to bed as he had intended when he got home. *Good,* she thought. *I'm going to talk to him about Mike right now.*

She went inside and straight upstairs, not even stopping to let Barney out. She knocked on Tighe's door.

"Yeah?"

"Can I come in?" Lilly asked.

"Yeah."

She opened the door and stepped into his small, neat bedroom. She glanced around at the posters that had hung on the walls for years, at the bedding she had bought him early in high school, at the heap of laundry lying on the floor. Tighe was sitting at his desk, typing something at his computer, his back to her.

"We need to have a little talk," Lilly said, sitting down on the edge of the bed. She noticed his back stiffen.

"What's up?" he asked. He didn't turn around.

"Look at me when I'm talking to you, please."

He turned around slowly. "What's the matter?" he asked.

"I want to talk to you about Mike." Did she just see his shoulders relax the tiniest bit?

"What about him?"

"I just found him in the shed at Mrs. Laforge's house. He was trying to steal power tools to sell." She let that sink in for a moment.

"Why were you at Mrs. Laforge's house?"

"Is that your takeaway from what I just said?" Lilly asked.

"No, no. Sorry. So you must have talked to him."

"Yes. I saw him come out of the shed and I confronted him. Is he in some kind of trouble?"

"Not that I know of."

"But you two have been spending a lot of time together. He hasn't said anything to you about needing money? Can his family afford food?"

"Yeah. Don't worry, Mom. Mike's fine, his family's fine, everyone is fine."

"Don't get smart with me, Tighe. I'm worried."

"About Mike?"

"Yes! Who else would I be talking about?"

Tighe shrugged.

"And what's with you lately?" Lilly asked. She might as well get all the issues out of the way as long as they were having this talk. "You haven't been yourself."

"Who have I been?" Tighe's laugh faded to a lame chuckle. "Sorry."

"I mean, you haven't been around very much, you haven't been eating meals with me and Laurel,--"

"There was just that one dinner," he said.

"True. But I still get the feeling something is off."

"I'm fine. I promise." Tighe looked her in the eyes.

Lilly was silent for a moment, wondering whether continuing to ask questions would do her any good. She didn't believe him, but there was no other way to get him to talk to her.

"Okay, if you're sure. But remember that you can always talk to me about anything."

"I'll remember," he said. Lilly could see that he was itching to get back to his computer.

She kissed the top of his head and went downstairs, where she called Hassan.

"How was your day?" he asked. "Sorry I didn't get a chance to stop by, but Dad and I were busy all day. He's thinking of buying a vacation home here."

"That's great!" Lilly smiled. She knew Hassan would be more comfortable visiting Juniper Junction if his parents were around more often. He sometimes worried that his sister didn't have enough time to spend with them, and they were a close-knit family.

"We talked to a realtor today and she's going to show us a couple houses tomorrow."

"Wow! I didn't realize he was going to look for something so soon."

"Once he told me about it, he wanted to get started right

away. I guess he and my mother have been talking about it since last Christmas." Lilly remembered how much they had enjoyed the house they rented the previous winter.

"You'll have to tell me all about the houses you visit," Lilly said. "I'm so happy for them!"

Hassan promised to keep her posted. "What did you do today?"

Lilly sighed and told him about Mrs. Laforge, then about her talk-that-went-nowhere with Tighe.

"I remember when I was his age," Hassan said. "During that last summer before I went to college, I didn't want much to do with my parents. I think it was my way of separating from them before I left so it wouldn't be so hard when I was away from home."

Lilly sighed. "I hope you're right. I'd hate to think that he's just changing and this is what our relationship is going to look like from now on."

"That's not going to happen, trust me," Hassan said. "If I could have that summer back to do over, I'd spend every minute with my family. I'm sure Tighe will realize the same thing someday."

"I hope so," Lilly said.

CHAPTER 22

The next morning Lilly was at work when the phone rang.

Harry answered it. "Juniper Junction Jewelry. How can I help you?"

A look of confusion passed over his face, then his brow furrowed in concern. "Okay. Hold on, I'll get her."

He handed the phone to Lilly. She raised her eyebrows in question. He covered the phone with his hand. "Noley," he whispered.

Lilly's heart plummeted into her stomach. She reached for the phone with a hand that had turned clammy. Why did Harry look like that?

"Noley?" she asked.

There was strangled mumbling on the other end, followed by a heavy breath.

"Noley?" she repeated.

"Yes," came the strangled response. "I'm at the bistro. The police are here. They're talking to Armand and looking at me. What do I do?" Noley asked in a panicked whisper.

"First of all, take a deep breath. They could be looking at you for a thousand reasons. Have you talked to Bill?"

"No. I don't want to drag him into this. If he's not here, there must be a good reason."

Lilly had to admit Noley was right. She would call Bill herself.

"Do you have any idea what they're talking about?" Lilly asked.

"I can't imagine that it would be anything other than the investigation into Cerise's death. They must have found something." Noley's voice was low, urgent.

"Do you want me to come over?"

"Would you mind?" Noley asked. "I hate to ask, but I'm afraid I'm going to need someone here in case the police want to talk to me next."

"All right. I'll have Harry look after the shop and I'll be over in a couple minutes."

Without giving a reason, Lilly explained to Harry that she had to run over to the bistro and didn't know how long she would be gone. She hurried out the door just a few moments after getting off the phone with Noley. Two police cruisers were parked on the street in front of the bistro, possibly explaining why the line of customers so frequently a fixture around the bistro was nowhere to be seen.

As much as she had hurried, Lilly didn't get to the bistro before the police turned their attention to Noley.

When she entered the bistro, two customers were hurriedly making their purchases. From their movements, it was clear they wanted to get as far away from the bistro as they could. Armand was charging the second customer's credit card. He handed the card back to its owner with a shaky smile and a terse *merci*.

The two women left with a last glance at Armand. Lilly approached the counter after the door had closed.

"How's everything, Armand?"

"I really do not know," he answered in his accented English.

"Are the police talking to Noley?"

"*Oui.*"

"I guess I should wait for her out here."

Armand gestured toward the empty tables. "Take your choice," he said.

"Could I get a cup of coffee?" she asked.

"*Oui.* I will bring it to you."

Lilly chose the table closest to the kitchen and while she waited for her coffee she strained her ears to hear what Noley and the police might be discussing. Their voices were too low, though, and she heard only rumblings.

Armand brought a French press to the table, along with a white cup and saucer. The aroma was strong and bracing.

"Thanks, Armand. Have you heard anything about Cerise's cause of death?"

He nodded. "I think you had better ask your friend."

Uh-oh. Lilly's stomach immediately started churning and she lost interest in the coffee. She twisted the ring on her right ring finger and her leg jiggled up and down. It seemed like an hour before the police finally emerged from the kitchen of the bistro. No customers came in during the entire time.

They nodded to Lilly, probably assuming she was a customer, and left the restaurant. Lilly stood up. "Armand, can I go back there?"

He nodded briskly. "I think you should."

Lilly pushed the swinging kitchen door and the first thing she saw was Noley, tears streaming down her face. She had her hand over her chest and was heaving breaths.

"Noley! What's wrong?" Lilly hurried to her friend's side.

"I, I…"

Lilly's eyes searched the kitchen for a paper bag. When she didn't see one after just a second or two, she opened the kitchen door and called to Armand.

"Armand, get me a paper bag, quick!"

He reached for one of the take-out bags under the counter

and handed it to Lilly. She turned and handed it to Noley after bunching up the top of the bag.

"Put this up to your face and breathe into it," she directed.

Noley breathed into the bag, inflating and deflating it several times, each inflation a little slower than the one before it, until she was breathing normally again.

She sat down on the floor with her back against the wall.

"Thanks," she said in a shaky voice.

Lilly sat down next to her friend. "What happened?" she asked.

Noley closed her eyes and gulped. "The police got the results from the lab that did the tests on the food I served at the July Fourth reenactment."

"And?" Lilly could feel her heart start to beat a little faster.

"There was cyanide in her salad. And I'm the one who served it to her."

"Cyanide!" Lilly exclaimed.

Noley buried her face in her hands. "I didn't put cyanide in the food, I swear."

"Of course you didn't," Lilly declared.

"I'm going to be arrested. I just know it," Noley choked, then she started sobbing. "What am I going to do?"

"Did the police say they were going to charge you with anything?"

"No." Noley gulped again. "They were just asking me questions."

"I'm sure they won't charge you with murder," Lilly said, hoping she was right. "Are they sure the lab didn't make a mistake? It's just bizarre that only one person, out of everyone who ate that day, got sick."

Noley nodded. "I know. And I said that to the police. But they said they're checking up on every angle. They seem to think I had it in for Cerise because she and Armand were trying to hone in on my catering gig."

"That's ridiculous," Lilly said.

"I know, but that's what they think." Noley gasped and her eyes widened as she had a sudden thought. "Armand is going to think I killed his wife."

"I'm sure Armand knows you didn't kill anybody," Lilly said in a soothing voice.

Just then there was a light knock on the swinging door that led to the kitchen from the main room of the bistro.

"May I come in?" Armand called through the door.

"Yes," Lilly answered.

Armand came over to where the two women were sitting on the floor. He crouched down until he was at Noley's level.

"Noley, the police told me about the food at the reenactment. I want you to know that I don't think you killed Cerise."

Noley started to cry. She cried so hard she couldn't speak for a couple minutes. Lilly and Armand watched her with tears in their own eyes, though probably for different reasons. Lilly couldn't bear the thought of her friend's suffering; Armand was probably remembering his wife and thinking of her last painful moments. Finally Noley wiped her nose with her sleeve.

"I'm so sorry about everything, Armand. Thank you for believing in me."

Armand nodded, overcome with emotion, tears glistening in the corners of his eyes.

"But I can't stay here, obviously," Noley continued. "When it gets out that there was cyanide in the food I provided and that's what killed Cerise, you'll be out of business if I keep working here."

"Unfortunately, I think you are right," Armand said, straightening up and leaning down to help Noley to her feet. "It would probably be best if you left work now. I will pay you through today, of course."

"Thanks." Noley's voice was small and quiet. She reached for her knives, which she took everywhere with her when she cooked, and her favorite apron, which she had brought from home. Lilly held the door open for her and she walked out into the summer sunshine, blinking.

"Want to come to the store for a little while?" Lilly asked. She didn't know what Noley would do there, but she didn't want her friend going home to an empty house.

"No, thanks. I've got to go home."

"Are you sure?" Lilly asked. "I don't think it's a good idea for you to be alone right now. At least at the store you'll be with me and Harry."

"I can't," Noley said. "I appreciate what you're doing, but I need to think this through. Get my affairs in order."

That sounded grim.

"What do you mean, get your affairs in order?" Lilly demanded.

"You know, in case I go to prison."

The look Lilly turned on her friend was full of sympathy and love. "You're not going to prison. If I have to figure out for myself who put the cyanide in the food, I'll do it to keep you out of prison."

Noley hugged Lilly and walked slowly to her car. "Want a ride back to the shop?" Noley asked.

"No, thanks. I'll walk. I'll call you later," Lilly said.

Noley didn't answer, but gave a limp wave as she pulled away and headed home.

As soon as Noley had turned the corner, Lilly whipped out her cell phone. She dialed Bill.

"Bill? Have you heard what's going on?" she asked breathlessly when her brother answered.

"Yeah," he said in a weary voice. Lilly could practically see him raking his hand across his haggard face.

"You know Noley didn't do anything wrong," Lilly said.

"Of course I know that. But if I want to keep my job I can't interfere with an investigation. I have to let it take its course."

"Why do you always say that?" Lilly whined. "Can't you

just tell the people working on the case that they need to come up with some more leads that make sense?"

"Lilly, I'm not in charge of the investigation for obvious reasons. I can't tell them what to do. Everyone knows about me and Noley--for God's sake, she sent in a ton of food for everyone who had to work on Memorial Day. Everyone loves her food. They want nothing more than to find good leads, trust me."

Of course Bill was right. He knew what he was doing and he would do everything he could to make sure Noley wasn't arrested for Cerise's murder.

But Lilly wanted the police to find the real killer *now.*

CHAPTER 23

Lilly was relieved and happy to see Hassan come into the shop later that afternoon. There was a comforting familiarity in their routine--he would kiss her and ask how her day was and she would respond and then ask him what he did. Boring and simple, but comforting nonetheless.

Hassan couldn't believe it when Lilly told him what had transpired at the bistro that morning.

"No one actually believes Noley put cyanide in the food that Cerise ate, do they?" he asked.

"I'm sure the police don't believe it, and Armand says he doesn't believe it, but that doesn't really matter if they can't figure out who did it," Lilly said miserably. "Plus, if her name is associated with a cyanide poisoning, even though she didn't do it, no one is going to want to have anything to do with her cooking."

"I hope the police find the person who did this, and do it quickly," Hassan said.

"Me, too. Are you and your dad going to look at houses today?" Lilly asked.

"Yes. There are two on the schedule for this afternoon, and then a whole slew of them tomorrow."

"Call me tonight," Lilly said, and Hassan left. Lilly checked the clock about a hundred times until it was time to lock the doors and put the displays away. She couldn't wait to get home to call Noley.

She called Noley as soon as she got home from the shop.

"How's everything going?" she asked when Noley picked up the phone.

"About as well as you'd expect," Noley said. "I can't even call Bill because I don't want to get him in trouble. And he hasn't been over. I'll bet there are people watching him at work to make sure he doesn't contact me."

Lilly didn't know what the policy was when it came to officers dating persons of interest. "Tell you what. Let me invite Bill for dinner tomorrow. Then you can come over and the two of you can talk here. I'll make myself scarce and make sure the kids go somewhere. That way you can have some privacy to talk about everything."

"That would be great. I don't want to drag him down if I get in more trouble."

"Nol, you're not in trouble. Just because the police questioned you doesn't mean that you're going to be arrested."

"You wait. I just know it'll happen."

Hassan called Lilly later that evening. "Dad found the house he wants," he announced. "He can't wait to bring my mother here to show her."

"That was fast!" Lilly was thrilled to finally hear some good news. "Where is it? What's it like?"

"It's a small house not far from your mother, actually. It's on a cul-de-sac with only a few other houses. It's pretty small, but they don't need much space if they're just going to visit once in a while."

"I can't wait to see it," Lilly said. At least one thing was going right--she was happy with Hassan and now that his parents were planning to spend more time in Juniper Junction, she would get to know them better, too.

Before bed she gave Bill a call to invite him for dinner the next evening. He asked her how Noley was doing.

"I've tried calling her, but her phone is always off," he said. "I haven't had a chance to stop over at her house yet."

"I'm sure she's got the phone off so you can't call," Lilly said. "She's so afraid that you're going to get in trouble if you have any contact with her."

"She should let me worry about that," Bill said.

"You can tell her that yourself tomorrow at dinner," Lilly replied.

"All right. See you then. And thanks."

The next morning Lilly got up late, so she missed breakfast and was cranky by eight o'clock. She left the shop, where she had been doing paperwork in her office, to run across the street to the diner to grab something to eat.

Orson was behind the counter when she entered.

"Hey, Lilly. How's everything?" he asked in a subdued voice.

"Not bad, Orson. Everything okay with you?"

He shrugged. "I heard a rumor this morning about Noley. Maybe you can confirm or deny it?"

"I can try. What is it?" Lilly asked, her heart sinking. She had a feeling she knew exactly what the rumor was about.

"There were a couple cops in here this morning getting breakfast before their shift started and they were saying Noley is a person of interest in Cerise's death. Is it true?"

Lilly was in an awkward position. Should she tell Orson that Noley was a person of interest and feed the rumor? Should she deny it outright?

She decided on the diplomatic approach.

"The police talked to her yesterday, that much I know. Whether she's been named a 'person of interest,' I don't know the answer to that." It was technically true.

"She obviously had nothing to do with it," Orson said, his

brow furrowing. "What could possibly make them think she was at fault?"

Now he was asking more specific questions, getting into territory that made Lilly squirm. "I'm not exactly sure, Orson. I guess we'll have to wait and see what the police have to say."

He shook his head in disgust. "I feel terrible for Noley."

"So do I."

"What brings you in here this morning?"

"I'm starving," Lilly replied with a smile. "Can I get a cup of coffee and an egg sandwich to go?"

"You got it," Orson said, and he disappeared to give Lilly's order to his line cook. When he returned he said, "It'll just be a few minutes."

"Thanks." She paid for her meal.

"Say, there were a couple real estate agents in here having a late lunch yesterday and they mentioned Hassan's name," Orson said as he handed over her change.

"Hassan's name? Why?" Lilly asked in surprise.

"One of them showed a house to his father. I didn't know Hassan's father was moving to Juniper Junction."

Is nothing private in this town? Lilly thought.

"They were saying how much he loved one of the houses he looked at."

"He's not moving here permanently," Lilly said. "He's looking for a vacation home for himself and his wife. Hassan did mention that his father found a house yesterday that he really liked."

"Sounded to me like it was more than that--sounded to me like he's ready to put an offer in."

Lilly shrugged. "I don't know. Hassan didn't mention that." This conversation was making her uncomfortable. Didn't realtors have confidentiality rules or something that they had to follow?

Orson left to check on Lilly's order and she was happy to stand by herself in the doorway of the diner, waiting for her food without having to answer any more questions. Presently Orson returned with a paper bag.

"Here you go, Lilly. Enjoy," he said.

"Thanks, Orson." The door jingled behind her as she left to go back to work.

In the jewelry shop Harry was perusing the morning paper before unlocking the doors. "Have you seen this article?" he asked, handing her the paper and pointing to an article above the fold on the first page.

Lilly hadn't had a chance to look at the paper yet, so she scanned the article he indicated. It was about the rash of fires in Juniper Junction; the police had no leads on the arsonist or arsonists, and folks in town were getting more jittery the longer it took to find the firebug.

"It's really scary to think they can't catch this person," Lilly said, handing the paper back to Harry. "You just have to wonder what's next."

Harry nodded, but didn't say anything else because the first customer of the day had come through the door, and she was followed by a steady stream of customers and window shoppers the rest of the day. Lilly heaved a sigh of relief when she locked the doors that evening.

"Long day," she said. "But long days are sometimes the best because they mean we're busy." Harry nodded his agreement.

"Oh!" she cried. "I almost forgot! I'm supposed to have Noley and Bill over for dinner. I'd better hurry home."

She stopped at the grocery store on her way and picked up ingredients for a simple dinner of subs. Laurel and Tighe were home when she arrived, but they both had plans for the evening.

"I'm going to a concert in the park with Nick," Laurel said.

"Mike and I are hanging out with some people from work," Tighe put in.

"That's fine," Lilly replied. "I'll go over to Hassan's house for a little while after dinner to give Noley and Bill some privacy."

"That sounds gross," Laurel said.

Lilly grimaced. "They need privacy because Bill doesn't want people in the police department to know he's seeing her right now."

"Why not?" the kids asked in unison. Lilly realized that they weren't aware of Noley's troubles.

"The police talked to her because some of the food at the July Fourth reenactment was contaminated."

Her announcement was greeted with a chorus of questions and exclamations.

"Contaminated with what?"

"Do they think it's her fault? Is that why Uncle Bill can't go see her?"

"She couldn't have done it!"

"Someone must have made a mistake!"

Lilly held her hands up, pleading for quiet.

"Of course we don't believe she has anything to do with it, but they don't have any leads. As for Noley and Uncle Bill coming over tonight, they just want to keep their relationship on the down-low right now. They obviously have some things to discuss. I think Noley has a lot of questions that Bill might be able to answer."

"Poor Noley," murmured Laurel. Tighe nodded his agreement.

Bill arrived first, as Lilly had known he would. He wasn't one to be late for dinner. Noley wasn't far behind.

"What's for dinner?" Tighe asked.

"Subs. It's make-your-own-dinner night," Lilly replied as she set out the fixings for the meal. Everyone lined up and helped themselves to the sandwich ingredients on the counter and Lilly placed a big bowl of chips and a plate of sliced peaches on the table. She instructed everyone to get their own drinks and eventually the group sat down together.

The meal was quiet, considering there were five people gathered around the table. Noley and Bill exchanged nervous glances, but neither one said anything. Lilly knew they were waiting until all the onlookers cleared out of the kitchen. Laurel fidgeted throughout the meal, and Lilly knew she was eager to meet Nick. Tighe was quiet, too.

As soon as dinner was over Lilly stacked the dishes in the sink while Laurel and Tighe made haste to get out of the house before she could ask them to do the dishes.

"You two leave these dishes alone." Lilly used her best mom voice to instruct Noley and Bill before leaving for Hassan's. "I'll do them when I get home. The point of this is for you two to sit and relax and talk."

At Hassan's house they sat in the backyard with his father. Lilly wanted to know all about the houses he had been seeing.

"I've seen so many," Amir sighed. "It's hard to keep track. There's one in particular that I love, though. I saw it yesterday. It's perfect for us. It's small, but that's what we want. That way when our relatives visit, they'll have to go home sooner because there won't be enough room for them!" He laughed.

"There's plenty of room at my house, Dad," Hassan reminded him. "Everyone could always stay with me."

"Be careful what you wish for, my son," Amir said with a smile and a wink.

"So when do I get to see it?" Lilly asked.

"Why not right now?" Amir replied.

Hassan smiled. "Works for me. Lilly?"

"Sure! That sounds fun," Lilly said.

"I'll drive," Hassan offered.

It was still bright outside when the three pulled up in front of the house Amir liked so much. Lilly loved it.

"It's charming!" she exclaimed from her seat in the back. Amir turned around and smiled at her.

"Do you think we can get out?" Amir asked his son.

"I don't see why not," Hassan replied. Everyone got out and started up the front walk. There were countless delightful details, such as the woodwork on the front porch, the cornices, and the cozy front door.

"I just love it, Amir," Lilly sighed.

"Thank you. I do, too," he answered. "I know Basra will love it."

"So has Basra seen it at all, or is she just trusting your good judgment?" Lilly asked in a teasing voice.

"Oh, my dear, she has insisted upon seeing photo after photo of every house," Amir said with a chuckle. "I don't make a move without her okay." Hassan smiled.

"Let's go look at the backyard," Hassan suggested.

"Do you think we should?" Amir asked.

"I'd love to see it," Lilly said. The three trooped around the side of the house. The backyard spread ahead of them, full of mature trees. It sloped gently downward from the back of the house; a wooden bench sat at the bottom of the small hill under a leafy oak tree.

"It's beautiful, Amir," Lilly said. They turned around and headed back to the car.

"Lilly, shall we swing by your mother's house and say hello?" Hassan asked, turning around to glance at Lilly.

"I'm sure she would like that. She hasn't seen your dad in a few months."

Hassan drove to Bev's house and pulled to a stop out front. Lilly knocked on the door and was about to let herself in when the door opened. Bev stood in the doorway with a smile on her face.

"Lilly! I'm so glad you came by. And who are these gentlemen with you?"

CHAPTER 24

Lilly looked over her shoulder and exchanged glances with Hassan.

"Mom, you know Hassan. And remember his father, Amir?"

Her mother's face clouded. "I don't think I remember them," she said. "But if you say so…"

She led the way into the living room and sat down with her hands primly folded in her lap.

"So what brings you here?" she asked.

Lilly didn't know how to handle this. Should she just talk as if her mother remembered Hassan and Amir? Should she reintroduce them?

She decided on a hybrid approach. She gestured toward Amir. "Amir, Hassan's father, is planning to buy a house in Juniper Junction. We just drove over to have a look at one he especially likes. It's right near here."

"Oh? That's nice. This is a lovely neighborhood. You'll like it. Where are you moving from?"

Amir played along. "My wife and I live in Minnesota and we're looking for a vacation home, so we've decided to buy one here to be closer to our son and to Lilly, of course."

Bev gave Lilly a blank stare. "Why does he want to be close to you?"

Lilly swallowed. "Because Hassan and I have been dating for a while now, Mom. Amir and his wife are very nice and love Juniper Junction. Hassan has a house on the other side of town, too."

Bev looked from Lilly to Hassan. "You two are dating?" she asked, her voice tinged with incredulity.

"Yes, Mom," Lilly answered. Hassan merely nodded. He didn't seem to know how to respond to Bev.

"Well, that's news to me. Why didn't you say anything?"

"I did. Maybe you just forgot," Lilly said quietly. Her insides were churning like a storm at sea and her throat was dry. She had been waiting for this day--fearing it--since her mother had started getting confused many months ago. It was heartbreaking.

"I must have forgotten," Bev said, nodding. "Would anyone like some huckleberry lemonade?"

"That would be very refreshing," Amir said. "Thank you."

"I'll help you, Mom," Lilly offered. The two women disappeared into the kitchen. Bev opened the refrigerator door and stood looking inside.

"I don't know where I put it," she said.

"The lemonade?" Lilly asked.

"Yes," her mom said, turning around and searching the room with her eyes. "I made it early this morning."

Lilly looked around, too, opening the fridge door again and peeking inside, just in case her mother missed it. It wasn't there. She wandered over to the sink and looked out back.

There was the clear glass pitcher of lemonade on the patio table. A glass of the lavender-colored drink sat next to it.

"There it is!" Lilly exclaimed, her relief almost palpable knowing that her mother wasn't mistaken about making the lemonade.

"Oh, that's right," Bev said, snapping her fingers. "I was

sitting out there before you came over and I went inside for a cookie. I didn't even get a sip."

"I'll go out and get it," Lilly said. She went out the back door and was back inside just a moment later carrying the pitcher and glass.

"The lemonade in the glass is already getting warm," Lilly told her mother. "I'll pour you a new glass. Want to get a tray out and we'll take the drinks into the living room?"

While Bev got a tray out of one of her cupboards, Lilly poured four glasses of the lemonade, thinking about how many years her mother had been making this particular recipe. It was one of Lilly's favorites.

Bev grabbed a box of cookies from the counter and carried them into the living room. Lilly followed with the tray of drinks. She handed out the glasses and sat down next to Hassan on the sofa.

Amir took a sip of the lemonade and Lilly was raising her glass to her lips when she saw a look of shock move fleetingly across Amir's face. Her brow furrowed and she took a long gulp of her drink.

She started choking, purely by reflex, and set the glass down on the end table next to her. Bev watched the entire scene and took a tiny sip of her lemonade. Only a couple seconds had passed since Amir took his drink, but the damage was done.

"Oh, dear," Bev fretted. "This tastes terrible. It tastes like I used salt instead of sugar."

Lilly hurried into the kitchen for a pitcher of water and several glasses. She poured water for everyone and passed the glasses around.

"How could I have made such a mistake?" Bev asked, her eyes blinking rapidly. "Lilly, gentlemen, I'm so sorry about this."

"That's perfectly all right," Amir assured her. He gave her

a broad smile. "Mistakes happen to everyone, and it's easy to confuse salt and sugar."

"Absolutely," Hassan agreed.

Lilly couldn't say anything. She was blinking back tears, too. Her heart went out to her mother, whose distress and embarrassment were obvious. She had never made a mistake like that before.

She recovered as quickly as she could, talking brightly about Amir's house hunting, the weather, and the kids' summer jobs. She was careful not to mention Noley or Bill or any of their troubles.

Bev listened politely to Lilly, but she wore a faraway gaze and seemed preoccupied. Lilly knew what her mother was thinking--how could she have made such a mistake preparing the lemonade she'd been making for decades? Lilly wanted to do something to take her mom's mind off her embarrassment.

"Mom, how about coming over for a sleepover tonight? We can watch a movie and make popcorn. It would be fun. I'm sure Laurel would join us," she added, knowing the mention of one of the grandchildren might tip the scales in her favor.

But she was wrong this time.

"I don't think so, Lilly. I need to do some cleaning and there was a television show I wanted to watch tonight."

"What show?" Lilly asked. "We could watch it at my house."

"I don't remember off the top of my head," Bev said. It was the way she said it that sent the signal to Lilly--there was no show. Bev wanted to be by herself.

"Okay. But if you change your mind, give me a call," Lilly said, getting up to gather everyone's glasses. She put them in the dishwasher and rinsed out the pitchers before kissing her mother good-night and leading the way back to the car.

Bev stood on her front porch and waved as Hassan pulled away from the curb. Lilly turned to watch her through the back window of the car. Everyone in the car was silent; the only sound came from the *click* of the turn signal whenever Hassan turned a corner.

When they arrived at Hassan's house, Lilly was the last one out of the car. Her mind was busy, trying to decide what steps to take. She would certainly have to share these new developments with Bill, as much as she hated to add more stress to his life. She should probably reach out to her mother's doctor, too, to discuss possibilities.

Amir went into the house ahead of Hassan and Lilly. Hassan wore a pensive, almost sad, expression on his face.

"Are you all right?" Lilly asked him, reaching for his hand.

He sighed. "I guess so. Why do you suppose she forgot me?"

So that was it. It hurt him that Bev didn't remember him.

"I think there's no rhyme or reason to whom a person forgets when they're dealing with dementia," Lilly said softly. "The day will probably come when she doesn't know me, either." The very thought of it was enough to send Lilly's stomach into spasms.

"I mean, if she forgot my father, that's one thing. She rarely sees him," Hassan said. "But do you think it means she just doesn't care about me?"

"I don't think that at all," Lilly assured him, and it was the truth. She had heard stories of patients knowing friends from decades past when they didn't recognize the people who lived with them.

She squeezed Hassan's hand. "I should go," she said. "I need to get home so I can talk to Bill about Mom. Hopefully he and Noley have had some time to talk about what happens next."

"I'll call you tomorrow," Hassan said, kissing her.

When Lilly arrived home Bill and Noley were sitting next to each other on the front porch swing.

She parked the car in the driveway and walked around the

house to where her best friend and her brother sat, holding hands. She smiled at the sight of them.

"Everything okay?" she asked. She dragged a rocking chair over to the swing and sat down facing the couple.

"For now," Noley replied, looking at Bill. "We just have to wait and see what happens, and Bill doesn't know what that's going to be. Or when." Bill nodded.

"He's also convinced me to do a little cooking," Noley continued. "Especially now that I'm not working for Armand, I need to maintain my income stream. I had been debating whether I should cancel the assignments I have from a few different sources, but Bill helped me decide to go ahead and work on them." She smiled.

"And that's why I should get going now," she said, standing up. "I've got work to do." She smiled again at Bill and he stood up next to her.

"I'll head out, too," he said.

"Actually, Bill, can you come into the kitchen with me? There's something I need to talk to you about," Lilly said.

His eyes narrowed. "Okay. I'll be right there." Lilly took her cue to go into the house so the two lovebirds could say good-night. A few minutes later Bill came into the kitchen.

"It sounds like things went pretty well between you and Noley," Lilly said.

He nodded absentmindedly. "I guess. I tried to be as positive as I could, but the truth is that the detectives aren't getting any closer to anyone else who might have put the poison in the food. It's not looking good for Noley right now."

"You didn't tell her that?"

"I couldn't. It would scare her to death. She'd be paralyzed into not cooking, not doing anything, not going anywhere."

Lilly knew he was right, though she wished they didn't have to keep the truth from her friend.

"Will the detectives come and talk to you before they go talk to Noley again?" she asked.

"I don't know. They'll certainly tell me first if they're going to arrest her," he said. "But they might not tell me if they're just going to talk to her again."

He paused. "What do you need to talk to me about?"

"Mom."

"Uh-oh. What about her?" he asked.

"Hassan and I and his father went over there to see her while you and Noley were talking. She didn't know Hassan."

Bill closed his eyes for a long moment and took a deep breath.

"I was afraid of this."

"Me, too. And that's not all. She made her huckleberry lemonade with salt instead of sugar. She's never made a mistake like that. Amir and I both drank it before I realized what had happened. Mom was upset."

"I'll bet she was."

"I think we need to notify her doctor," Lilly said. Bill nodded. Lilly knew they were getting closer to the time when their mother would need more care, and she knew Bill knew it, too. There had always been an unspoken agreement between them that they would share the responsibilities of taking care of her as her condition worsened, but she had hoped her mother would be able to cook for herself for a long time to come. Cooking was the one thing, besides her grandchildren and Fred, that brought her a great deal of joy.

"I'll call him tomorrow," Lilly offered. She was often the one who took her mother to doctor appointments because she had a more predictable schedule than Bill.

"Thanks. Let me know what he says," Bill replied.

Lilly leashed Barney and went for a walk after Bill left. She wished her mother had taken her up on the offer to spend the night, but she was also grateful to have some time to herself to think things through.

Her mother was declining further, that much was obvious. And on top of that, there was the situation hanging over Noley's head--would she be charged with poisoning Cerise, or would the police find another suspect? One thing was sure: Noley didn't poison anyone, not even accidentally. Someone had deliberately tainted Cerise's food with poison.

And there was Tighe, too. He was growing further and further away from her as the summer wore on, and though her logical mind knew he was pulling away because he was sprouting wings to fly from her nest, her emotional mind wanted everything to go back to the way it had been when he was a little boy. When he needed to hold her hand to cross the street, when he would hug her every time he had been away from her, when he would always tell her he loved her. She swallowed as she choked on a single sob. Barney turned around to look at her and she managed a smile for him.

"I'm okay, boy."

Then there were the house fires. What was going on in Juniper Junction this summer? Though none of the fires had had any direct effect on her, they contributed to a general sense of unease among the population. People talked about them all the time, people watched their neighborhoods more closely, and people were nervous. Everyone hoped the fires had stopped because there hadn't been a fire in a few days, but Lilly had a feeling they wouldn't stop until the culprit was behind bars. And she refused to even admit to herself that Tighe had always been out of the house when the fires were set.

CHAPTER 25

The next morning Lilly called the doctor's office as soon as it opened. She had to leave a message for the doctor and was told he wouldn't be able to call her back until lunchtime or even later. She spent the entire morning fidgeting and unfocused.

"What's the matter with you today?" Harry asked.

"I've just got a lot on my mind," she answered. "Everything from my kids to my mother to my brother to my best friend."

"Uh, don't look now, but you might want to add one more name to that list," Harry said in a warning tone.

Lilly looked up as Beau walked into the store. He wore a hideous pair of cutoff denim shorts and a muscle shirt; his hair was in a man-bun.

"Harry," he said tersely, nodding his head toward the young man.

"Lilly, we need to talk," he said.

"Why? What's going on? And why did you get all dressed up just to come see me?" She shouldn't have said anything, but she couldn't help herself.

"Very funny," he said. He motioned toward her office in the back of the shop. "Can we talk in there?"

"Sure," Lilly said, leading the way. She couldn't imagine what had gotten him worked up enough to come into the store.

She closed the door behind her and faced Beau. "What's this all about?" she asked.

"Laurel tells me that Tighe is drinking," Beau said. If he had hit Lilly right between the eyes, she couldn't have been more surprised.

"What?" she exclaimed. "I don't know what you're talking about!"

Beau seemed to calm down then. "I'm sorry if this is the first you're hearing about it. Laurel and Nick came to see me last night and she let it slip that Tighe has spent a lot of time out at night, drinking."

Aside from being furious that Laurel lied to her about going to the concert the previous evening with Nick, she was shocked that her daughter would share information like this with Beau instead of her.

"I can assure you, this is the first I'm hearing about Tighe drinking," she said, her mind spinning. Was alcohol responsible for Tighe's behavior lately? Was that why he was spending so much time away from home, squirreling himself away in his room whenever he was home, and not wanting to have much to do with her?

It was all starting to make sense. Maybe leaving the nest and pulling away from his mother weren't the only reasons Tighe was spending so much time out with his friends.

"It sounds like he has a problem," Beau said.

Lilly recalled a few incidents early in their marriage when Beau over-imbibed and she suddenly recognized some of the behavior she had been seeing from Tighe--the evasiveness, the desire for privacy. She could have kicked herself for not noticing the signs earlier. And to be told by Beau—that was the ultimate insult! Why couldn't Laurel have come to her? Why go to the man who had abandoned the family for so many years and start spilling secrets to him? Lilly couldn't decide if she wanted to scream or cry.

But she did neither. She sat down at her desk and motioned for Beau to sit down across from her.

"I'll have to talk to him," she said.

"I think we should do it together," Beau countered.

Lilly hadn't thought of that. She had always dealt with problems on her own. She hadn't even considered the idea that Beau, now that he was back in town, might want to take a more active role in the kids' lives, for better or worse.

He had really grown up in those fifteen years.

"You're probably right," she conceded. "What are you doing tonight?"

"Got a dinner date at five," he said smugly.

On the other hand, maybe he hadn't changed so much, after all.

"Are you willing to reschedule or postpone it until later tonight?" Lilly asked. "Tighe gets out of work at five and he's supposed to go home to let Barney out. We can ambush, er, meet him then. I'll get Harry to watch the shop."

"Yeah. I suppose I can do that."

"Thanks, Beau. Hopefully it won't take long to talk some sense into him."

"I'll see you at your house around five," he said, and stood to leave.

"Uh, by the way, what time was Laurel at your house last night?"

"I dunno. It was about seven thirty, I guess. She said she had just finished dinner at your house."

"Okay, thanks," Lilly said with a nod. "See you later."

Wasn't life supposed to get easier as the kids grew older? Lilly heaved a sigh of frustration as she walked into the front of the shop.

"Everything okay, boss?" Harry asked. His attempt to lighten the mood in the shop was met with a smile from Lilly.

"Everything will be," she said. "Harry, I hate to ask you to do this, but could you look after the shop for an hour before closing? I need to run home, but I'm hoping to be back in time to help close."

"Sure," he answered. Lilly suspected he wanted to ask why she was just leaving for an hour, but she didn't offer any details.

At precisely ten minutes to five that afternoon, Lilly got in her car to drive home. She wanted to be in the house, prepared and waiting, when Tighe got home.

She pulled her car into the garage, which she didn't normally do. It was a tight squeeze between bikes and the lawn mower and all kinds of garage-style junk.

She was in the kitchen when there was a knock at the back door. Turning around, she saw Beau standing on the steps. It looked like he had changed his clothes--thank God. The last thing Lilly wanted was for Tighe to be distracted by his father's distasteful appearance.

She let him in, noting that his car wasn't in the driveway. Barney, who was used to seeing him on occasion, came up to sniff him. When Beau passed Barney's test, the dog wandered back to the living room to sit in front of the window, his favorite spot.

"Did you park out front?" she asked.

"The woman I've got the dinner date with, Nikki, dropped me off. She'll run a couple errands and be back for me when I text her."

It wasn't long before Tighe came in through the back door. Barney raced into the kitchen to greet him, and while Tighe was rubbing the dog's head he looked at Lilly and Beau in surprise.

"What are you guys doing here?" he asked.

"There's something we need to talk to you about," Lilly said. Beau nodded.

"What is it?" Tighe asked, the suspicion growing in his voice.

"I heard that you've been doing a lot of partying this summer," Beau said.

Tighe stiffened ever so slightly.

"Who told you that?"

"A little birdie," Beau answered. "Care to explain?"

"Not really."

"Well, you have to," Lilly said. "Because you haven't been yourself since you graduated and I think I know why."

"Did Laurel squeal?" Tighe asked, his hands balling into fists. "I'll kill her."

"I told you, it was a bird," Beau said. Lilly breathed a silent sigh of relief that he didn't rat out Laurel.

"So what if I've been drinking a little?" Tighe asked in a challenging voice. "In Colorado I can drink legally on private property. At least I'm not smoking weed."

"First of all, it's only legal for eighteen-year-olds to drink on private property with parental consent. You know you don't have our consent. And second, it's a good thing you're not smoking weed because I'd wring your neck," Lilly said. Then her tone softened just a bit. "I know everyone does it, and I get that. But you seem to have gone overboard. I wouldn't be surprised to learn you've been drinking too much and too often."

"Have you been talking to Mike's mother?" Tighe asked. "Is she the one who told you all this?"

"So you've been drinking with Mike?" Lilly asked.

Tighe sighed as he realized he had given his best friend away. "Yeah. But don't tell his mother. She'll kill him."

"And what do you think we're going to do to you?" Lilly asked. Beau lifted his brows and awaited Tighe's response.

"Hopefully nothing," Tighe said with a nervous chuckle.

"Sorry, pal," Beau said. "This can't go unanswered. Believe me, boy, I was in your shoes one time and it's not pretty."

"What do you mean?" asked Tighe.

"I mean, I drank when I was a teenager and I got to the point where I did stupid things--stupider than usual--and as I got older it became harder to go through a day without a drink."

"So you're saying I'm an alcoholic." Tighe's voice was flat.

"I doubt it," Lilly said. "But the more you drink, the harder it is to stop. We just want to keep you safe and out of trouble with the law, that's all. That's our job."

"I'm an adult," Tighe said.

"You may be an adult, but that doesn't make you smart," said Beau. "You have to earn the right to be treated like an adult."

"Here's what I'm worried about," Lilly said. "For several weeks now I've seen some changes in the way you act. You go out of your way to avoid time alone with me, you're spending more and more time in your room, you're going out all the time. I worry that if you're drinking every time you're out, that's a lot of alcohol."

Tighe didn't say anything.

"Do you ever drive when you've been drinking?" asked Beau.

"*I* don't," Tighe answered. Meaning someone else did.

"Does Mike?" Lilly asked.

Tighe shrugged. "He's done it once or twice."

"And what happened?" Lilly asked.

"Really nothing," Tighe said.

"What's that supposed to mean?" Lilly demanded. She was losing her patience trying to drag answers out of her son.

"It means, no one got really hurt. It's nothing to worry about."

Lilly's voice went up an octave. "What do you mean, *no one got really hurt*? Either someone got hurt or they didn't. Out with it, Tighe."

"Mike hit someone, but it was a really gentle hit."

Lilly felt like she was losing her mind. She sat down hard at the kitchen table. Beau pulled out a chair and sat down across from her. He waved his hand toward another chair, inviting Tighe to sit down. It wasn't so much of an invitation as a silent order.

Tighe sat down with a *thud*, knowing he was in trouble now.

"Tell us everything," Lilly said.

"Mike was driving one night last week. He was going really slow. He backed into someone."

"Was the person badly hurt?" Lilly asked.

"I don't think so. I wasn't in the car." *Thank God,* Lilly thought. The last thing this family needed was more trouble.

"So how do you know all this?" Beau asked.

"Mike told me. But you can't tell his parents."

"We'll worry about that later. Right now I want to know what happened to the person he hit."

Tighe didn't say anything. He looked at his hands and picked at his fingernails.

"Tighe? Answer me."

"Mike hit Mrs. Laforge."

"Oh, my God," Lilly said, putting her hands over her face. "I can't believe it."

"He only tapped her," Tighe said.

Lilly stared at her son, incredulous. "She was unconscious when I found her!" she shouted. "She's an old lady! She wound up having to go to the hospital by ambulance!"

Beau looked from his son to his ex-wife. "You found her?" he asked Lilly. "And you didn't know she had been hit by a car?"

"She was on the strip of grass between her lawn and the street, unconscious," Lilly explained. "Actually, it was Barney who found her. She was lying almost under a bush. She didn't remember what had happened and by the time Barney found her there were no cars around."

"What happened to her?"

"She sustained a concussion and some very bad bruising," Lilly said, staring daggers at Tighe. "She couldn't walk. That's why she had to take an ambulance. There was no way to get her into my car to take her."

"Mike didn't know who it was," Tighe offered.

"I don't care. He knew he hit someone, right? Otherwise he wouldn't have told you. He was wrong to leave her lying there. That's a serious crime, Tighe." Lilly shook her head, her eyes closed. She knew what she needed to do--she needed to tell the police that her neighbor had been the victim of a hit-and-run. She knew, too, that Mike needed to accept responsibility for what he had done.

And as for Tighe...he needed to accept responsibility for his role in the debacle. He had kept a crime a secret to protect his friend.

Lilly couldn't believe this was happening.

She opened her eyes to find Beau and Tighe staring at her. "What next?" asked Beau.

"First of all, you need to get Mike over here," Lilly said, pointing to Tighe. "Call him. We need to talk to him tonight."

"Who are you going to tell?" Tighe asked, his voice getting higher.

"*I'm* not going to tell anyone. You and Mike are. You're going to start by telling the police, then you're going to apologize to Mrs. Laforge, and finally you're going to tell Mike's parents. And I'm going with you to make sure you do it."

"Oh, my God," Tighe groaned. "This sucks."

"And stop saying *sucks*," Lilly shot back.

CHAPTER 26

Mike arrived about a half-hour later. Beau was still there, having texted his girlfriend that he would have to give her a raincheck on dinner. This was more important, he had told her. Lilly was pleased beyond all reason that she didn't have to handle this particular crisis by herself.

She called Hassan to tell him what was going on. She had hoped to see him that evening, but she had to deal with this mess first. Then she called Harry, apologized for taking so long, and asked him to close up the shop for the evening. He agreed and voiced his hope that everything was all right. Lilly hung up without answering him.

When Mike got there Lilly opened the back door for him and motioned for him to have a seat at the kitchen table, where Tighe was already sitting. Tighe gave his friend a dark look and Mike looked at Lilly and Beau nervously.

"What's going on?" he asked.

"Tighe, you tell him," Lilly instructed.

"They know you hit Mrs. Laforge, our neighbor, with your car the other night after you had been drinking."

Mike looked down at the table. "How'd they find out?" he

asked Tighe in a low voice. As if Lilly and Beau couldn't hear him.

"I had to tell them," Tighe said. "They were breathing down my neck." Not exactly true, but if that was how Tighe wanted to play it, that was fine with Lilly.

Mike sighed and looked up at Lilly and Beau. "Are you going to tell my parents? Or the police?"

Lilly shook her head. "You are."

"I can't tell them. They'll kill me," Mike said, his eyes widening.

"You could have killed Mrs. Laforge," Lilly pointed out. "Admitting to what you did is the least you can do."

Mike swallowed. "If I don't tell my parents, I suppose you're going to?" he asked Lilly and Beau. They both nodded solemnly.

"This is your chance to do the right thing," Beau said. Lilly glanced at him, secretly impressed by his handling of this crisis.

"What about Mrs. Laforge?" Mike asked.

"What about her?" Lilly countered.

"Is she okay?"

"She's improving. She suffered a concussion and some bad bruising on her legs and hips, but she's going to be fine. It's a miracle she wasn't hurt worse."

Mike reddened. "I can't believe I was so stupid. I'll tell her what I did and apologize. Are you guys going to tell the police?"

Lilly and Beau exchanged glances. "We really should, but I think that's a decision for you and your parents and Mrs. Laforge," Lilly said.

"With the knowledge, of course, that we know what happened and we can go to the police if necessary." Beau nodded.

"All right. I'll go home and talk to my parents tonight,"

Mike said, pushing his chair back from the table. "I'm really sorry about this, Mrs. Carlsen, Mister Carlsen."

"You're young, Mike. And this goes for you, too, Tighe, even though you weren't in the car when it happened. This is a pretty potent lesson about what can happen when you drink too much. Mike, you and your parents will have to decide what your family's consequences are for underage drinking and then driving under the influence, but for Tighe there's going to be a steep price to pay," Beau said, raising his eyebrows in Tighe's direction.

"Like what?" Tighe demanded.

"Watch your tone, young man," Lilly warned with a glare at her son. "You're not really in a position to be disrespectful, are you?"

Tighe clamped his mouth shut and slumped back in his chair. "It's better that you learn this lesson now than when you're in college, when things have a tendency to get out of control quickly," Lilly said.

Mike stood up and shook hands with Beau. "Again, I'm really sorry for all of this, Mister Carlsen." Then he turned to Lilly. "Same to you, Mrs. Carlsen."

"I'm sorry we had to have this conversation, but hopefully everything will turn out all right," Lilly said. "Let Tighe know what you and your parents decide to do."

Mike nodded and reached for the door handle.

"Wait a sec, Mike," Lilly said. "The night I found you in Mrs. Laforge's shed--did you need money to buy alcohol?"

Mike glanced at Tighe and nodded. "A guy we know has an ID and he gets it for us."

"Who is this guy?" Lilly asked.

"You don't know him," Tighe murmured.

"What's his name?" Lilly asked.

"Ed."

"He's Jimmy's brother," Mike supplied.

So that's why Tighe had been hanging out so much with Jimmy.

"No more hanging out with Jimmy, then," Lilly directed.

"Okay," the boys said in unison.

Mike left and Lilly shifted her attention to Tighe, who was still seated at the table. He looked at her expectantly. Beau seemed content to let her do the rest of the talking.

"Now for you. I'm going to turn off your cell phone service until the day you leave for college. And you're going to offer to do Mrs. Laforge's yard work for free until you leave. And finally, your new curfew is ten o'clock at night, no exceptions."

One would be forgiven for thinking Tighe had been stabbed in the heart. "What?" he cried, half standing in his shock. "You can't do that!"

"I just did," Lilly said. "And you're lucky I stopped there."

"How am I going to talk to people?"

"In person."

"But how am I going to know where and when to meet people?"

Lilly pointed to the landline phone that hung on the kitchen wall. Tighe looked at her like she had three heads.

"You're kidding. I am not using that thing. Mom, no one talks on the phone anymore!"

Lilly shrugged. "You're going to learn to love it. Tighe, I wish I didn't have to do this, but it's for your own good. It's better to suffer through these indignities now than wait until something much worse happens."

Tighe realized this was a fight he was going to lose. "All right," he grumbled. "I'm going to bed." He left his phone on the table, then stalked up the stairs. Lilly and Beau listened as his bedroom door slammed. It wouldn't even be dark for another two and a half hours.

"Teenagers are no picnic," Beau said, shaking his head. Lilly could have laughed out loud at his world-weary view of teenagerhood, given that he hadn't even experienced his own children's teenage years until eight months ago, but she kept quiet. She was just glad he had agreed to show up for the showdown with Tighe.

"That's for sure," was all she said.

"I'll text Nikki and ask her to come get me," Beau said. "I don't really feel like doing anything tonight. I think I'll go home and watch television."

"Sounds good to me," Lilly agreed.

Beau pulled out his phone and dashed off a quick text. While he waited to hear from Nikki, Lilly invited him to sit down again at the kitchen table.

He sat down. "You know, Lilly, I'm impressed with the way you handled Tighe. I am learning a lot from you."

"Thanks. What are you learning?" she asked.

He sat back in his chair and laced his fingers together. "For one thing, I'm learning that I was probably a pain in my mother's neck at Tighe's age. For another thing, I'm learning how to deal with my own kids. I take my cue from you. If I had had to reprimand Tighe tonight, he'd still have his phone and he wouldn't be mowing anyone's lawn."

"He has to feel the punishment if it's going to make an impression on him," she said. "I had to do all that to make sure he knows we mean business."

"Well, thank you," Beau said.

"I'd say 'my pleasure,' but there's nothing pleasurable about it," Lilly said. "It stinks to have to discipline him, especially right before he goes off to school, but there was no choice."

"Let me know if you need any help enforcing your law," Beau said, checking his watch and standing up to leave. "I'm a good enforcer."

After Beau left Lilly made herself a cup of tea and whistled for Barney to go outside with her. She sat out on the patio, letting her tea cool while she wondered why she had chosen a hot drink when it was so warm outside. Then she realized it was a comfort decision: when her life was in turmoil, as it was at the moment, she turned to comforting things to feel better. She leaned her head back against the cushion of the chaise lounge and closed her eyes.

She could hear several bees enjoying the evening warmth. Barney snuffled happily among the flowerbeds and the street was quiet. She must have dozed, because she was startled awake by the sound of a single bark from Barney.

"What's up, boy?" Lilly asked, lifting her head.

"Lil?"

It was Bill. He was tapping on the back gate.

"Oh, hi. I'm out here. Come on in."

Bill unhitched the latch on the gate and walked over to where Lilly still lay on a chaise lounge. He pulled a chair near to her and sat down.

"What's wrong?" she asked, her heartbeat quickening. Something in Bill's demeanor, his silence, was raising alarm bells.

"Bad news, I'm afraid," Bill replied. "I just got word that Noley is going to be arrested and charged with Cerise's murder."

Lilly sat up straight. "Oh, no," she breathed. Barney started whining, sensing something wasn't right. Bill reached over and patted his head.

"I couldn't stop it." Bill said. "All the evidence points to her, even though I know she didn't do it."

"This is awful. I never really thought it would happen," Lilly said.

"I suppose I didn't, either. I kept thinking we'd turn up some evidence that would exonerate her."

"So what happens next?" Lilly asked.

"The thing is, I could lose my job if I give her a heads-up. Likewise if you tell her and you got the information from me."

"We have to give her a heads-up somehow, Bill. She can't just be taken by surprise," Lilly said.

"That's why I came here to talk to you. Do you have any ideas? She'll have every right to quit talking to me forever if she finds out about this when they show up at her door to take her down to the station."

Lilly thought for a minute. "I can go over there and kind of hint around that she needs to be prepared for something."

Bill shrugged. "Maybe."

Lilly banged her fist on the small table next to her. Barney barked at the sound. "We all know she didn't do it! Why are they arresting her? Shouldn't they be looking for the person who really did it?"

"Like I said, every lead has led nowhere, and they're getting pressure to make an arrest. All the evidence points to her, so she's the most logical choice. They're still building a case."

"I'm leaving now," Lilly said. Bill stood up to go. "Wait!" she cried. "What am I going to tell her about you?"

"Tell her the truth. I'll do everything I can to help. But I won't be able to go see her." Lilly could see the pain in her brother's eyes even in the waning light. He turned around and left.

"Inside, Barn," Lilly directed. Barney leapt up the back steps and Lilly handed him a treat in the kitchen. She grabbed her purse from the counter and left.

Lilly drove more slowly than usual on her way to Noley's house. She dreaded the conversation she was about to have and she had to think through exactly what she wanted to tell her best friend. When she arrived she sat in her car at the curb for a few minutes, gathering courage and rehearsing what she was going to say.

A moment later she knocked on the door. Noley opened it and her face lit up when she saw Lilly.

"I'm so glad you came over!" Noley exclaimed. "I was just

going to make some popcorn. Can't screw that up and kill anyone with it. Want some?"

Lilly didn't. Her stomach was in knots. But she accepted and waited in the kitchen while Noley poured a little oil in a pan, heated it, and dropped a handful of kernels into it before putting the lid on top. Then she swirled the oil and corn around until the characteristic popping sounds started bursting from the pan. It smelled so good.

"Heat a little butter in the microwave, will you?" Noley asked, still swirling the pan around. Lilly put a bit of butter into a small dish and microwaved it until it was completely melted. Noley poured the creamy-white kernels into a big bowl and held out her hand for the butter. When she had drizzled the butter over the top of the corn, sprinkled on some salt, and mixed it all with a big spoon, she turned to Lilly and smiled.

"This is my favorite snack," she said. "Come on." She led the way into the living room. The two women sat across from each other and Noley placed the bowl of popcorn on the coffee table between them. Despite not wanting anything to eat, Lilly found that she reached into the bowl again and again for handfuls of popcorn. She knew she was procrastinating.

"So what brings you here tonight?" Noley asked. "Kids both working?"

"Yes, they're both working late," Lilly fibbed. She hesitated for a moment, then decided she hadn't spent those minutes in the car rehearsing for nothing. She took a deep breath.

CHAPTER 27

"Nol, have you ever seen one of those television shows about survivalists?"

Noley gave her friend a confused look. "I think I've seen a few minutes of a couple shows. Why?" she asked. Her eyes narrowed, as if she was getting suspicious.

"You know how those people prepare for the worst even when it doesn't seem possible that disaster will strike?"

"Yeesss...," Noley said, drawing out the word. "What are you getting at?"

"I just think they might have the right idea. You know, preparing for the worst and all that."

"Are you trying to tell me something?"

"In a way, yes. I just want you to be prepared for anything that might happen."

"Oh, my God. What am I supposed to be prepared for?" Noley's eyes were like saucers and her mouth was agape. "Is Bill dumping me?"

"No, nothing like that."

"Then what is it?"

Lilly couldn't come right out and tell Noley what was

going to happen. She didn't know what to say. She took a deep breath…

And didn't have to say anything because Noley figured it out.

"Oh, my God. They're coming to arrest me for murder."

Lilly didn't say anything, but looked at her hands, which were interlaced in her lap.

"They are. I knew it. I didn't do it, Lilly, I swear." Noley buried her face in her hands.

"Listen to me, Noley. There isn't a single person who believes you did it."

"Someone must. Why else would I be getting arrested? When are they coming?"

"I don't know. But soon."

"I was just wondering why Bill hadn't called today. Now I know why." Noley stood up and went to the window, peering up and down the street as if the police cars would materialize any second. Which, Lilly supposed, was a possibility.

"Bill doesn't want to jeopardize anything for you. He doesn't want to be accused of helping you in any way, because that would be bad for both of you. And as long as he's got his job, he can share things with me that you might not otherwise find out. And I can share those things with you. Like the thing I came over to hint to you."

"That they're coming for me," Noley said miserably. "I don't even have a lawyer. I should get one, shouldn't I?"

"Definitely," Lilly replied. "I can give you the number of my lawyer. She's really good."

"Thanks." Noley had been holding it all together until that moment. But suddenly she started to cry.

"What am I going to do? This will ruin my entire future, not to mention Bill will never look at me the same way again," she sobbed. Lilly stood up and put her arms around her friend.

"This isn't going to ruin your future, you'll see. And as for

Bill, he thinks the sun rises and sets with you. We know you didn't do this, and the truth is, according to Bill, that the police don't really believe you did it, either. But the district attorney is all over this. The problem is that they don't have any other leads and you're the best suspect at the moment. But that's going to change even if I have to find other suspects myself. You're going to call that lawyer and tell her what's going on and then you're going to have positive thoughts."

Noley couldn't stop crying. Lilly led her to the couch, where she sat with her elbows on her knees, her tear-stained face in her hands.

"Is there anything you'd like me to tell Bill?" Lilly asked. "He feels terrible about this whole mess."

Noley shook her head. "Don't tell him anything. I'm so embarrassed to be in this position that I don't even know what to say to him."

"That's okay. I don't think he expects you to have anything to say. But I want to make sure you know that he knows you're innocent."

"And he can't talk to the detectives on this case?"

"He's talked to them, of course, but he's in a weird position. He can't do anything that would interfere with their investigation if he wants to keep his job."

"And here I was wondering what it would be like if I ever married him," Noley said in a choked voice. "When all the time I should have been wondering what it's like to live in prison." She started crying afresh, her tears coming faster now.

"Noley, snap out of it," Lilly directed. Her voice sounded harsher than she meant it to. "You're going to get through this with my help and with the help of everyone who knows you. Get a grip on yourself and try to think positive thoughts. You can't be crying when the police get here because they'll wonder how you found out they were coming."

Noley nodded and wiped her nose with her sleeve. "I'm

sorry. You're right. I didn't do anything wrong--I'll just have to trust the judicial system to work the way it should." She sat up a little straighter.

"That's the spirit," Lilly encouraged her. "And if the judicial system needs a little nudge, then that's what I intend to do. Don't worry about anything right now. Do you want me to stay for a while?"

"Would you mind?" Noley asked. "I don't want to be alone when the police get here. I'll be scared to death."

"I'm happy to stay," Lilly said. "Just let me text Laurel and Hassan and let them all know where I am." She pulled out her cell phone, texted the necessary recipients, called Tighe, and reached for the popcorn as she sat back on the sofa.

"What do you suppose the food will be like in jail?" Noley mused.

"Stop it!" Lilly exclaimed.

"I was just wondering," Noley said. She sounded hurt and Lilly regretted her reply.

"It'll probably be awful," Lilly said. "Maybe you can teach them how to cook."

"Maybe if I can teach them how to cook I'll get time off for good behavior," Noley said with a giggle. It was macabre, but if that made her feel better, then Lilly was more than willing to participate.

"You could teach them how to bake a file into a cake and make the cake still taste good," she suggested.

"Or you can teach them how to make breakfast muffins--call 'em your Break-Out-Fast Muffins." Noley was laughing so hard she had to hold her sides.

She opened her mouth to say something else when there was a knock on the door. Immediately all traces of a smile vanished from Noley's face, as did her pink complexion. She turned ashen and took a shaky breath.

"I can't stand up. My legs are like jelly," she told Lilly. "Can you answer the door?"

Lilly nodded wordlessly and went to the door. Two uniformed officers stood there, grim-faced and serious.

"May we come in?" one of the officers asked.

Lilly was weepy and sick to her stomach when she went home just a short while later. The officers had taken Noley to the police station (without the need for handcuffs, thank God) and Lilly had promised to visit her as soon as possible. One of the officers suggested that she wait until the next day, since it was already late and the booking process would take some time. The arraignment was to be first thing in the morning.

Noley had gone bravely, once she was able to stand up, and Lilly locked the door behind them when they departed. Noley only faltered once, when Lilly called after her, "I'll see you soon--love you!"

She collapsed on the sofa when she got home. She knew the kids were upstairs, but she didn't even call up to them to say hello. Barney came over and, seeming to sense that something was amiss, jumped up onto the sofa, curled up with his head in her lap, whimpered once, and was still.

She stroked his head as thoughts tumbled around in her own. How was she going to help Noley? What would Bill do if he found out she was trying to do the job of the police?

It didn't matter what Bill thought. She was going to have to forge ahead and figure out who the real killer was. Noley didn't deserve to spend a single moment locked up in a cell.

She grabbed a pencil and pad of paper from the drawer in the end table next to the sofa, trying not to disturb Barney, and started writing down the people she would need to speak to and the questions she would have to ask them.

1. *Armand. What was his relationship with Cerise like? Were*

there any people who didn't like her? Why, exactly, did they leave New York City to come to Juniper Junction?

2. *The students who helped Noley at the reenactment. Have the police talked to them? Did they see anyone hanging around the food longer than necessary? Were they aware of any ingredients that were in the van that they didn't recognize?*
3. *Kathleen Deveau. What was her relationship with Armand and Cerise? Did she suggest that they come to Juniper Junction? Had she discussed with them her dislike for Noley?*

Writing down a plan for trying to find out the identity of the real killer gave Lilly hope and a little bit of courage. She sat for a while longer, stroking Barney's fur, until Laurel came downstairs.

"What are you doing, Mom?" she asked, looking into the living room.

"Just sitting here, resting," Lilly replied.

"Are you sick? You never just sit down to rest."

Lilly smiled. Laurel had a point. Sometimes she would sit down to watch television or read, but she never just sat still and did nothing but think.

"I'm not sick. It's been a long day. Noley was arrested tonight and charged with Cerise's murder."

Laurel gasped and came to sit on the edge of the sofa. "You're kidding. What happened?"

"Bill gave me the heads-up that other officers were coming to her house to arrest her, so I went over and I was there when they arrived."

"Thank God."

"I think Noley was glad to have someone there. She is confused and upset because we know she didn't kill anyone. She's one of the gentlest people I know."

"So why do the police think she did it?"

"Because they're stuck and the evidence *does* seem to point to Noley. I think they were under pressure to make an arrest and she was the closest person they had to a suspect."

"Uncle Bill must know she didn't do it."

Lilly nodded. "Of course he knows she's innocent, but he can't stand in the way of an investigation or he'll lose his job."

"Can he visit her in jail?"

"I'm sure he won't. That would look pretty bad for both of them."

"What can we do to help her?" Laurel asked.

Lilly didn't want to reveal her plan to start talking to witnesses and other interested persons, so she just gave Laurel a tired smile.

"We can go visit her as often as possible, for one thing. And though she keeps her house nice and clean, we can give it a thorough cleaning before she comes home so she doesn't come home and have anything to do."

"I can help with all that. And I'm sure Tighe will help. Even Nick will help."

"Thanks, honey. I think I'm going to go to bed. It's been a very long day."

"Tighe told me what happened. With him and Mike, I mean," Laurel said as Lilly was trying to move Barney to the other end of the sofa.

Lilly stood up and locked eyes with Laurel. "Dad didn't tell him where he got the information about Tighe's drinking. But I'm glad you said something. I didn't recognize the signs, though I should have, and now we can hopefully get him on the right path."

"I'm worried about him. That's why we fought outside those times you and Mrs. Laforge complained about us. His friends come by and they drive really fast, too. That's why Mrs. Laforge complains about the car noise. I was trying to get him to stop," Laurel said. "I didn't want to tell on him, but I figured it was for his own good."

"You did the right thing," Lilly assured her. She gave her

daughter a hug, an act that was becoming far too infrequent. "Thank you."

"You're welcome, Mom. Just don't let on that I ratted him out."

"I won't, I promise."

Laurel went out into the kitchen, helped herself to a glass of water, and went back upstairs.

Lilly wasn't far behind. She let Barney out in the backyard, locked up, and went upstairs. She peeked into Tighe's darkened room.

"Tighe?" she whispered.

"Yeah?" came his voice from under the covers.

"Is everything okay?"

"Everything's just great, Mom. Why do you ask?" The level of ugly sarcasm in his voice made Lilly wince.

"You know, we're doing this to help you."

"I know. Good night." He turned his back to her and didn't say anything else. She longed to give him a kiss on his forehead, like she had done when he was little, but she knew that would most certainly not be welcome.

She turned around and went to her own room. Barney followed, faithful as always. She climbed into bed, made a little place down by her feet where Barney would spend the night, and lay back against her pillow. Though she feared she wouldn't get any sleep after the stressful day she had had, she fell asleep almost immediately.

CHAPTER 28

First thing the next morning, Lilly went to the shop. She had the opening work done before Harry got there, in part to thank him for closing the shop the night before.

"How's everything?" he asked when he came in.

"Everything could be better," Lilly began, then proceeded to tell him what had happened the previous evening. Harry was shocked when he heard the developments.

"How's Noley doing today?" he asked.

"I don't know. I looked online and found the visiting hours for the women's side of the jail, so I'm planning to head over there today. I was hoping you'd keep an eye on things while I'm gone."

"You know I will."

"Thanks. I won't be gone for long. Visitors are only allowed fifteen minutes each."

"Will Bill be able to go visit her?"

"I'm sure he would like to, but it would be better if he didn't. No one wants him or Noley accused of trying to interfere with her case." Her own words rang in her ears--*interfere with her case*. Wasn't that exactly what she was planning to do?

Yes, but she banished the thought from her mind. Her

interfering couldn't be as bad as Bill interfering. That reminded her-she needed to get that list out and make a plan of attack for talking to the people she had chosen to target for her own questioning.

Back in her office, she found the list. Studying it, she decided to start at the beginning, with Armand. He might be able to provide lots of information, and she might even be able to talk to him without him realizing he was being questioned.

Right before lunch Lilly asked Harry to watch the shop while she ran over to the county jail to visit with Noley for a few minutes. She got in her car and sped to the jail, eager to see her friend, but anxious about what condition Noley might be in.

But when she arrived, she found she wasn't the only person there to visit Noley. She would have to wait her turn.

She had been sitting in the waiting room for about five minutes when a thick metal door clanged open and Noley's parents walked through it. Noley's mother, Melissa, held a tissue to her eyes and her father, Russell, was stone-faced.

She rose to greet them.

"Lilly!" Noley's mother cried. She hugged Lilly and Lilly could feel the sobs coming from her frame.

"It's a terrible thing," her father said. "My poor girl in there, suffering. And there's a murderer out there! They don't even care about finding the right person now, since they've got someone in custody."

"They do care, though," Lilly tried to assure him. "And I'm going to do a little digging around myself, to see if I can find something the police may have missed. We're not going to let Noley stay in here for long."

At this, Melissa, who had managed to stem the flow of tears, started up again. Russell put his arm around his wife. "Keep us posted, Lilly. We'll let you get in there now to see her."

Melissa and Russell left and a guard ushered Lilly into a small empty room. She sat at a utilitarian Formica-topped table and waited for Noley. She waited less than a minute.

"Hi," Noley said glumly, walking past the guard in the doorway. "Did you see my parents out there?"

Lilly nodded. "They were upset, as you'd expect. But I told them to hang tight, because we're going to get you out of here."

Noley sighed. It seemed her entire person had changed overnight. Her normally bouncy hair had lost its luster and hung in stringy strands off her shoulders. There were large dark gray circles around her forlorn eyes and her cheeks looked sallow and sunken.

"Did you get any sleep last night?" Lilly asked.

"No way," Noley said. "It was so noisy all night long. It's certainly not like being at home."

"Maybe you can get a nap today," Lilly suggested. She was finding it difficult to think of things to say.

"What, so I can lie awake again tonight?" Noley asked with scorn. "No thanks. I'll stay awake." Lilly nodded.

"How are the kids?" Noley asked. It seemed that she, too, was finding it hard to think of things to talk about.

"They're good. They'll both be in to visit you at some point," Lilly said. "We have to figure out exactly what the rules are about visitors, then we'll set up a schedule."

"And Bill?" Noley asked hopefully. Lilly assumed Noley already knew that it would be impossible for Bill to visit her in jail.

"He's doing about as well as you'd expect," Lilly said noncommittally. The truth was, she hadn't talked to Bill since before she went to Noley's house the previous night, but she didn't want Noley to think they weren't in constant communication.

They talked for a few more minutes about the weather, the food (so far Noley hadn't felt like eating anything), and the morning traffic, then it was time for Lilly to leave. She wanted so badly to hug her friend, but she knew it wouldn't be allowed. So she gave Noley the brightest smile she could muster. Noley tried to smile in return, but it was hard. Lilly could see her swallowing several times, as if trying to keep the tears from flowing.

Lilly made up her mind on the way back to the shop that she would eat lunch at Armand's bistro later that day in order to get the ball rolling with her own questions about the case. Since she and Harry took turns taking care of the shop while the other went to lunch, it would give her the perfect opportunity to interrogate Armand--pleasantly, of course--without having to keep asking Harry to watch the store for her. She made a mental note to give him a bonus for being such a huge help.

Harry went to lunch first. When he returned Lilly told him she wasn't hungry yet and wanted to wait a while before going to get something to eat. She wanted to wait until the lunch crowd was completely cleared out of the bistro and she could have Armand's complete attention.

It was past mid-afternoon when Lilly finally told Harry she was getting hungry and would be back in thirty minutes. In truth, she was starving.

She ordered a croissant and a cup of coffee when she got to the bistro, just so it wouldn't appear strange that she went in and didn't order any food. As she had hoped, she was the only customer in the bistro at that hour.

Armand rang her up at the counter. She lingered over taking the change from him, hoping to engage him in conversation enough so he would want to sit down with her to talk while she ate.

"So how are *you* doing, Armand?" she asked, her voice warm.

"I have some hard days, that is certain," he replied. He closed the register slowly as he handed over her change.

"I'm sure you do. It must be very hard. And now this, to have no pastry chef. How are you managing without a pastry chef?" She was being careful not to mention Noley's name.

She pretended to rummage through her handbag before reaching for the change.

"I am working from morning until night trying to get all the food cooked myself, but you're right. It is hard to manage without a pastry chef. So many of my customers are coming in here for the desserts and the special breakfast pastries. But I am managing somehow."

Lilly's ruse, such as it was, worked. When she took her change and sat down at the table closest to the register, Armand came and sat down with her.

Score one for Lilly, she thought. *I should have been a detective. This is easy.*

"I suppose you've heard that Noley has been arrested?" Lilly asked, taking a sip of her coffee and watching him over the rim of the mug.

"*Oui*, I did hear that. The police came to tell me this morning."

"Do you think that will affect your business?" Lilly asked.

"I do not know, but I hope not," Armand replied. "Word hasn't really gotten out yet, so people don't realize why she's not here. The regulars are used to seeing her in here already. But only one of them asked me about her today."

Lilly sighed. "Poor Cerise. None of this would have been necessary for you if she hadn't met with such a terrible end."

Armand shook his head sadly. "Yes, I miss her very much. Her parents have been staying with me and they like to talk about her. But I do not. I am not ready for that yet."

"How long had the two of you been married?" Lilly asked.

"Only two years," Armand answered.

"Practically newlyweds," Lilly said, her tone sympathetic and sorrowful.

"That is correct."

"I actually found the first two years of my marriage very trying," Lilly confided. "My husband and I--actually, now he's my ex-husband--fought a lot simply because I think we were still getting to know each other."

Armand nodded, a faraway look in his eyes.

"Have you ever felt that way?" asked Lilly.

Armand gave her a look that was unreadable. "I suppose I have," he said, nodding slowly. "Anytime one changes one's lifestyle to accommodate another person, there is bound to be a little bit of, how do you say it, tension?"

"And of course to start a business as newlyweds, that must have added more stress to the relationship," Lilly prompted. She hoped she wasn't being too obvious, but Armand kept talking.

"*Mais, oui,*" he said. "Naturally we didn't have identical ideas about how to run our business, so we had some, shall I say, lively discussions about it."

"Those 'lively' discussions," Lilly began, her fingers in air quotes, "can be good for a marriage."

"Yes, you are right. I suppose they can."

"But I know, as a business owner myself, that I don't want anyone telling me how to run my shop. I assume you and Cerise both feel--I mean, felt--the same way." Her statement was calculated to get him talking more about his relationship with Cerise.

It worked.

"Cerise thought we should be exclusively a pastry shop, but I disagreed. I thought we would be more successful if we served savory foods for *petit dejeuner* and *dejeuner*--um, breakfast and luncheon--too. Foods that people could enjoy as full meals. Cerise's passion was making pastry, but I had to explain to her that if we were going to stay in business, we had to broaden our menus."

"Eventually you must have persuaded her, since you now serve two meals a day."

"Yes, I did persuade her," Armand said.

"You don't have any children, do you?" Lilly asked. She wondered if she was going a bit too far.

"No. Cerise wanted children, but I wanted to wait. She was unhappy about that."

Suddenly he stood up. "I really must get back to work. Please, I must let you enjoy your croissant and coffee in peace."

Lilly said goodbye and Armand disappeared into the kitchen.

That had been like taking candy from a baby. Lilly finished her food, returned to her shop, and spent the rest of the day helping customers.

That evening she sat down with her pad of paper and jotted down notes from her "interview" with Armand. She figured she should keep the pad with her for future interviews, just to make sure she remembered everything while the information was still fresh.

Before she went to bed she gave Hassan a quick call. He apologized for not calling her earlier in the day, but said he and his father had been busy all day with realtors.

"My dad put an offer on the house we all went to see the other night!" Hassan exclaimed.

"That's wonderful! Has it been accepted yet?"

"Yes. He is so happy. We're just waiting on all the formalities now."

"I'm so happy for you and your parents. You must be exhausted from all the house hunting on top of trying to work, too."

"I am," Hassan admitted. "I can't wait to see you again." Lilly smiled at the warmth in his voice.

She waited up until ten o'clock to make sure Tighe came home on time, and sure enough, he walked through the door at nine fifty-nine.

She smiled at her son. "Well done."

"Thanks." If she wanted him to sit and chat with her for a while, though, she was disappointed. He went straight up to his room. Laurel was already home and sleeping, since she had to get up early for work.

The next day Lilly visited Noley again. She looked a little pinker than she had her first day in the jail, and Lilly hoped it was because she was getting some hope back in her thoughts. And maybe eating, too.

"I talked to Armand yesterday," Lilly said in a low voice once the guard had moved away to stand by the door of the little visitors' room.

"What did he have to say?" Noley asked, her eyes lighting up just a bit.

"Only that he and Cerise had some kind of a disagreement over how the bistro should be run. Cerise thought it should be a pastry shop, Armand thought it should be more of a restaurant. I guess we know who won that argument."

Noley nodded thoughtfully. "You know, I remember hearing one of Cerise's relatives grumble something about a pastry shop when we were in the receiving line at her funeral. I wonder if there was more tension between them than they let on."

"It's possible. No one really knows what goes on behind closed doors in any relationship. Maybe they fought like cats. And the problem is that the relatives are probably back in France by now. It's not going to be easy for the police to question them."

"It would be sad if they fought over the bistro," Noley said.

"Maybe so, but it would be good for you," Lilly pointed out. "If they were fighting, that would throw at least a little bit of suspicion on Armand. And the husband is always the first one to be suspected. You know that."

"Yeah, but the police have obviously cleared him. Otherwise he'd be sitting in here and I'd be at home, making muffins or some kind of roast or working on a new cheesecake recipe."

"But maybe the police didn't ask questions with a business person's mindset. They may have asked Armand about fights between him and Cerise, and if they didn't actually *fight* about the bistro, he might not have thought to share that information with them. He would think of it more as business discussions, but they can still put a lot of stress on a couple," Lilly pointed out.

"Don't worry," she continued. "We'll have you home making muffins and roasts and cheesecake in no time," Lilly assured her friend. Noley looked skeptical.

"Just don't get hurt," Noley said. "I don't want that guilt hanging over my head, too."

"Don't worry about me. Just remember that I want a dozen of your blueberry muffins if I figure out who did this."

Noley gave her friend a genuine grin. "Deal," she said. "Now when am I going to see those kids of yours?"

"Hopefully this afternoon," Lilly replied. "I checked the visiting schedule and people are allowed to come in for fifteen minutes later in the day. They'll both be out of work by then, so I'll have them stop by. They want to see you for themselves, to make sure you're all right."

"I miss them," Noley smiled sadly. "How's Hassan?"

"I think he's tired. He's trying to work while he's in town, plus his father is visiting, and he's been taking his father around to look at houses on the market. He needs a break."

"Things will calm down for him," Noley said. *It's just like her to be trying to make me feel better*, Lilly thought. *No wonder she's my best friend.*

"I need to get back to the shop," Lilly said. "I'll do some more hunting as soon as I can." She gave Noley a little wave and left.

CHAPTER 29

That evening when Lilly got home from work, both kids were in the kitchen.

"How did your visits with Noley go?" Lilly asked, tying on an apron to protect her work clothes.

"We couldn't go in together," Laurel said.

"I know. I should have mentioned that before you went," Lilly said, reaching for a bunch of carrots in the refrigerator.

"So Tighe and I each only had a few minutes with her. She cried when I left," Laurel said. The corners of her eyes glistened.

"She looks better than I expected," Tighe said, looking away. Were there tears in his eyes, too?

"She's definitely better than she was yesterday," Lilly agreed. "Her cheeks are pink, and it looked like she'd had something to eat and maybe even a shower."

"She must be hating the food in there," Laurel remarked.

"I'm sure the food isn't the only thing she hates about being in there," Lilly said. She was busy slicing pork tenderloin for a quick stir-fry.

Lilly's cell phone rang and she looked at the caller ID. Bill.

"Kids, I need to take this. It's Uncle Bill. Can you finish

the stir-fry?" Both her kids were competent in the kitchen, thanks to years of being friends with Noley. They both nodded and got to work.

Lilly took the phone into the living room and sat down on the edge of the sofa. "I'm here," she told Bill. "I just wanted to get out of the kitchen."

"How is she?" Bill asked eagerly, ignoring what Lilly had said.

"She's okay, I suppose. Not happy, certainly, but not in despair. And the kids and I were just talking about her--she's much better than she was yesterday."

"How can you tell?"

"Her coloring, her eyes. She just looks better."

"Did she ask about me?"

"Your name didn't come up today, but she asked about you yesterday. I think she was harboring some hope that you could visit her in jail, but I told her that wouldn't be possible."

"It might," said Bill.

"What do you mean?"

"I'm thinking about taking a leave."

"Why on earth would you do that?" Lilly asked, incredulous. "You're the one on the inside--the one person who can give us a little more information than the cops working on the case. You can't leave your job now."

"I'm pretty useless here, to be honest with you. I can't focus on work, I can't seem to complete any paperwork. I'm a mess."

"I'm so sorry, Bill. But I really think it would be best if you stayed at work. What would you do with yourself all day if you didn't have your job to keep you busy?"

He didn't answer.

"I thought so," Lilly said. "Nothing. You'd drive yourself nuts, and probably me and Mom, too. And she doesn't need to be driven any further down that road."

Bill heaved a loud sigh on the other end of the line. Lilly knew he was running his hand through his thinning hair.

"I suppose you have a point. But if I'm not able to concentrate on what I'm doing, I'm going to start making mistakes. And then I'll get fired and then I'll be home anyway, worrying about Noley and driving you and Mom nuts. Or nuttier."

"So you need to really focus on your job right now. I know you're worried about Noley, but the best thing you can do right now for her is to stay at work, keep your job, and keep your ears open for any information that might lead to more suspects."

"I know how to do my job, Lilly," Bill said testily.

"A minute ago it didn't sound like it," Lilly retorted. "And now that I have your attention, I need you to tell me everything you know about Noley catering the reenactment."

"Lilly, don't even tell me you're investigating this, too," Bill said in a stern voice. "You know we can both get in big trouble for that."

"I know, but we won't," Lilly answered with forced cheerfulness.

"What if you get hurt? There's a crazy person out there and if you start nosing around where you're not wanted, you could be in real danger."

"Don't worry, I'm only asking questions to try to get things straight in my own mind. There has to be someone who saw something. Don't you agree? I mean, the place was packed with people. You can't just pour poison on someone's food without another person in the crowd seeing *something*."

"So what do you want to know from me?" Bill asked. Judging from the tone of his voice, Lilly knew he was resigned to her asking questions.

"I want to know what the detectives learned when they talked to Armand."

"What difference does it make? They've obviously cleared him of suspicion."

"I talked to him yesterday and he mentioned that he and Cerise had argued about the bistro. Cerise wanted it to be exclusively a pastry shop; Armand wanted to serve actual meals. Clearly, Armand won that argument. I'm wondering what he told the police about their, um, discussions. Were they heated? Were they no big deal?"

"We already know that they disagreed because Cerise wanted to start a family and Armand wasn't ready. What if that was the reason Cerise wanted just a pastry shop—to have more time for a family?"

"I don't know, Lil--" Bill began.

"And what if Cerise nagged Armand about everything to the point that he killed her?" Lilly's voice was rising.

"Whoa. Slow down, Lilly. There's absolutely no evidence that anything like that happened. You're getting pretty far afield," Bill warned.

"But it's a possibility," Lilly urged.

"Look. I'll see if I can get a look at the notes in the file. They're doing a pretty good job of keeping me out of the loop on this one. I don't know why, since they kept me informed about what was happening last Christmas when you were the one under suspicion."

"I guess almost-family can be a little hairier than actual family when someone has been accused of a crime," Lilly replied.

"Who said anything about almost-family?" Bill asked. Lilly could hear the smile in his voice.

"Oh, please. We all know you're head over heels for Noley. Let's just cut the nonsense about her being almost family."

He chuckled. "You got me there."

"When you get married, I'm taking full credit for it," Lilly said, momentarily changing the subject to something happier.

"When we get married, I'll let you," he laughed. "But we're not married yet. We have to get her out of jail and cleared of these charges before that can happen. Before either of us can even think about that happening, in fact."

"Okay, let's get back to business," Lilly said. "I have a plan to talk to some of the other people who were around the day of the reenactment. Your job is to talk to the detectives investigating this case and get some info from them."

"All right. How come you're the better cop this time?"

"Because it's Noley," Lilly answered simply. "She may be my best friend, but I can still look at this with more detachment than you can."

"I guess you're right. Let me know what you find out, and be careful. There's a murderer out there."

"You do your job and let me do mine. And speaking of that, I *do* have a shop to run, too, so let me get some sleep."

"Goodnight."

The next morning Harry was already at work when Lilly arrived.

"What are you doing here so early?" she asked.

"I stopped to get breakfast at the bistro," he said. "Normally there's a really long line, so I wanted to get there early so I'd get to work on time. But there were only a couple people in line today. So I was in and out of there in no time. I figured I might as well come in early and get things set up for the day."

"Well, thank you. That was nice of you," Lilly said. "What did you get for breakfast?"

"A *tartine* with plum jam and a large *cafe au lait*," he said. "I wanted the *pain au chocolat* so badly, but I'm trying to watch my waistline," he said with a grin.

"Any particular reason?" Lilly asked.

"Maybe," he answered cryptically.

"What's her name?" Lilly asked with a wink.

"Alice."

Lilly was shocked. She hadn't really expected him to answer and she had never known him to have a girlfriend.

"Ooh! What's she like?" Lilly asked.

"She's really nice. She's blonde, medium height...I don't know. What do you want to know?"

Lilly feared she was making Harry uncomfortable, so she decided to end his misery.

"Just knowing she's really nice is enough for me, Harry. I don't want you to be hanging around anyone who's not nice," Lilly said. She smiled at her assistant.

He was blushing. He turned around and took a bite of *tartine*, probably so he wouldn't have to say anything else.

Suddenly the full force of what Harry had said struck Lilly.

"There were almost no customers in the bistro this morning?" she asked. "I wonder if people are staying away because they know Noley worked there and now she's been charged with Cerise's murder."

Harry shrugged, his mouth full.

"They say there's no such thing as bad publicity, but I disagree, at least when it comes to food and restaurants," Lilly said. "And the quicker we can find out who killed Cerise, the quicker Noley can recover from all the bad publicity she's gotten."

Lilly knew what she had to do next.

She went back to her office and pulled up the website for the local community college. Before long she had located the number for the culinary arts department and placed a call to the director of the culinary arts training program. Upon being told that the woman was on vacation, Lilly was transferred to the assistant director, Kathleen Deveau, the woman she was trying to avoid because of her history with Noley.

When she explained that she was hoping to talk to the students who had worked with Noley, Ms. Deveau was at first reluctant to allow her to do so.

"It seems like Noley may have bitten off more than she could chew," Ms. Deveau said.

"How do you mean?" Lilly asked.

"I mean, maybe the responsibility of such a large catering job was just too much for her," Ms. Deveau said. Was Lilly mistaken, or was there an undercurrent of glee in Ms. Deveau's voice?

"Noley was more than capable of doing the job," Lilly said, the ice dripping from her voice.

"Perhaps not, given the outcome of the event," Ms. Deveau said in a mild tone. Lilly could feel her blood pressure ratcheting up like a geyser.

"Ms. Deveau, would you prefer that I speak with the department head?" Lilly inquired.

"That won't be necessary," Ms. Deveau said in a tone that would freeze molten lava.

"You'll help, then?" Lilly asked.

"The head of the department is on vacation. I will make arrangements for you to speak to the appropriate students."

"Can I just get in touch with them myself?" Lilly asked, not wishing to involve this woman any more than absolutely necessary.

"Unfortunately, I can't give out any contact information," Ms. Deveau answered. "But I can get in touch with them myself and ask them to meet you. I believe there were six students who helped Noley at the reenactment. Would you like to meet with them separately?"

"I think that would be best, yes," Lilly replied.

"I will contact each of the students and you will have to be here when they are available. You understand, of course, that I can't make them come in. And you will talk to them in my office for fifteen minutes each. No more, as they are all busy and I certainly am, too."

Both women knew Kathleen Deveau had Lilly over a barrel.

"Thank you," she said through gritted teeth.

"You know the police have already talked to each of them,

right?" Ms. Deveau asked. "I can't imagine what you can extract from them that the police haven't."

"Let me worry about that," Lilly said. "I'm hoping one of them might remember something they didn't think of earlier. Plus, I thought they might find it easier to talk to me since I'm not with the police. I'm just a friend trying to help a friend."

"What time of day works best for you to meet with the students?" Ms. Deveau asked.

"Later in the evenings is best. That way I can close up my shop and not have to worry about getting back to work in a hurry," Lilly answered. Too late, she realized Ms. Deveau would most certainly schedule the meetings for mid-day now that she had that information.

"Let me talk to the students and I'll get back to you," the woman said.

Lilly hung up feeling drained and angry. But since she was finally doing something that could really help Noley, she tried to forget the odious Ms. Deveau. She shouldn't be thinking of her own inconvenience at a time like this, anyway--she needed to keep Noley uppermost in her mind. She hated to think of her friend, stuck in that jail cell and not knowing what was going on in her absence.

While she was sitting there, Bill called. He spoke in low tones, as if he didn't want to be overheard.

"I got a quick look at some of the notes on the case," he said without preamble.

"And?" Lilly asked excitedly.

"Armand and Cerise had been arguing a lot because Cerise believed Armand was having an affair. He swears he wasn't, but she didn't believe him. Prior to that, they were fighting because Cerise wanted to start a family and Armand didn't."

"That's interesting," Lilly said. "Do you suppose he could have killed her because he was sick of being accused of being unfaithful?"

"I doubt it," Bill said softly. "That's no reason to kill someone."

"Is there a good reason?" Lilly asked. Bill didn't answer.

"Anything else?" she asked.

"Yeah. The students all posted so many selfies that afternoon, right around the time of the murder, that they're not under suspicion. They wouldn't have been able to poison Cerise, based on how close in time all the photos were to the time she was killed."

"All right. Anything else?"

"No. I'll keep trying," Bill answered.

Sighing, she rejoined Harry in the shop.

"A woman came in while you were in the back. When I offered to go get you, she said not to. She had some errands to run, then she was going to check back for you in a little while."

"Do you know who it was?" Lilly asked.

"She didn't leave her name."

CHAPTER 30

When the woman returned about a half hour later, Lilly almost didn't recognize her. It was Debbie Foster, Mike's mother, and she looked haggard and tired. "Hi, Debbie. How have you been holding up this summer?"

"Hi, Lilly. Can I talk to you for a minute in private?"

"Sure. We can go back to my office. What's up?"

Debbie didn't answer as she followed Lilly to the back room. Lilly motioned for her to take a seat and Lilly sat behind the desk.

Up close, Debbie looked even worse. She was wearing too much make-up and her hair looked thin and straw-like.

"Is everything okay, Debbie?" Lilly asked.

"It's going to be, I think."

"What's going on?"

"I just came in to thank you for talking to Mike. He talked to his father and me and we're so grateful to know what the problem is. I didn't notice the signs that he had been drinking, but I knew something wasn't right with him."

She looked down and then back up at Lilly again. "That's the reason for my weight loss. I've been so worried about him that I haven't felt like eating since before the summer began. Not the best way to lose weight, I'm afraid."

"It's not," Lilly agreed. She had lost weight like that after Beau disappeared all those years before, so she winced knowing what Debbie had been going through.

"I wish you had called me or that I had called you, or something," Lilly said, folding her hands in front of her on the desk. "It's embarrassing. It feels like I'm the only one going through it, and even when I realized Mike was drinking too much, too, it still didn't occur to me that you might be going through the same things."

Debbie sighed. "I also wanted to tell you that Mike has talked to your neighbor and she doesn't want to press charges against him. What a wonderful lady."

Mrs. Laforge, a wonderful lady?

"Well, I'm glad he talked to her," Lilly said, trying to conceal her surprise at this revelation of Mrs. Laforge's character. "I've told Tighe that he will be taking care of Mrs. Laforge's yard work for the rest of the summer, *gratis*."

Debbie nodded. "She asked Mike to clean out her shed. It'll take days. Have you seen it?"

"Yes, the night I found Mike in there," Lilly said with a grin. "It's in pretty rough shape."

"Well, my husband and I are going to see to it that Mike makes it look brand new."

"I must confess, I was a little bit nervous when I saw you come in here. I was afraid you were here to read me the riot act about confronting Mike."

"Not at all. I'm just glad that everything is out in the open. It's always easier to solve a problem when everyone has all the facts." Debbie stood up. "So thanks again for everything." She turned to open the office door, then turned back to Lilly.

"Say, how did you realize Tighe had been drinking?"

Lilly smiled. "A little birdie told me."

Kathleen Deveau called later that afternoon.

"I've contacted all the students who helped Noley on the fourth of July," she said. "One of them can meet you at noon day after tomorrow. Can you be here?"

Lilly gripped the phone a little tighter and took a deep breath. She should have known better than to tell Ms. Deveau evenings were best.

"Yes, I can be there," she finally said.

"Good."

"While I have you on the phone, Ms. Deveau, can you tell me how you know Noley?" Lilly asked.

There was a sigh on the other end of the line.

"I met Noley in cooking school," she said tersely.

"Am I correct that you and she are not friends?"

Kathleen let out a harsh laugh. "You are correct."

"May I ask why?"

"She's an arrogant cheat, that's why."

Lilly didn't want to push too hard, or she feared Kathleen would refuse her access to the students who had helped Noley, so she let the matter go for the moment.

"All right. I'll be there at noon the day after tomorrow," she said.

That evening when she visited Noley, she got right down to business.

"First of all, I talked to Bill last night. I had to talk him out of taking a leave of absence from the police force."

Noley's eyes grew wide. "What? Why would he do that?"

"He's so sorry that this has happened to you that he can't focus on his work."

Noley's eyes grew moist almost immediately. "He's so sweet."

"Sweet, maybe. But we can't afford for him to be away from the office right now. He needs to get some information so we can help you."

"What kind of information?" Noley asked.

"We need to know what Armand told the police about his disagreements with Cerise over the future of the bistro."

"Okay," Noley said.

"How's the lawyer working out?"

Noley shrugged. "Fine, I guess. She's sure she can get a jury to find lots of reasonable doubt that I killed Cerise, but I don't want it to get that far. She's doing some investigating of her own, but she has lots of other clients and she can't focus only on me."

"That's what I'm here for. And Bill. And anyone else I can find. We're trying to get you out of here before this has a chance to go any further."

Noley gave Lilly a grateful look. "I just wish I could help more."

"Don't worry. When we need information from you, I'll tell you. In the meantime, keep your chin up. How's the food?"

Noley finally smiled. "They're letting me work in the kitchen. It gives me something to do and a lot of women are coming up to me, telling me how much better the food is after just a few days and asking how I learned to cook."

It was Lilly's turn to smile. "See? I knew you'd made a splash in here somehow."

"A lot of the women in here are really nice. They're not people I would have met otherwise."

Lilly stood up and pushed back her chair. "Oh, I almost forgot. I have an appointment scheduled day after tomorrow at noon with one of the students who helped you cater the reenactment. I'm meeting with them each separately. Anything I need to know?"

Noley looked thoughtful for a moment. "There was one, Stacy, who didn't like being 'bossed around,' as she put it. She was kind of a pain in my neck."

"I'll watch out for her. And speaking of being a pain in the neck, that Kathleen Deveau is no picnic."

"I'm telling you, she hates me," Noley said. Lilly couldn't imagine anyone hating Noley. She blew a kiss to her friend and left. She met the kids, who had visited Noley before Lilly arrived, at the diner for dinner that evening.

"Hey, Carlsen family," Orson greeted them when they walked in. "How's everything going?"

"Everything is definitely going," Lilly responded with a grim face. "I'm sure you've heard about Noley. We're doing everything we can to get her out of there."

Orson shook his head. "It's terrible. I feel so sorry for her."

"We all do," Lilly said, indicating her kids with a sweep of her hand. "We've been visiting her every day to help keep her spirits up. I think that's probably the most important thing right now."

Orson was leading them to table while they talked. There were only a few other people sitting at tables on the far side of the restaurant, so Lilly didn't worry about being overheard.

"Orson, you hear a lot of things in here, I'm sure. Would you try to keep your ears open and let me know if you hear anything about Noley or about Cerise's murder?"

"You bet," he answered with a nod. He handed menus to Lilly and the kids. "I'll be back to take your orders."

They didn't really need to look at the menus because they already knew what they wanted. When Orson returned Lilly chose a half a club sandwich and a small salad. Tighe and Laurel both ordered burgers with all the fixings.

Orson chuckled. "If Noley were here I'd be a half hour taking her order, with all the special instructions she has." Everyone laughed.

After they had eaten, Lilly and the kids went home. Barney was beside himself with joy at seeing his family again. He danced in circles when Lilly asked him if he wanted to go for a walk.

When she and Barney were out front of the house and Barney was furiously sniffing around for any signs of recent four-legged passers-by, Lilly was admiring the red, white, and blue bunting on the house across the street when she heard a soft cough.

She whirled around at the same time Barney lifted his shaggy head and let out one bark. Mrs. Laforge was standing on her front lawn, in her pajamas.

"Mrs. Laforge! You startled me. How are you feeling?" Lilly asked.

"Much better. I saw you out here with that dog and I wanted to come out and thank you for helping me the night I, uh, fell down."

"That's what neighbors are for, Mrs. Laforge." The old lady looked as if she wanted to say something, so Lilly waited.

"I also want to thank you for sending Tighe over here to help with the yard work. That's been a big help."

"I'm glad to hear it. I understand Mike Foster is helping you clean out your shed, too."

"He is. I declined to press charges against him."

"That's pretty nice of you. I don't know that I would have been able to be so nice."

"Mrs. Carlsen, I've got sons. They did stupid things when they were young and the people who were affected by their actions didn't press charges. I'm merely paying it forward."

This woman is full of surprises, Lilly thought.

"Well, Beau and I appreciate it, and I know Mike's parents do, too." There was an awkward silence.

"When are these fires going to stop?" Mrs. Laforge asked suddenly.

Ah, perhaps that was why the older woman wanted to talk. She was afraid.

"I hope they catch the person who's setting the fires very soon. It's unsettling to have a firebug on the loose, isn't it?" Lilly asked.

"It sure is. I hope whoever it is stays out of this neighborhood."

"I've got to get going, Mrs. Laforge. Can Barney and I walk you to your house?"

"Nope," the lady answered in her back-to-normal gruff tone. "You think I can't make it home by myself?"

"No, of course I don't think that," Lilly mumbled, tugging on Barney's leash. He had thankfully left Mrs. Laforge alone during the brief encounter, choosing instead to sniff the ground relentlessly.

She left, only turning back once to assure herself that Mrs. Laforge was safely up her front steps. *Why does that woman make it so hard to like her?* Lilly thought with frustration.

When she and Barney returned home from their walk, Lilly fell into bed and spent a luxurious evening reading a book she had borrowed from the library. Hassan called to talk, and hearing his voice put a smile on her face. Amir had postponed his trip back to Minnesota, and Hassan was determined to spend as much time with his dad as he could.

Lilly knew both kids were home and in their rooms and though she faced worries about Noley, her mother, and the arsonist on the loose, Lilly went to sleep with a feeling of calm. It really was comforting to know the kids were okay.

CHAPTER 31

Lilly slept so well that she got off to a late start the next morning, so she decided to skip breakfast at home and stop in at the diner before going into the shop. As usual, Orson was there to greet customers and take orders.

"Do you cook, too, Orson?" Lilly asked with a smile. "You do everything else around here."

"No," he answered with a smile. "I let the experts do the cooking.

"Speaking of experts, I've been thinking about Noley, sitting there in jail. I feel so sorry for her. A woman that special shouldn't be locked up," Orson said. Then he winked and added, "You know, if she weren't dating your brother, I'd ask her out myself."

Lilly didn't know quite what to do with that remark, so she just smiled and looked down at the menu he had handed her.

"Do you have any of the overnight oatmeal left?" she asked. "I know you only make a few containers of it each night."

"I think there are some left. Let me check," Orson offered, and went into the kitchen. He returned a moment later. "We've got the Elvis Special, which is banana and peanut butter, and the Christmas in July, which is cinnamon and dried cranberries."

"I'll take the Elvis Special," Lilly said. She waited while Orson retrieved her breakfast from the back and put it in a takeout container for her.

He returned and rang up her sale, but the credit card machine wasn't working.

"Sometimes it takes a minute to warm up," he said. He tried her card again, then waited for a few moments when it didn't work the second time.

While he waited he greeted another customer and showed him to a table.

He returned to the register and put Lilly's card in the reader again. While he waited to see if the third time was the charm, he chatted with her.

"It's a shame that Noley couldn't get the entire catering job for that reenactment. It's not fair to let her do just a part of it and let the owners of the bistro swoop in from New York and take over the rest."

"Actually, she did snag the entire job," Lilly said, now getting a little annoyed at having to wait for her purchase to be rung up.

"She did?" he asked.

"Yes. Armand and Cerise asked the Chamber of Commerce if they could take part in the catering. The Chamber reached out to Noley to ask if she would mind and she said it would be fine with her if they did the ice cream bar."

"Oh, I see. So that's all they did?" he asked.

"It is. Noley did all the rest." Despite all that had happened, Lilly couldn't help the hint of pride that crept into her voice when she talked about her friend's work.

"But she wasn't there that day," Orson said.

"She was there, but she had help from the culinary arts students at the community college. She spent much of the afternoon running back and forth between the college's vans, which she used to transport all the food, and the back of the tent, where a lot of the prep was set up."

The register finally started beeping with success at having charged Lilly's credit card for her breakfast, so Lilly took the container of oatmeal Orson proffered and headed over to her shop.

When she went inside she found that Harry was already at work.

It was getting close to the shop's Christmas in July celebration and sale, so Lilly set Harry to work taking down July Fourth decorations and setting up Christmas decorations that day. By the time they left that evening, the shop had turned into an enchanting winter wonderland. And since all the shops on Main Street participated in the event, the other shopkeepers had put out their Christmas decorations, too. It was a beautiful sight—all that was missing was a blanket of snow.

Lilly smiled to herself as she drove over to the jail for her visit with Noley. She loved the town's celebration of Christmas in July and couldn't wait for the summer to be over. There were a lot of people in the Rocky Mountains who loved summer, but she was one of the ones who waited--sometimes impatiently--for fall to arrive, bringing with it chilly temperatures and occasionally even snow.

Noley was in muted spirits when Lilly arrived at the jail.

"Were the kids here this morning?" Lilly asked when she sat down opposite her friend in the visiting room.

"Yeah," Noley answered.

"What's up? You seem more discouraged today."

"I am," Noley said with a sigh. "I feel like I'll never get out of here. And it's almost Christmas in July. I always make Christmas cookies in summer shapes for it. I'll miss it this year."

"Who knows? Maybe someone will stumble on something

that'll prove your innocence. In the meantime, guess who has a crush on you?"

"Who?" Noley asked wearily.

"Orson Weaver."

"Orson? What makes you think that?"

"He told me so."

"You're kidding. Doesn't he know I'm dating your brother? At least, I hope I'm still dating your brother."

Lilly rolled her eyes. "No, I'm not kidding. And yes, he knows. And yes, you're still dating my brother. I'm waiting for my invitation to the wedding."

Noley rolled her eyes this time. "The last person your brother wants to marry is a jailbird."

"Okay, okay. Enough of that talk. Now, have you thought of anything that might help in my investigation?"

"No." Noley's tone had gone from weary to miserable.

"Well, I'm talking to the student at the community college tomorrow at noon. Maybe he or she can remember something they had forgotten. I should get going. You keep your chin up, huh?"

Noley gave Lilly the best smile she could muster. "I'll try."

The next morning Harry was already at the shop when Lilly arrived for work.

"What brings you in so early today?" she asked.

"There was a fire in my neighborhood last night and I couldn't get back to sleep after all the fire trucks left."

Lilly whirled to face him. "There was another fire?" Her mind went, unbidden, to where Tighe had been. He had gone out again with Mike.

"Yeah, but I don't think the arsonist did it. This home wasn't for sale or even empty."

Lilly covered her mouth with her hands. "Oh, no. Was anyone hurt?"

"No. Luckily they got out in plenty of time. And the fire

trucks got there so fast that they were able to put it out without a total loss of the home."

Lilly breathed a sigh of relief. "Thank goodness. It wasn't on the news this morning. I had the radio on when I drove over here."

"Probably because they don't think the arsonist did it."

"How did it start?"

Harry shrugged. "I haven't heard. Probably electrical. It was an old house. What's really interesting is that there was a house for sale right next door. If the arsonist had set the fire, that's probably the house that would have burned."

"I hope you're right," said Lilly.

It wasn't long before Lilly was driving up the winding road leading to the community college just outside town. She was glad to have something to take her mind off the fire, even if it did involve dealing with Kathleen Deveau. Kathleen was waiting in her office when Lilly arrived just before noon.

"I've scheduled all the students. You've got one at noon today, one at four, and one at eight tonight." The schedule couldn't have been worse. It took every ounce of restraint Lilly had to keep herself from slugging Kathleen.

Instead, she smiled. "Thank you. I appreciate that." *I'll kill her with kindness*, Lilly thought.

When the first student, Erica Simon, arrived, Ms. Deveau left her office so Lilly and Erica could talk privately. Lilly asked a number of questions about what Erica may have seen the day of the reenactment. Erica remembered that Noley had been very tired, but that her fatigue hadn't seemed to stop her from working hard. Erica, being the first person on the sign-up list, had been chosen to help Noley preparing food. That meant Erica hadn't witnessed what happened to Cerise.

Lilly made her way back to the college two more times that day to interview two more students. Neither was able to shed any further light on the events leading up to Cerise's death.

The following day wasn't much different, at least in terms of Lilly's schedule. Kathleen had scheduled students for ten o'clock, one o'clock, three o'clock, and five o'clock. Each time Lilly drove out to the college she hoped Ms. Deveau would choke on cafeteria food.

On the second day of interviews, the first student, Ben, was slightly more helpful. He seemed eager to help--Lilly guessed that he, like Orson, probably had a crush on Noley.

"So Ben, can you tell me everything you remember from that afternoon?"

"Sure. I mean, I told the police already, but I'm more than happy to help you. I hate to think of Miss Appleton sitting in jail."

Lilly nodded and smiled, encouraging him to begin his story.

"I was at the pulled pork table. My job was to place the pork on a roll and ask customers which sauce they wanted, then another student, Jim, would serve the plates. I was reaching for another stack of plates when I heard a commotion coming from the end of the salad table. I looked up and saw a woman clutch at her throat and I figured she was having an allergic reaction to something in the food."

Lilly realized she had been leaning forward while Ben talked. She sat back and tried to relax.

"So the woman was lurching backward, just like something you'd see in a movie death scene. Another lady next to her started screaming."

"And then what happened?" Lilly asked.

He swallowed, then continued. "Then she fell to the ground. I went over there to see if there was anything I could do to help. A bunch of people had already called nine-one-one on their cell phones. The woman stopped moving and a couple men knelt next to her to see if she was breathing. But she wasn't. That was when all hell broke loose--sorry for the language--and more people started screaming and yelling. It was awful."

"Okay, so then what did you do?" Lilly asked.

"I stood there with everyone else, waiting for the cops."

"Do you remember anything else? Do you remember seeing anyone you recognized standing there? Do you remember the woman coming through the line for pulled pork?"

Ben shook his head. "I would have remembered her in my line because she was dressed in serving clothes. I would have wondered why she was dressed like that because the rest of us were in black pants and white shirts. Plus, I hadn't seen her earlier. I remember recognizing a couple people just from being around town, you know, but nobody I actually know. Wait. I also remember there was a kind of commotion a few minutes before she clutched her throat and fell. Of course, I hadn't seen her at that point."

"What kind of commotion?" Lilly asked, suddenly on alert.

"I don't know for sure, but I think someone tripped someone else. I heard someone yelling at someone else to be careful because they had knocked some guy right to the ground."

"Who was it that fell?"

Ben shrugged. "I don't know who it was. He couldn't have been hurt that badly because everything quieted down a minute later."

"And you didn't see it happen? Do you know who tripped the man?"

Ben shook his head. "Sorry. I didn't see it."

"That's okay, Ben. You've been a big help. Did you tell the police about this?"

"No, because I just remembered it while I was speaking to you a minute ago. Should I let them know?"

"I'll tell them," Lilly said. "If they need more information, they'll follow up with you, I'm sure.

"One more question, if you don't mind," Lilly said. "Can you remind me where the salad table was in relation to all the other tables?"

"It was the first table in the tent, in the left-hand corner."

"So anyone could have entered the tent, put something in her food, and then left quickly. Is that right?"

"Yeah. That sounds right. I never thought of that. Do you think that's what happened?" His eyes were wide with shock.

"That's what I hope to find out."

Later that day Ben's table partner, Jim, came to be interviewed. He couldn't shed any more light on the goings-on than Ben had. Nor could the third student of the day.

There was just one more student to interview, and it had to be Stacy, thought Lilly as she drove to the college for the fourth time that day. And since talking to Noley, she had considered herself warned.

And indeed it was Stacy. A tall young woman with spiky green hair, Stacy sat with her arms folded, waiting for Lilly to speak.

"Stacy, I'm just here to ask a couple questions about Noley Appleton."

"So? What are the questions?" she asked in a surly voice.

Her attitude flustered Lilly. All she could think of for a moment was that she'd bean one of her own kids for talking to an adult that way.

"Um, I'm just wondering what you saw at the reenactment."

Stacy made a show of thinking, looking at the ceiling, sighing, squinting her eyes.

"Nothing," she finally said.

"You didn't see the woman who died?"

"Yeah, I saw her, but only after she was dead."

"Where were you before she died?"

"Behind the tent."

"And what were you doing back there?" Talking to this young woman was worse than trying to give Barney a bath.

"Talking to Ms. Deveau."

"Ms. Deveau was there?"

"Yes. She came by to see how things were going. She had her doubts about Noley's ability to carry out the whole thing. Frankly, I did, too. And obviously we were both right."

Lilly suppressed the urge to reach out and slap some manners into this young woman, but she intertwined her fingers and refrained.

"So Ms. Deveau discussed her concerns with you?"

"Obviously."

Lilly closed her eyes for a moment, counting to ten.

"What else did she say?"

"Just that Noley has always gotten jobs by doing 'favors' for people." She used her fingers to make quotation marks in the air as she spoke.

Lilly couldn't help the gasp that escaped from her mouth. Ms. Deveau was spreading filth like that to students? That must have been what she meant when she said Noley was arrogant and a cheat.

"I happen to know that Ms. Appleton has gotten her jobs based on nothing but superior ability," Lilly said.

Stacy shrugged. "That's not what I heard."

"Stacy, is there anything else you can tell me? Maybe where Ms. Deveau went after you talked to her?"

Stacy shrugged again. "I dunno. Noley asked me to do something and I had to do her bidding."

It was clear Lilly was not going to get any more information out of Stacy. She couldn't wait to get away from the college.

Before she left, though, she had to talk to Kathleen Deveau.

CHAPTER 32

Kathleen told Lilly she could afford five minutes of her time to talk. Lilly sat down across from Kathleen at her desk and took a moment to organize her thoughts before proceeding.

"I don't have all evening, Ms. Carlsen," Kathleen said in an acid tone.

"I know. Thank you for answering my questions," Lilly said.

"I haven't answered them yet," Kathleen pointed out.

Lilly swallowed and glanced at the notebook in her lap. "Kathleen, I didn't realize you were at the food tents the evening Ms. Deveau died."

"Is that a question?"

"What were you doing there?" Lilly asked.

"Checking up on the students, obviously. I was concerned that Noley wouldn't be able to handle the event and I was there to make sure the students didn't get a negative reputation because of Noley's shortcomings."

"Were you still there when Cerise died?" Lilly asked.

"Apparently I was," Kathleen said. "I didn't realize it at the time, of course."

"I'm just wondering because by that time Noley had gone back to the van," Lilly said.

"All the more reason to have someone responsible present," Kathleen said dryly.

"Did you happen to see someone being tripped a few minutes before Cerise fell to the ground?" Lilly asked.

"I really don't recall that. Ms. Carlsen, I think you'd better go." Kathleen gave Lilly a dark look and Lilly could feel the shivers starting at the nape of her neck.

She stood up and left the office after thanking Kathleen tersely for her time.

As she drove home, Lilly realized there was something bothering her. It was just out of reach in the back of her mind, and she couldn't quite figure out what was wrong.

But she couldn't dwell on it for long, because as soon as she got home the phone rang. It was Bill.

"I'm at Mom's house. One of the neighbors called the police because Mom was outside wandering and didn't seem to know where she was. I think you'd better get over here."

A feeling of doom dropped right into the pit of Lilly's stomach. "Is she okay?"

"She's okay. I found her a couple blocks away. The sergeant who responded to the call got in touch with me because he knows the situation."

"I'll be right over."

"Over where?"

Lilly spun around, not realizing Tighe had come into the kitchen and heard her speaking.

"Over to Gran's house. Uncle Bill found her wandering around her neighborhood. She didn't know where she was."

Tighe was silent for a moment. Then he looked at Lilly. "She's getting worse, isn't she?"

"I'm afraid so." A wave of nausea swept over Lilly.

"What's going to happen to her?"

"I don't know. It's something Uncle Bill and I need to

discuss with her at some point. I think it had better be soon, though. Do you want to go over there with me?"

"Do you think I should?"

"You and Laurel are her favorite people in the world. If anyone can talk to her, you can." She waited, holding her breath, wondering if he would decide to do the right thing.

"Okay. Let me grab my sneakers." Lilly smiled in spite of the seriousness of the situation. Was it possible she was getting her son back?

"Where's Laurel?" Lilly asked as she and Tighe climbed into her car.

"Out with Nick, I guess."

Lilly handed her phone to Tighe, since she had confiscated his. "Text her, will you, and tell her where we're going."

Tighe texted Laurel and sat back in the seat. "I don't want Gran to die."

Lilly almost hit the brakes at Tighe's words, but she stopped herself. Her heart constricted until Lilly felt like it might stop beating. She didn't want to even think about it. No one had mentioned Gran dying, but she supposed it was natural to wonder about it.

"Gran's not going to die anytime soon," she told Tighe. "She's strong and healthy, with the exception of her mind."

"That's the worst part, don't you think?" he asked. "Her body will keep living while her mind dies."

Lilly wanted to close her eyes to let the tears recede back into her tear ducts, but she couldn't because she was driving. Three tears slipped down her cheek. Tighe looked over at her when she didn't answer him.

"I'm sorry, Mom. I didn't mean to make you cry."

"It's okay," Lilly replied with a loud sniff, wiping her eyes with her sleeve. "It's something we have to deal with, right?" Tighe nodded, but didn't say any more.

When they arrived at Bev's house, Bill met them outside.

"Is she in there by herself?" Lilly asked anxiously.

"No. Mildred is in there with her."

"How is she doing? Any better?"

"She knows where she is, but she doesn't remember leaving the house."

Lilly closed her eyes and shook her head. "What do you think we should do?" Tighe had been listening and he spoke up.

"Why don't we take turns staying with her? That way she can't leave the house without someone knowing about it."

Lilly smiled at her son. "I think it's a wonderful suggestion, but I also think it's time to look at a more long-term solution. You're going to be leaving soon and Bill and I both work, and Laurel is in school. And then she's leaving in another year. I think it's time to think about hiring outside help." She looked at Bill and he nodded.

"We have to see how Mom feels about it before we do anything," he said.

"Today may not be the best time," Lilly said.

"But what if she just gets more and more confused?" Tighe asked. "Then what? Then it'll be too late to talk to her about it so she can understand what's going on."

"You know, Tighe, you might have a point there," Lilly said. "Maybe we should use this whole thing as a springboard to talk to her."

"But she doesn't remember leaving the house," Bill pointed out.

"Do you think she'd believe us if we told her that's what happened?" Lilly asked.

Bill nodded. "I think so."

"Then what do you think? Should we talk to her about it now?"

"Yeah, I guess we probably should," Bill said. He opened the door and held it for Lilly and Tighe, who preceded him into the living room. Bev and Mildred sat in chairs facing each other.

"Hello, Lilly," Mildred said, getting up and reaching for Lilly's hands. "It's nice to see you, dear."

Lilly kissed Mildred's soft cheek. "It's nice to see you, too, Mildred. Thanks for staying with Mom."

"It was no trouble. You know that," Mildred said. "You all probably have a lot to discuss, so I'll be going home. I'll come back later to check on her."

"You're a doll, Mildred. Thanks again." Lilly walked Bev's friend to the door and watched as she navigated the front steps, then she returned to the living room, where Tighe sat on the floor next to Bev's chair and Bill sat on the sofa.

"Well, this is a nice surprise," Bev said with a smile. "We're just missing Laurel. Where is she?"

"She's out with a friend," Lilly said. She took a deep breath. "Mom, do you remember what happened earlier today?"

"Why, of course," Bev replied. "I went to the grocery store to pick up a steak for your father's dinner."

Bill and Lilly exchanged glances. Tighe looked at his hands.

"I'm not talking about that, Mom. I mean that you left the house and when Bill found you, you didn't know where you were or why you had left the house. A neighbor had called the police because you were so confused."

Bev tilted her head and looked at Lilly from under a wrinkled brow. "I don't remember doing anything like that," she said.

"You did, Gran," Tighe put in.

Bev blinked several times, trying to understand what her daughter and grandson were saying. "I'm so embarrassed," she murmured.

"Don't be embarrassed, Mom," Lilly said, swallowing hard to keep from crying. She paused to compose herself. Why wasn't Bill saying anything? She looked over at him and saw that he was clenching and unclenching his jaw, swallowing repeatedly.

He was trying not to cry, too.

"These things happen sometimes," Lilly said after a moment. "What we need to figure out is how to keep you safe."

"I should think I'm safe in my own home," Bev said. A slight note of indignation had crept into her voice.

"You are, no doubt about that," Lilly agreed. "But it's when you leave your house that you may not be safe. I mean, when you leave the house and don't remember it."

Bill finally spoke. "Mom, we don't want you to get hit by a car or not remember your address or how to get home."

Bev looked from her daughter to her son. "What are you saying?"

"We're saying that maybe it's time to think about hiring someone to stay with you. You know, to run errands with you and go for walks and things like that. Just to make sure you're okay."

"You want to hire a babysitter for me." The pain in Bev's voice was obvious.

"Of course we don't want to hire a babysitter for you," Lilly said. "We were thinking more of a person who can help with household chores and can take you wherever you'd like to go."

"It sounds like a babysitter to me," Bev grumbled.

"Gran, it's just a person who's going to make sure you don't go off on your own," Tighe said. "Just so we don't worry about you all the time."

Bev smiled at her only grandson and rested her hand, criss-crossed with blue veins, on top of his head. He was still sitting next to her on the floor. "You don't have to worry about me," she said with a smile. "I'm just fine here. Your grandfather takes good care of me."

Tighe looked from Lilly back to his grandmother. "But

when he's not here, you need someone to make sure you're safe. Please, Gran?"

No one made a single sound then. Lilly and Bill and Tighe watched Bev, but she was looking down at her hands, which were now folded in her lap.

"If someone comes to help me, do they have to stay here?" Bev asked in a small voice.

"Do you want them to?" Lilly asked. She already knew the answer, just from the way her mother asked the question.

Bev shook her head.

"Okay, let's start with having someone here just in the daytime," Bill suggested. Lilly nodded.

"We'll find the perfect person, Mom. Don't worry about anything," Lilly said.

"I don't want someone in this house who's going to steal from me," Bev fretted.

"Mom, if someone comes in this house and steals from you, they're going to have to answer to me and the rest of the Juniper Junction police force. We're not going to let anyone steal anything," Bill promised.

"All right, I guess we can try it," Bev said. Her shoulders slumped and she looked to Lilly like she had aged ten years in the short time they had been talking.

"Gran, can I spend the night?" Tighe asked. Lilly looked at him in surprise.

"Of course you can, dear. But don't stay just because you're worried about me," Bev answered. "I'll be fine."

"It's not that," Tighe said. "It's just, that's what we used to do. It was fun. Maybe Laurel can come, too." Lilly looked at her son and for the umpteenth time that day, tears sprang to her eyes. The lump in her throat hurt.

"Mom, can I borrow your phone again?" he asked. She handed it to him.

He dashed off a text to Laurel, then held the phone until it buzzed with her reply. "Laurel's coming over too, Gran," he said with a smile, then handed Lilly the phone. "We should make popcorn." Gran couldn't say no to popcorn.

"That sounds delicious," Bev said.

"I think my work here is done," Lilly said, kissing her mother on the cheek. "I'll call later on to see how everything is going."

"All right, dear," Bev said.

Lilly needed to see Hassan, to talk to him, to vent to him, to soak in his level-headedness for a while. It didn't matter whether Amir was there--she just needed someone to talk to. She missed being able to pick up the phone and call Noley whenever she felt like it.

Noley. Just the thought of her best friend, stuck in that miserable jail, made Lilly's heart race with frustration. She had to find out who poisoned Cerise before Noley could be made to suffer any longer.

She drove over to Hassan's house and found father and son in the backyard, each nursing a gin and tonic. She plopped down into the empty seat across from them on the patio and Hassan immediately stood up and went to the outside bar and mixed her a drink, too.

"It looks like you could use this," he said as he handed her a tall glass with a lime garnish.

"I sure could," she said, closing her eyes and taking a sip. "Mmm. Hassan, you can make my gin and tonics anytime."

He smiled. "What's up? I missed talking to you today."

"I spent various parts of the entire day--and yesterday--talking to the students who helped Noley cater the reenactment," she answered. "I talked to each of them and I learned a few new things. I don't know how useful the information is, though."

"What did you learn?" Hassan asked.

Lilly began with Ben's information. "I learned that anyone could have entered the tent, poisoned Cerise, and gotten out fast without being seen. She was close to the corner of the tent, where there was an exit, when she fell. And the poison was on her salad." Lilly sighed.

"Then I learned that the assistant director of the culinary program was at the event when Cerise was murdered. She is open about her hostility toward Noley because Noley has gotten a couple jobs that they were both competing for.

"I don't know where we go from here. Something's not right, but I can't seem to put my finger on it," Lilly concluded.

"Maybe if we're both trying to figure it out, we'll get somewhere," Hassan said.

"What's worse, though, is that I got a call from Bill a while ago," Lilly continued. "Mom had wandered away from her house and didn't know where she was or what was going on."

Hassan and Amir wore matching frowns. "Is she okay? I assume you've found her?" Hassan asked.

Lilly nodded. "Bill found her. A neighbor had called the police and was trying to keep an eye on her as she walked around."

"Does she remember what happened?" Amir asked.

"No," Lilly said, shaking her head sadly. She took another sip of the gin and tonic. "She's just taking our word for it that she left the house by herself."

"Should you be over there with her?" Hassan asked. "I'm not trying to get rid of you, but I'm concerned about her."

"Tighe went with me over to her house and he asked Mom if he and Laurel could spend the night," Lilly said. And before she knew what was happening, she choked on a sob. Tears spilled from her eyes and she set the gin and tonic on the patio flagstone.

"I'm sorry," she mumbled. "I don't know what's wrong with me. Excuse me." She stood up and hurried into the house, where she locked herself in the bathroom just off the kitchen and sat down on the toilet seat. She started weeping and couldn't stop.

CHAPTER 33

After several minutes the tears began to slow. She took a deep breath and heard a faint knocking on the bathroom door.

"Lilly? Are you okay in there?" It was Hassan. Lilly had thought she heard him puttering around in the kitchen after she escaped to the bathroom, and she knew he had waited to hear the crying stop before coming to talk to her.

"I'm okay," she said, wiping her nose with a tissue. She ran the cold water and splashed her face with it before leaving the bathroom.

"I'm sorry," she said again. "I don't know what's gotten into me."

"I do," he said, gathering her to his chest and holding her while he spoke. "Your mother isn't well, your best friend is in jail, your town is on fire, and your son is leaving for college soon. And to top it all off, your normally-attentive boyfriend is spending all his time with his father."

He held Lilly away from him. "You have nothing to be sorry about. But I do. I've been neglecting you and I'm so sorry." He hugged her again. "I think I'll tell Dad it's time for him to head back to Minnesota."

"No," Lilly said, leaning back and gazing at Hassan. "If there's anything I've learned from my mother's troubles, it's that you should spend all the time you can with your dad before he doesn't know who you are or he's too frail to enjoy your company."

"You want him to stay here?"

"Yes," she said firmly. "I can't help you because I've got a lot on my plate right now, but if your father is here and wants your help with house-buying particulars, then that's what you need to do. Just try to squeeze in a little time for me once in a while." He leaned down and kissed her as Amir stepped into the kitchen.

"Ahem," he said with a cough. "Lilly, Hassan, I've been thinking. I am going to head back to Minnesota while we wait to close on the house."

"Amir, Hassan and I have just been talking about that," Lilly said. "I don't want you to leave now, and especially not because of me and my troubles. I would feel worse if I thought you were leaving because of anything I'm going through right now."

"Is this true?" Amir asked his son.

"Yes, Dad. I think you should stay until the inspections are over, then head back home and bring Mom to see it." Hassan smiled at his father.

"If you are sure you don't mind, then," Amir said reluctantly.

"I'm sure." Hassan put his arm around Lilly. "I think I can handle both of you," he said. Lilly and Amir laughed. Lilly didn't remember the last time she laughed, and it felt good.

Lilly drove home that night, exhausted and still worried. Though seeing and talking to Hassan and Amir had calmed her down a bit, she couldn't shake the feeling that her mother's situation was deteriorating and the good days would be fewer and farther apart. When she got home, she should have gone to bed.

Instead, she turned on the computer and spent a mind-boggling hour researching home health aides. There were so many options, so many aides out there looking for clients. *Wouldn't it be best to find someone who's already busy with clients? They must be the best ones.*

On the other hand, would someone like that have time to take care of Mom the way she deserves? Maybe it would be better to go with someone who's just starting out and looking for clients.

Or maybe it would be better to go with an older person. An older person might have more empathy for the things Mom is going through.

Lilly's mind reeled. She pushed herself back from the computer and closed her eyes, leaning her head back again the chair. What she needed was Bill's input. He was the only other person who knew exactly what she was going through right now.

She called him and he picked up on the first ring.

"I was going to call you," he said.

"Are you at work?" she asked.

"No, so I can talk. Listen, I learned a little more about this Kathleen Deveau, who seems to hate Noley so much. The detectives talked to her up at the college."

"And what did they find out?"

"She's Armand's cousin. You probably knew that already. She was the one who suggested they come to Juniper Junction to open a bistro. Her hope was that it would do really well and they would eventually need her to help run the place. She is desperate to leave her job at the college because apparently she hates it, but it pays well."

"So she would have no reason to kill Cerise," Lilly reasoned. "Without Cerise to create all those pastries, the bistro might not do as well and there wouldn't be a need for Kathleen's help running the place.

"Unless she wanted to be the pastry chef," Lilly said suddenly, sitting up straighter in her chair. "Do you think that's possible?"

"I don't know. I wasn't privy to the discussions with her. I suppose it's possible. It would be nice to see her behind bars, wouldn't it? She's a shrew."

"I would love to see her behind bars," Lilly agreed. "But in the meantime, we need to keep looking for information. Oh, before I forget, I talked to one of the students who helped at the serving tables," Lilly said. "He said there was some kind of commotion a few minutes before Cerise fell to the ground."

"Did he give you any details?"

"He said there was some grumbling because someone apparently tripped someone else, but that was it. But it's something that the police might like to follow up on," she said.

"All right. I'll let someone know and they can talk to the kid. What was his name?"

"Ben."

"Thanks." Bill hung up.

When the phone rang a few minutes later, Lilly sat up with a start, whacking her knee on the leg of her desk.

"Ouch!" she exclaimed as she hobbled to the phone. It was Beau.

"How is everything going with Tighe?" he asked.

"All right, I guess," Lilly answered. "He's spending the night at my mom's house."

"Why?"

"Because she had a bad spell today and he's worried about her."

"What kind of a bad spell?"

Nosy. "She forgot where she was when she left her house. But she's okay now," Lilly hastened to add. Why did she mind so much telling Beau about her mother's problems?

"That is bad," he said.

"I know," Lilly replied with a hint of testiness in her voice. "Do you want me to tell Tighe you called?"

"Sure. I was just checking in with him. I do that sometimes." *Always the compassionate father,* Lilly thought with a little sneer. Then she checked herself. At least Beau was making an effort, however small it might seem to her. Should she really be dumping on him?

"Say, as long as I've got you on the line, I was thinking you and me and the kids could get together for coffee in the next couple days. I'd like you to meet my girlfriend," Beau said. *So that's why he called. I was wondering why he didn't just call Tighe's cell.*

"The kids don't drink coffee."

"That's not the point," Beau answered.

"Um, do I really need to meet your girlfriend?" Lilly asked. "You're a grown-up. You can date whomever you please."

"I'm not asking for your permission, Lilly," Beau replied with a hint of frustration. "I just thought, you know, since I'm seeing this woman, that the kids should get to know her. And as long as they're going to be spending time with her, I figured you'd like to meet her, too."

Lilly sighed. "I've got a lot going on right now, Beau. Can it wait a bit?"

"It's only coffee. I'm not asking you to spend the week with us."

Lilly often found herself biting the inside of her cheek to keep from saying something snarky to Beau, and this was one of those times.

She paused as she tasted blood, then said calmly, "Well, I'm sorry, but it's going to have to wait. You can get together with the kids, but I cannot meet your friend right now."

"Fine. I'll call them," Beau said, and he hung up.

"Honestly, that man," Lilly said to Barney, who had wandered into the room. "Want to go outside, Barn?"

The dog jumped and danced around, then ran to the door and thumped his tail repeatedly against the wall while he waited for Lilly to turn off the computer and join him. While she sat on the patio in the waning light of the evening, Barney went rummaging through the flowerbeds to see what he might find.

Lilly yawned and closed her eyes again. They were burning from exhaustion. With her eyes closed, she could focus on her thoughts about Cerise's murder and who might be responsible for it. If only she could figure it out…

She must have dozed, for Barney's barking jerked her fully awake a few minutes later. He had cornered a rabbit behind one of the shrubs and was having a thrilling time playing with it. Lilly stood up and hurried over to where the poor little rabbit was being tormented and spoke sharply to Barney.

"Come, boy," she said. "You leave that rabbit alone." Barney turned to her, giving the rabbit a chance to scamper off to safety through a hole under the corner of the fence.

Perhaps her mind had crystallized an idea while she rested, or perhaps it was seeing the rabbit run away and duck under the fence into the neighbor's yard, but Lilly was suddenly reminded of the scene of Cerise's murder. There had been an opening in the corner of the tent, giving the murderer a chance to get away quickly after poisoning Cerise's food.

But that wasn't all Lilly had been thinking about.

She had figured out what had been bothering her.

CHAPTER 34

Orson Weaver had said that Noley hadn't been present at the time of the murder.

But Orson had said also said he had been in the diner during the entire reenactment.

So how could he have known Noley wasn't there?

Because he must have been there.

As Lilly stood in the corner of her backyard with Barney whining at her feet in the hope that the bunny would come back, everything started to become clear to Lilly.

Why would Orson have lied about being at the diner at the time of Cerise's death? It wasn't as if he was going to be fired if someone found out he wasn't at work--he owned the diner. And the bistro owned by Cerise and Armand had taken away so much of his business…

Lilly's breath came faster and faster as her heart beat increasingly harder. She needed to talk to Bill.

She called Barney, who had wandered off in search of another playmate in the shrubs, and they went inside. She sat down hard in one of the kitchen chairs and dialed Bill's number.

"Hi, Lil," he answered.

"I know who did it," she said.

"Did what?"

"Killed Cerise!" She spoke as if he were hard of hearing.

"Oh. Okay, who do you think did it?" he asked in his best I'm-humoring-you voice.

"Don't talk to me like that, Bill, or I won't tell you."

"Okay, okay. I'm sorry. Who did it?"

"Orson Weaver. You know, the owner of the diner."

Bill was silent for a moment.

"But I thought he was in the diner at the time of Cerise's death," he finally said. "I would have to check the notes in the file."

"I thought he was, too, but he knew somehow that Noley wasn't at the tent when Cerise died. It would have been easy for him to get out quickly through the corner of the tent after poisoning Cerise's food. No one would have known he was there."

She had Bill's full attention now.

"I'll call you right back." He hung up without saying another word.

She didn't have to wait long before hearing from him. "The notes say that all the business owners on your block of Main Street state that they were in their stores, but their statements haven't been verified yet. So it's possible that Orson Weaver is our guy."

"So what happens next?" Lilly asked. Her heart had finally stopped beating so fast, but it was starting up again.

"We go talk to him. Nothing is certain, Lil," Bill cautioned. "Don't go celebrating yet. There's a lot of investigating to be done before we can arrest him."

"Believe me, I'm not celebrating. I don't want it to be Orson," Lilly said. "I like him. He has a crush on Noley, you know."

"I didn't know that," Bill said.

"Yeah." Lilly paused. "And you know what? This didn't

occur to me when he told me, but he mistakenly thought Cerise and Armand had swooped in and taken over part of the catering job for Noley."

"So you're saying that he has a thing for Noley and he might have killed Cerise out of anger that she was taking away Noley's job."

"Yes," Lilly said excitedly. "So not only was he mad that the bistro was taking so much of his business, but he was upset because he thought they were taking work from Noley, too."

"I've gotta run. I'll call you later when we know more." He hung up abruptly.

Lilly paced the house with Barney at her heels for several long minutes. She thought about trying to go to bed, but she knew she would be too keyed up. She thought about going to the shop to do some lingering paperwork, but she knew she wouldn't be able to focus, especially with the diner right across the street.

She checked her phone several times to make sure the ringer was on and to make sure she hadn't missed a call from Bill, even though the phone had been in her pocket since she hung up.

"Barney, let's go for a walk," Lilly finally said. The dog's tail started its typical furious wagging and Lilly laughed. "You knew all along we would end up going for a walk, didn't you?"

She clipped on his leash and they headed outside. She turned in the general direction of her mother's house, with her face lifted to the evening breeze. It felt good to get outside and walk off some of her nervous energy.

They walked several blocks until they came to Bev's house. Lilly knocked on the door and Tighe opened it.

"Mom! What are you doing here?" he asked.

"Barney and I were just taking a walk and this is where we ended up," she answered with a smile. She and Barney went into the house, where Fred launched himself into a frenzy of excitement over the appearance of his friend. The two dogs danced in circles around the living room until they were able to calm down and lie down together next to Laurel, who sat on the floor in front of the sofa.

Bev sat in an armchair, laughing at the dogs. Lilly smiled broadly watching her mother. It had done Bev good to have her grandchildren over to spend the night.

"We made popcorn," Bev said. "Care to join us?"

Lilly couldn't bear the thought of sitting down. She was too agitated--what she needed was to get back outdoors. She looked at Barney, who was happily ensconced against Fred's furry body.

"No, thanks. I'd like to keep walking for a little while. Can I leave Barney here?"

"Of course," Bev replied.

"Do you want me or Tighe to go with you?" Laurel asked.

"No, you stay here with Gran," Lilly said.

Barney didn't even try to follow her. He was too tired from his walk and he loved being curled up next to Fred.

Lilly struck off from Bev's house in no particular direction, but before long she realized that her footsteps were leading her in the direction of the house Amir was planning to buy. She followed the darkened sidewalks until she came to the block where the house was located. The houses on the block, much like the ones in Hassan's neighborhood, were spread out. They were all built in a similar style, and there were even a couple picket fences like one might see in a painting.

She looked around. There were only a few lights on in the homes on the street. She looked behind her. It was suddenly a little spooky out here by herself. She wished she had brought Barney. He wasn't much of a guard dog, but he would at least let her know if there were other people around.

She walked to the end of the block, her shoes making shushing noises on the sidewalk. When she came to the house Amir wanted to buy, she paused out front, looking at the Craftsman-style home and imagining Amir and Basra living in it. She and Hassan would hopefully visit often whenever his parents were in town.

Using the flashlight on her phone, she shone a beam of light ahead of her as she walked into the backyard. The scent of summer flowers wafted around and she took a deep breath, knowing there was a profusion of roses somewhere nearby. There was a fence along the back of the property, but both sides were open to the neighbors' properties.

She turned off her flashlight and stood in the backyard looking up at the sky. It looked like navy blue velvet sprinkled with tiny fairy lights. She sighed contentedly. This was part of the reason she loved living in a small town in the mountains--she found beauty there that she wouldn't find anywhere else.

She turned on her flashlight again and began moving very slowly and almost noiselessly through the grass, which was probably how she was able to hear a faint hissing sound coming from behind her. She spun around and flashed the light all around, but nothing--or no one--was there. *Probably just an animal rustling in the grass,* she thought. She shuddered, hoping it wasn't a snake.

She took a deep breath and continued forward, scolding herself for being such a sissy. But then she heard the noise a second time. She whirled around again, and this time she thought she saw a faint light coming from inside the empty house.

Uh-oh, Lilly thought. *Someone's inside. I'd better get out of here before they see me out here and call the police. I didn't think there was anyone living here.*

Still using the flashlight, she began making her way around the side of the house. The house was still almost completely dark, so Lilly wondered who had turned a light on.

Then she saw it, and it wasn't a light at all. It was a flame, licking its way into one of the rooms on the side of the house.

The house was on fire.

Lilly broke into a run, still using her flashlight to guide her steps. She stumbled a few times, but kept running. When she reached the sidewalk in front of the house she turned off the light and dialed nine-one-one.

She breathlessly told the dispatcher where she was and what was happening. The dispatcher warned her away from the house and Lilly was only too happy to follow the dispatcher's orders. The flames were growing brighter now and Lilly could hear one of the windows on the side of the house shattering. The fire was visible throughout the downstairs of the home now. Lilly was amazed at how quickly it was spreading.

She was running toward the small grove of trees on the far side of the house, between it and the home next to it, when she heard a different noise and looked over her shoulder.

Someone was clattering down the front steps of the house and, as she watched, the person ran toward her. She could tell it was a man, and apparently he hadn't seen her yet. She ducked into the trees, worrying that the flames from the house would eventually fly over to where she stood and set the trees on fire, but she didn't want the man to see her, to know *she* had seen *him*.

She hid behind a particularly large oak tree and peered around the trunk of it as the man ran past. Though it was dark outside, there was a street lamp shining on the sidewalk and street at this end of the block.

Lilly squinted to get a better view of the man so she could describe him to police.

But she wouldn't need a description--she could give them his name. It was Orson Weaver.

CHAPTER 35

Lilly stifled the urge to call out to him, to stop him from running away. Her mind reeled in confusion--was Orson the arsonist who had been terrorizing Juniper Junction since the beginning of the summer? Why else would he be here, in this neighborhood, running from the scene of a fire in a house in which no one lived?

Lilly remained hidden behind the tree until Orson was out of sight, but she came out when she saw the police and fire trucks scream down the block, their lights flashing and sirens blaring to wake everyone in town.

Before a full minute had passed, the firefighters had jumped from the trucks and were pulling large hoses from hooks. They trained the hoses toward the house and thick streams of rushing water began to soak the home and the ground around it, fighting the flames as hard as it could.

Neighbors had by now gathered outside to watch the horrifying spectacle. Police were keeping everyone back, ordering everyone to stay as far away from the fire as possible. Lilly searched frantically for Bill, but he wasn't there. She ran up to the closest officer and tapped him on the arm. He whipped around, ready for whatever action was necessary.

"Please, officer, my name is Lilly Carlsen and I called in the alarm. I--" she began.

"You have to get out of this area. Now," he barked.

"I know. I am, but--"

"Did you not understand me?" he asked. "I said right now."

"But I know who did it!" Lilly cried. "I'll go stand over there, but I have to talk to someone so they can catch the man who did this!"

The officer beckoned another officer over and asked him to accompany Lilly and take a statement from her.

When Lilly and her escort were safely away from the fire, he took a notebook from his pocket and began questioning her.

"What were you doing here tonight?" he asked, a stern look on his face.

"My, um, boyfriend's father is trying to buy this house and I was just walking around, looking at it," she answered.

"Did it ever occur to you that this is trespassing?"

"No."

The officer grimaced. "Did you go in the house?"

"No." *I'm not a burglar,* Lilly thought.

"How did you see the fire?"

"I saw it through one of the downstairs windows. At first I thought someone was inside and had turned on a light."

"And you were the one who called nine-one-one?"

"Yes. I--"

"And then you stayed?"

"Yes. I'm--"

"Why did you stay?"

"I ran away from the house, but while I was running I saw someone else leave the property."

"Why didn't you say something about this right away?"

"I've been trying to! You won't let me get a word in edgewise." She knew it was disrespectful, but this man was starting to annoy her.

"All right. Tell me about the person you saw."

"It was Orson Weaver, the owner of the Main Street Diner."

"You know this person?"

"Yes. I own the shop right across the street from him."

"Just a minute." He stepped away from Lilly and spoke into the radio which was clipped to his shoulder. Lilly heard the words "Orson Weaver" and a lot of static.

The officer turned his radio down and spoke to Lilly again.

"Did you see Mister Weaver set the fire?"

"No, but he ran down the front steps of the house just after the fire was set."

"You also ran away just after the fire was set," the officer pointed out.

"Yes, but I was there for a different reason. I don't set fires."

The officer shook his head, and not in an endearing way.

"Where do you live?"

Lilly gave him her address, but explained that her mother lived just a couple blocks away and that she had been to see her mother before coming over to the new house.

"I'll give you a ride to your mother's house to get your dog," the officer said. "I'm sure someone will contact you again tomorrow to have you give an official statement."

He led Lilly to his cruiser and drove her to Bev's house. When they arrived there was another police car parked out front.

The officer with Lilly spoke into his radio again, then listened to the response.

"That's Officer Carlsen's car. Any relation?"

"He's my brother."

"Why didn't you say so?"

Lilly rolled her eyes and didn't bother answering.

The officer reminded her that she would have to go to the police station to give an official statement, then drove off. Lilly trudged up the walk and Bill opened the door before she even reached the top of the front steps.

"Where have you been?"

"Don't ask."

"Why did you go over there? That was stupid!"

"If you knew where I went, then why did you ask me?"

Bill ignored that. "I hear Orson Weaver was over there," he said.

Lilly nodded, suddenly too tired to talk. She sat down in a chair opposite her mother, who had remained uncharacteristically quiet while her children argued.

"A couple officers are headed to his house right now to talk to him," Bill said.

Lilly just looked at him. "Orson started that fire, Bill."

Bill nodded. "You're probably right. But they'll see what he has to say about it."

"And what about Cerise's murder? Have you found out any more about where Orson was at the time of the murder?"

"I checked the files and no one had followed up yet with the employees of the diner. Someone was headed over to do that about an hour ago. I asked them to put a hustle on it because we had information which indicated Weaver might not have been in the diner when he claimed to be."

Lilly jumped up. "I can't believe I didn't even think to call Hassan yet and tell him about the house!"

She dialed Hassan's number and broke the news to him as soon as he answered, figuring it was better to get it over with as quickly as possible, like pulling off a bandage.

"I can't believe this," Hassan said. "Are you all right? What on earth were you doing over there at night and by yourself?"

"I was just out for a walk and Barney didn't want to come. I was perfectly safe," Lilly explained.

"I disagree. Why didn't you take someone with you?"

The truth was that Lilly wanted the kids to stay with Bev to keep an eye on her, but she couldn't say that out loud--not with Bev listening.

"I just didn't think to. It won't happen again, I can promise you that."

"Good. Now, I have to tell my father the bad news. He'll be very disappointed because he loved that house. He even had my mother all excited to see it."

"I'm so sorry, Hassan."

"I know you are. But thanks to you being there, maybe the firefighters could save part of the house. We'll find out. I'm going to make some calls as soon as I tell Dad. I'll call you tomorrow. I love you, Lilly."

"I love you, too."

"I'm glad you're okay." His voice was soft.

"Me, too."

When Lilly hung up she turned to her mother. "Mom, I'm going to take Barney and go home. It's been a very long day."

"I'll drive you," Bill offered.

Bev rose and kissed Lilly on the cheek. "I worry about you, Lilly," she said. Lilly hugged her mom. It wasn't often her mother spoke words like that to her, though she often spoke that way to and about Bill. Deep down, Lilly knew her mother loved her as much as she loved Bill, but it was nice to hear it once in a while, too.

CHAPTER 36

Lilly had a hard time falling asleep that night. She knew her kids were safe at her mother's house, and her mother was safe with the kids there, but she couldn't help worrying about all of them. It wasn't concern for their safety, really. Just concern for the future. Lilly didn't like to admit how much she relied on Tighe and Laurel to help with her mother, but she knew she'd feel a greater weight of responsibility when Tighe left for school.

She could also feel the moment approaching when Noley would be released from jail and her charges dropped. That filled her with a happiness and excitement which kept her awake, too.

And then there was the fire. This one had hit close to home--the house Amir planned to buy. How would the blaze affect his plans? He and Basra were lucky to have Hassan to help them through the looking and buying process.

And finally, Orson Weaver. If he was the arsonist *and* Cerise's murderer, what did the future look like for him? Pretty grim, Lilly thought. What would possess him to commit such heinous acts?

There was one more thought that Lilly tried to keep in the

back of her mind, just because if filled her with shame. There had been times she wondered if it were really possible that her son had been the one setting fires, and if Orson were really the arsonist, Tighe was in the clear. She chided herself for even entertaining the thought that he was capable of something so awful.

Some of Lilly's questions about Orson were answered the next day.

Lilly drove to work through streets that were typically quiet for such an early hour. She parked in the alley and entered the office in the back of her jewelry shop. When she opened her office door onto the rest of the shop, she saw through her huge display windows four police cars slide into position across the street in front of the diner.

She wanted to turn away, to go back into the office and pretend that none of this was really happening. But she stood rooted to the spot, mesmerized by the goings-on across the street.

As Lilly stared, two police officers exited their car and approached the front of the diner slowly. One used the radio on his shoulder to say something. Lilly could practically hear the squawking machine talking back. She scanned the cars to see if Bill might be among the officers at the scene, but she didn't see him.

The officers disappeared into the diner and Lilly realized she had been holding her breath. She exhaled loudly and continued staring out the window.

Several minutes went by before the officers came out of the diner. They weren't alone--Orson Weaver walked between them and they each held one of his elbows. He looked straight ahead and Lilly gasped. She had thought, until that moment, that Orson might not be the person the police were looking for.

But when he locked eyes with her, she knew her suspicions had been right. He was the one.

And Lilly knew for sure that Tighe had nothing to do with those fires. Lilly smiled to herself. *I raised a good kid*, she thought. Another worry in the back of her mind was gone.

She turned away from the window before Orson looked away and reached for her cell phone, which she had left on a display case. She dialed Bill, her fingers trembling. It took three tries to get his number right.

"Are you watching the show across the street?" Bill asked when he picked up the phone.

"Yes. Does this mean Noley can go home?"

"It sure does. It may take a day or two to get everyone on the same page between the police and the DA's office and the jail, but she should be going home very soon." Lilly could hear the smile in his voice, and it matched hers.

"I feel terrible about Orson, though," she said. "He's always seemed like such a nice person."

"I think he is a nice person--but one who made some mistakes and got desperate."

"Do you know why he burned down those houses?"

"Yes, but I can't tell you until I've been cleared to say something about it. Suffice it to say that you were instrumental in catching an arsonist."

"I wish I could say I'm happy about it, but I'm really not," Lilly said.

"I know. But you did the right thing in reporting him."

"As soon as Harry comes in I'm going to head over to see Noley and tell her the good news."

"Normally I'd tell you to wait, but I think that's a good idea. Tell her I'll see her soon."

Lilly hung up and continued watching the police until the car with Orson in the backseat drove away. She heard a noise and saw Harry standing in the doorway to the office at the back of the shop.

"Did you see what's going on over there?" he asked breathlessly. "What's happening?"

"Orson is being arrested," Lilly answered.

"Why?"

"I don't know what they're charging him with," Lilly said. It was cryptic, she knew, but she didn't want to betray any confidence of Bill's.

Harry looked at her shrewdly. "Are you sure? You know everything that goes on around here."

"Okay, I'll tell you what I know for sure. I saw him running away from the scene of a house fire last night."

"You're kidding. I heard about that fire this morning on the radio. What was he doing there?"

"He--"

"Wait! What were *you* doing there?"

"I was there because Hassan's father is trying to buy that particular house and I just wanted to look at it again. It was stupid, I know. And while I was there the house caught on fire and I saw Orson running from the property."

"You're kidding," Harry repeated.

"I wish I were," Lilly said. "Listen, I've got to run over to the jail to see Noley. Can you take care of things here for a little while?"

"You got it, boss."

When Lilly arrived at the jail she could hardly sit still waiting for Noley. And when she finally was admitted to the room where Noley sat, in her jail togs and her limp hair and her dejected face, Lilly started to cry.

"Lil! What's wrong?" Noley shot up and advanced toward Lilly, but the officer standing by the door made a move to get between the women.

Noley sat down immediately and gestured for Lilly to sit across from her.

"What's wrong?" she asked again.

"Nothing," Lilly said, laughing and crying at the same time. "You're getting out of here!"

"What?!" Noley cried. "You're kidding!"

"Why does everyone think I'm kidding? And no, I'm not," Lilly said, rolling her eyes as she continued to both laugh and cry.

But Noley didn't cry. She just squealed.

"Hey! Pipe down!" the officer barked.

"I'm sorry," Noley whispered toward him. She stared at Lilly. "What happened? Do they know who killed Cerise? Who did it?"

"As much as I wish it had been Kathleen Deveau or even Armand, they think it was Orson Weaver. But you didn't hear it from me," Lilly said, wiping her eyes.

"No way. Orson? I can't believe it."

Lilly nodded. "Remember I told you he has a crush on you? Well, it's more serious than we thought. He thought you were being upstaged by Cerise and Armand for the catering event, so he decided to take matters into his own hands. Cerise can't upstage your cooking if she's dead, right? Plus, the bistro had taken away a lot of Orson's business after that bad review."

Noley could only shake her head, her mouth agape and her eyes wide open.

"And I think he's being arrested for starting the fires in Juniper Junction, too."

"You're kidd--" Noley began. "I mean, why do they think he did it?"

"Because I saw him running away from a house fire last night."

"*You* saw him? How? What were you doing at a house fire?"

"I wasn't at the fire. I went to the house because it's one that Amir is trying to buy." Lilly explained her presence at the empty house for the fourth time in twelve hours while Noley listened, speechless.

"Long story short, you're getting out of here," Lilly said with a wide grin.

"And it sounds like I have you to thank," Noley said.

"Bill was a big help," Lilly said. "He made sure things moved quickly on the police side while I fed him information that the police didn't have."

"I can't thank you enough. When do I get out of here, then?"

"Bill said it might take a day or two to get everything coordinated, but it'll be soon. And he says he can't wait to see you, by the way." Lilly winked and Noley blushed.

"Remember, I get all the credit at the wedding."

Noley grinned.

"I have to get back to work, but I had to come tell you the news. I'm so happy for you!" Lilly said in a quiet squeal. The officer at the door shot the women a dark glance.

"Thank you!" Noley called as Lilly left.

CHAPTER 37

It was all over Juniper Junction the next day. Orson Weaver had been charged with four counts of arson and the murder of Cerise. His diner, finally, was buzzing with activity.

Lilly went into work early that morning. She was standing at her large front display windows, watching the crowds assemble in front of the restaurant. She shook her head in dismay. Where were all those people when Orson needed them?

The phone rang and she was glad for an excuse to turn away from the pathetic sight. It was Bill.

"Noley's being released later today. I'm going to pick her up and take her home," Bill said. The joy in his voice was unmistakable.

"I'm so happy for her," Lilly said. "I hope you can convince her to keep cooking, too. I'm starting to have withdrawal cravings for her blueberry muffins."

Bill laughed. "I think once she gets settled at home and really gives it a good think, she'll realize she was meant to be a chef. She'll start cooking again, I have no doubt."

Lilly turned around and glanced again at the people in front of Orson's diner.

"Bill, why did Orson burn the houses down? Can you tell me that yet? Orson just doesn't seem the type. *Is* there a type of person who commits arson?"

Bill was silent for a moment. "The one thing all the houses had in common were their age. They were all older homes with lots of architectural detail. Lots of woodwork, if you get my meaning."

"I don't."

"Well, remember a while back when the diner got a bad review in the newspaper?"

"Yes."

"It seems that Orson started to formulate a plan at that time. He knows what can happen in a small town when an influential reviewer pans a restaurant. It dies, or at least that's what happens in a lot of cases. So he was worried about the future of his diner, and then Armand and Cerise come into town and start taking away--"stealing" is the word he uses--what little business remained, and he started to panic. He made a plan to kill Cerise, not suspecting that Noley might be the one to serve the salad to Cerise and then end up taking the blame for her murder. He was so angry he just wasn't thinking things through, obviously."

"But there was one house that wasn't for sale. People were living there. Did he set that fire?"

"He did," Bill said in a grim voice. "He just got the address wrong."

"So how did he happen to be in the food service tents when Cerise was there?"

"He obtained the cyanide online from the dark web--apparently you can download the dark web software for free--and he went over to the town square knowing Armand and Cerise had an ice cream table. His plan had been to wait for Cerise to eat something, then sprinkle it in her food when she wasn't looking. He saw her in the line for salad dressing and did it then. He didn't realize Noley had served her the salad.

He created a diversion and did it while she was distracted. He was the one who tripped that man in line, and while people were up in arms over that, he sprinkled the cyanide on her food. He had a hat pulled low over his face, so no one recognized him. Then he was able to get out quickly through the corner of the tent and get back to the diner."

"Okay, that all is plausible. But why burn down houses?"

"Because he's a woodworker. I know he's used his woodworking skills at the diner. You've probably seen it. And he knew which houses were for sale and unoccupied because he would listen to the real estate agents who came into the diner."

Things were starting to fall into place. She *had* seen his work, and it was beautiful. And she had heard him talk about overhearing conversations among real estate agents.

Lilly continued the story. "So Orson thought he could get work as a carpenter in rebuilding the houses if things in the diner business didn't work out."

"Exactly. He was trying to plan for his future," Bill said.

"Part of me feels just terrible for him."

"I know what you mean. He just got handed a set of circumstances that he couldn't deal with, and he was just trying to find a way to earn a paycheck."

Lilly didn't know what to say.

"I'll have Noley call you when she gets home," Bill said.

"Thanks. And thanks for keeping me in the loop. Bye."

Lilly's feelings were at war with themselves. She wanted to feel utter happiness for Noley's good news, but she was devastated at the thought that Orson, her friend, had been so horrified and depressed at the thought of losing his livelihood that he turned to violent crime.

When the phone rang after five, Lilly knew it had to be Noley.

"Hello?"

"I'm home!" Noley exclaimed.

Lilly's face broke into a wide grin. "You must be so happy! Can I stop over after work?"

"How about I come over to your house? Bill's taking me out to dinner and we can stop and see you on the way."

"I'll be there."

They hung up and Lilly looked at her watch. The forty-five minutes until closing would drag.

But when she and Harry finally locked the vault and triple-checked it before leaving after closing up the shop, Lilly could only feel joy at the prospect of seeing her best friend free again.

And she was shocked when she saw Bill park in front of her house. Noley slid out of the passenger door wearing the gorgeous dress she had bought to wear to a special dinner those weeks ago. She wore her high-heeled sparkly sandals; her hair, which looked like it might still be wet from the shower, was piled in a chignon that looked beautiful.

So Bill had finally made those reservations. Too bad it only took his girlfriend's stint in jail to get him to do it!

Lilly ran outside and hugged Noley, tears coursing down their cheeks. Bill looked on with a smile. Lilly could have sworn she saw him wipe his eyes once or twice, too.

Allergies, he said.

"What about the necklace I was going to lend you?" Lilly asked.

"I'll wear it someday--don't worry," Noley assured her.

"She looks perfect without it," Bill said, smiling. He hadn't taken his eyes off Noley.

They couldn't stay long--just long enough to say hello and for the kids to come running outside and hug Noley. Then they were off to the fancy-schmancy restaurant in Lupine.

"I've already made blueberry muffins--I'll bring some over for you in the morning!" Noley called as she and Bill drove off.

So Bill had convinced her to start cooking again.

Hassan came over for dinner and brought Amir with him.

Lilly served good old American hotdogs and corn on the cob. They sat on the patio and Amir shared his good news.

"The house is not a total loss," he said. "I've spoken to the fire officials, an architect, the realtor, and a builder. I think we're going to go ahead and buy it and fix it up. I want it exactly the way it was. Basra agrees."

Lilly was surprised. She didn't think Amir and Basra would go through with the sale of a house that had been involved in arson.

"And we're getting a very good deal on it because of the fire and water damage. It's worth far less than it used to be. But the insurance company will make sure the current owners get what they deserve for the house. Everybody wins." He smiled broadly.

Hassan patted Lilly's hand. "And the culprit is behind bars because of you. Thank God you weren't hurt."

Amir stood up. "I will go for a short walk while you two get some time to yourselves. I'll be back soon."

Hassan smiled at his father--apparently this had been prearranged.

"I feel like I haven't seen you in ages," he said, turning to Lilly.

"I feel the same way."

"What do you say to taking a vacation with me?"

"You're taking a vacation?" That surprised Lilly more than the fact that he was asking her to go with him.

He tilted his head back and let out a hearty laugh. "Yes! Does that surprise you?"

"Definitely. Where are you going?"

"Wherever you want to go," he said, his eyes twinkling.

"Ooh. I would need to give that some thought."

"Take all the time you need to think and let me know. I'll make all the arrangements."

"You're wonderful, Hassan."

"So are you, Lil."

They were leaning into each other and were about to kiss when Hassan's phone rang.

He sighed and looked at it.

"It's Dad," he said. "Hello?"

He listened for a moment, his face becoming grave. He stood up and pushed back his chair, motioning for Lilly to do the same.

"What's going on?" she asked, keeping her voice low so she wouldn't disturb the call.

Hassan hung up. "It's your mother. Dad found her wandering around again. He's just walking with her right now."

"Oh, no."

Was this the way life was going to be? Frantic phone calls and mad dashes to her mother's house? Lilly had a feeling it was only going to get worse. She tried calling Bill, but his phone went to voicemail; not surprising. He had probably promised Noley that she would have his undivided attention all evening.

She and Hassan hopped into her car and drove quickly to her mother's neighborhood, where they spotted Amir and Bev about three blocks from Bev's house. Amir was holding Bev's elbow to make sure she didn't trip on the sidewalk.

Lilly pulled to a stop next to them.

"Thanks, Amir. Mom, what are you doing?"

Bev turned to her and smiled. "Your father and I are just out for a walk before dinner."

Lilly pursed her lips. "Mom, why don't I drive you and Dad home?"

"Nonsense. Walking is good for us." Amir nodded at Lilly over Bev's head. He would walk her home.

Lilly and Hassan waited at Bev's house for the couple to return. When they arrived home, Bev went indoors to start dinner. Amir turned to Lilly.

"She's really a lovely lady, though very confused. I am

afraid I didn't know how to answer when she asked questions that your father would have known the answers to. She seemed to be getting quite agitated."

"That's okay, Amir. Thank you for bringing her home. I think Bill and I need to decide sooner, rather than later, what we're going to do."

"Do you want us to stay?" Hassan asked.

"No, I think you'd better head back to my house. Take my car. I'll walk home later or one of the kids can pick me up."

"We'll walk. I'll call you tomorrow." Hassan kissed Lilly and he and his father set off toward Lilly's house.

She went inside and sat with Bev while Bev ate a dinner of a cheese sandwich and applesauce. Then they watched a game show and Bev fell asleep in her favorite armchair before it was even fully dark outside.

Lilly stood next to her mother, watching her sleep. The lines in Bev's face softened in slumber and her mouth was parted just a little bit. She looked the way Lilly remembered from years ago, when Lilly was little. She wanted to wrap her mother in her arms and keep her safe from everything that was coming as her mental health declined, but she didn't want to wake her mom from what might be a lovely dream.

Tighe came over when he got out of work and he offered to spend the night with his Gran. Lilly went home, dejected.

CHAPTER 38

A week later there were two big events, and Lilly wasn't sure how she felt about either one.

First, Tighe left for school. He had spent more and more time with his grandmother before he left for school and nothing indicated that he had had any alcohol. He got his phone back the day before he left. Lilly was so proud of him. She promised herself she wouldn't cry on the way there, but all bets were off on the way home.

She sobbed from the moment she waved goodbye to her son until Laurel, exhausted, pulled into their driveway.

"Mom, when are you going to stop crying?" she asked, exasperated.

"Probably never," Lilly said through her tears.

"Are you going to be this upset when I leave in a year?"

Lilly started wailing. "Don't even talk about that, please!"

Second, a nurse started spending her days with Bev. Lilly and Bill interviewed Nicole, of course, and found her to be sweet, caring, competent, and professional. She came with good references and seemed eager to work with Bev.

At the end of Nicole's first day, Lilly and Bill thought it

would be nice to take dinner over to Bev's house so the four of them could eat together and get better acquainted.

They picked up a stack of burgers and a whole bag of French fries, and Lilly brought a pitcher of unsweetened iced tea.

"Oh!" Nicole said when she opened the door.

"Surprise!" Lilly exclaimed. "We brought dinner. We thought it would be nice to get to know you and you can get to know us."

"That's so sweet of you," Nicole said. "The thing is, Bev said my boyfriend could come over for dinner." She looked at Bev.

"Of course he can," Bev said, waving Lilly and Bill into the room.

Lilly and Bill exchanged glances. Was this kind of thing appropriate? Should Nicole be inviting her boyfriend to dinner at a patient's house?

"Um, I suppose that's all right, as long as Mom agrees," Lilly said pointedly.

Bill frowned. "Mom, I'm not sure this is the best idea," he said.

"Oh, poo," Bev said.

The doorbell rang. Nicole excused herself and went to answer it. She came back into the room a moment later with a man's arm draped over her shoulders.

Beau.

"Hi, guys! Small world, isn't it? I see you've met Nikki," he said.

"You're Nikki?" Lilly stared at Nicole.

Nicole nodded. "I didn't realize when I took the job that Beau knows your mother," she explained. "I hope that's not going to be a problem."

"I like Nicole," Bev piped up.

That was all Lilly and Bill needed to hear.

"Okay, Mom. Nicole stays," Lilly said.

It looked like Beau was in Lilly's life to stay, too.

RECIPES

CHERRY CHIP COOKIES

¾ c. butter, softened
¼ c. shortening (Noley uses Crisco)
1 c. light brown sugar
½ c. sugar
1 t. vanilla
2 large eggs
2 ¾ c. flour
1 t. baking soda
½ t. salt
1 ¾ c. white chocolate chips (11-oz. bag)
¾ c. dried cherries (you can chop them if you want, but Noley leaves them whole)
Sanding sugar, if desired.

Preheat oven to 350 degrees. Line baking sheets with parchment paper or silicone mat. In a large bowl beat first 4 ingredients until fluffy, about 2 min. Add vanilla and eggs and beat well.

In med bowl whisk flour, baking soda, and salt.

Gradually add dry mixture to butter mixture, beating well. Fold in chips and cherries. The batter will be very thick. If it seems too soft, refrigerate the mixture for about 20 minutes. Form balls about 1 T. in size and, if desired, roll in sanding sugar. Place 2" apart on the baking sheets. Bake for 9-11 minutes, rotating baking sheets about halfway through cooking.

ALABAMA WHITE SAUCE

1 c. mayonnaise
¼ c. apple cider vinegar
2 t. brown mustard
½ t. salt
½ t. pepper
½ t. garlic powder
¼ t. onion powder
Dash hot sauce, to taste

Mix all ingredients in medium bowl. Refrigerate until ready to use. Tastes great on grilled meats and hearty grilled vegetables.

NOLEY'S BLUEBERRY STUDMUFFINS

¾ c. butter, softened
1 c. sugar, divided
2 large eggs
3 c. flour
1 T. baking powder
½ t. salt
1 1/3 c. reduced fat or whole milk
1 ¼ c. fresh or frozen blueberries
2 t. lemon zest, optional

Preheat oven to 375 degrees. Grease a standard 12-cup muffin tin or mini muffin tins (you can use cooking spray). In a large bowl, beat the butter and ¾ c. sugar until fluffy. Add eggs, one at a time, beating well after each addition.

In another bowl, whisk 2 2/3 c. flour with baking powder and salt. Add to dry ingredients, then add milk and mix batter just until moistened.

Place remaining flour in a plastic bag and add blueberries, tossing gently to coat. Gently fold berries and any additional flour in the bag into batter. If desired, fold in lemon zest, too.

Fill each muffin cup 2/3 full. Sprinkle the remaining sugar over the tops of the muffins.

Bake for 20-30 minutes, or until muffins test done.

Makes 12 standard-sized muffins. If using mini muffin tins, bake 8-9 minutes.

NEWSLETTER SIGN-UP

Please visit https://www.amymreade.com/newsletter to sign up to receive monthly news, updates, promotions, contests, and recipes.

ABOUT THE AUTHOR

Amy M. Reade is a recovering attorney who discovered, quite by accident, a passion for fiction writing. She has penned nine mysteries and is working on several others, including a Cape May County historical mystery series. She writes in the Gothic, traditional, contemporary, and cozy mystery subgenres and looks forward to continuing the two series she has begun since December, 2018. She also loves to read, cook, and travel.

She is the *USA Today* and *Wall Street* Journal bestselling author of *Secrets of Hallstead House*, *The Ghosts of Peppernell Manor*, *House of the Hanging Jade*, the Malice series, the Juniper Junction Holiday Mystery series, and the Libraries of the World Mystery series. You can find out more about her books at www.amymreade.com.